Rebound

Aga Lesiewicz

REBOUND

MACMILLAN

First published 2016 by Macmillan
an imprint of Pan Macmillan
20 New Wharf Road, London N1 9RR
Associated companies throughout the world
www.panmacmillan.com

ISBN 978-1-4472-8310-2 HB
ISBN 978-1-4472-8308-9 TPB

1 3 5 7 9 8 6 4 2

A CIP catalogue record for this book is available from the British Library.

Typeset by Palimpsest Book Production Ltd, Falkirk, Stirlingshire
Printed and bound by CPI Group (UK) Ltd, Croydon, CR0 4YY

Visit www.panmacmillan.com to read more about all our books
and to buy them. You will also find features, author interviews and
news of any author events, and you can sign up for e-newsletters
so that you're always first to hear about our new releases.

Rebound

✳

Dusk is settling on the Heath, making trees and grass lose their colour. The shapes become blurred and unreal, all detail suddenly gone. The sky is dimming its brightness and the first stars and planets appear above the horizon. There is a handful of people about, mostly carrying their blankets and baskets in the direction of a few cars still parked in Merton Lane. I run up the hill at full speed and I can hear my heart pounding in my head, my breath quick and shallow. Once I reach the top I slow down. I don't turn into the woods because it's too dark there already. I run down across the meadow, which is still getting enough light from the sky, then turn sharply left, making a loop. I reach the main path again and decide to cross it and continue in the direction of the Ladies' Pond. I hear footsteps behind me, regular and strong, another runner making the best of the twilight hour. I run across the South Meadow at a steady pace. The sound of footsteps is still behind me. There's no one else left on the Heath now. I try not to panic, thinking that whoever it is will change their direction soon. But the sound of trainers pounding the ground persists, going exactly at my speed, not trying to overtake me and not slowing down. I quickly glance back and see the dark silhouette of a man, about twenty paces behind me. I think of stopping and letting him pass me, but fear is pushing me forward, my muscles locked in the mechanical movement of my limbs. I try to breathe steadily, not to break my rhythm, not to show that I'm afraid. I turn right onto a path and he does the same. I check my pepper spray, still tucked safely in the pocket of my shorts. At least I have something to defend myself with, if he attacks me. But for now my flight or fight response is limited to flight. The Ladies' Pond, I think, maybe one of the guards is still there. I change direction and run towards the back gate of the pond. I pick up speed, hoping I'll shake him off, and for a moment I think I'm winning, his footsteps no longer audible behind me. I see the wrought-iron fence, the sign that says WOMEN ONLY, MEN NOT ALLOWED BEYOND THIS POINT, and for a split second I hope it'll stop him. I reach the gate and it's locked, a huge chain and padlock in place. I think I hear the footsteps behind me again and I grab the top of the gate and leap over it, half-climbing, half-vaulting. I'm on the narrow, overgrown path that runs behind the toilets and the guards' house. I slip in the mud, then keep running, reach the main path and turn left towards the swimmers' platform. I enter the square of concrete in front of the bathrooms and look hopefully at the guards' house. The door is locked and it's dark; there is no one here. I turn to keep running and there he is, standing on the path, blocking my escape route. I take a step back, my heart pounding, my hand on the spray. He moves forward, coming out of the shadow of the building into the moonlight, and I recognize him. My fear gives way to relief, to be instantly replaced by more fear. What is he doing here? Why has he followed me? Is he going to kill me?

Thirty-six Days Earlier

I know it is over as soon as the parcel lands on my desk. Something about the twee wrapping paper, about the pink ribbon, tells me it has to end. I simply can't let it go on. I pretend it isn't there, ignoring curious looks from my assistant, Claire. I go out to lunch, although I don't have time for it, buy myself a wilted sandwich and a cup of latte that tastes of tinned milk, get back to my office. The parcel is still there, sitting in the middle of my desk, looking ridiculously pleased with itself. It has to go. I resist the urge to throw it away, there and then. In my glass cubicle I am under the constant scrutiny of Claire and the girls from the production team, who peek through the see-through walls, pretending they aren't looking. It is getting unbearable. My laptop pings. Saved by the meeting. Then another one.

By the time I return to my desk the office is almost empty, cleared by the Friday-evening rush to the pub. Claire, the efficient one, left at five on the dot. She comes to work an hour early every morning, so she can leave early and head straight for the gym. There is, of course, a gym at our glass and steel office complex, run smoothly by Happy Workplace, the company that takes care of everything: the buildings, the car park, the carp in the pond, the grass we sit on during our lunch breaks, the air we breathe. Claire loves it. Sometimes I wonder if she has a secret vice, a drawer full of unwashed sex toys, something dysfunctional, dirty. But no, Claire is perfect. She probably spends her evenings ironing her knickers and baking her own good-for-you granola, which she sprinkles on her yoghurt every morning at 10 a.m. precisely. And she is a perfect assistant.

The parcel is still there. I tear off the pink ribbon and rip the wrapping paper open. There is a cardboard box inside, decorated with little pink hearts. At least it is colour-coordinated. I open the box. A brown furry top of the head, two furry ears and, yes, another pink ribbon. A teddy bear. I take it out of its box and sit it in front of me. It's cute, I have to admit, but that's exactly what's wrong with it. As it lands in the wastepaper basket I think of the guy who's sent it. The guy who prides himself on being my own living cuddly toy. 'Your *cagnolino di peluche*' he signs his emails to me. I found it funny at the beginning, sexy even, his Italian roots and Italian looks inherited from his feisty (but thankfully deceased) Italian mother. The novelty of *cagnolino di peluche* wore off when I realized that cute and cuddly is not what I need in my life. Although, of course, all the girls in the office, with Claire at the helm, think he's God's gift to women. Handsome. Caring. Rich. Well, perhaps not a millionaire, but better off than the average Tom, Dick or Harry you're likely to bump into at a Soho bar on a Friday night. James, my *cagnolino di peluche*, is an MD in – as he calls it – a financial information services company. Big office in the city, convertible Audi A5, a river-view loft in St George Wharf with twenty-four-hour concierge and security, underground parking, on-site gym. What more could a girl want from a man? The problem is this particular girl has just realized she doesn't want the whole package. I don't want the cute and cuddly James any more.

I log off my laptop, take the bear out of the wastepaper basket and leave the office, the furry toy under my arm. The office lift takes me straight down to the car park in the basement, the only way in and out of the building that avoids the hawk eyes of the receptionists and security staff on the ground floor. What they see on the security cameras is their business, but I can do without their matey comments tonight. My trusted 4x4 is one of the few cars left in the car park. Why save the planet in a politically correct hybrid if you can rule the road in a Chelsea tractor? Except I don't live in Chelsea. The hilly streets of Highgate almost justify my BMW X5, although I haven't bought it to do the school run. I bought it for Wispa.

Wispa is a five-year-old chocolate Labrador with serious weight issues. She's been my best friend and companion since the day I brought her home as an overgrown puppy with fat paws and melancholy eyes. Named after the iconic Cadbury's chocolate bar, she took their eightie's slogan, 'Bite it and believe it', to heart. It took a lot of persuasion to convince her that not everything in this life has to be bitten to be believed. She came on board two years before James. Wispa and I dreamt of bringing up a litter of bumbling furballs, having the house full of puppy porridge and love, but then Wispa had pyometra and our dream was shattered. After her hysterectomy Wispa's interest in sex got replaced by an interest in food. Any food. My dog walker Nicole and I fight a losing battle with Wispa's obesity. She hoovers up her carefully measured doses of the vet-prescribed Satiety Dog Food, supplementing her diet with any old rubbish she can find on the streets of Highgate. She is insatiable. These days, the back of my BMW X5 is the only car space Wispa feels comfortable in.

I throw the bear on the back seat of the car and drive out of the car park. I briefly consider giving the bear to Wispa, but I know she'd only try to eat it. I'll walk up to the village and drop it off at a charity shop tomorrow. My iPhone rings and the car's Bluetooth smoothly intercepts the call, transferring it to the speakers. James. I consider ignoring the call, but I know I'll have to bite the bullet sooner or later.

'Hey, babe, how was your day? Anything exciting happen?'

He means the bear.

'Yes, how sweet of you. What's the occasion?'

'Oh, nothing, just thought I'd brighten your day. Make the girls in the office jealous. Make you think of your . . . *cagnolino di peluche.*'

He actually growls it seductively instead of saying it. And to think I used to enjoy his vocal displays of masculinity. 'James, we need to talk.'

'Great, I booked us a table at Roka.'

I've imagined dumping him on my own turf, at home, but why not do it over a plate of sushi?

'Sure, I'm on my way.'

It actually went easier than I'd thought. There were some tears. On James's part. And some lies. On mine. 'It's not you, it's me,' kind of stuff. And the predictable, 'I need more space.' He disagreed, he bargained, he begged, but in the end he gracefully accepted defeat. I was impressed. He almost behaved like a true gentleman. I say almost because he took it out on a waitress, complaining about an imaginary drop of soy sauce she'd spilled on his jacket.

I get home late. Wispa is waiting by the door, pissed off. I know she slept on my bed, she always does it to spite me when I leave her on her own for too long. This time I let her get away with it and pour myself a glass of wine. A nice Rioja to mark the occasion. And then I call Bell.

'I broke up with James.'

'The twerp is gone! Great!' I can hear she's been drinking.

Bell is the only one of my friends who's never warmed to James. She calls him the twerp, Mr Goody Two-shoes or, in his case, loafers, which in her book is enough to dislike him. 'Never trust a man who wears loafers. It's a guy who gives you a hickey on the first date to mark you as his property. They're all psychopaths, hiding behind the facade of mediocrity,' she said. She was wrong about the hickey: James has never given me one, has never left any marks on my body. He is a gentle and considerate lover. Perhaps too gentle and considerate. But she is right about the loafers. I've never quite got used to the sight of him slipping his feet into the tasselled horrors. Thankfully, he always wears socks with them. Bare feet in loafers would be too much to bear.

'Promise me one thing.' Bell pauses and I can hear her taking a gulp of white wine. She only drinks white. 'You won't jump into bed with the first guy that comes along.'

'Since when have you become my mother?'

'You know what I mean, Anna. I want you to stay single for a while, to give yourself some time to ask questions of an existential nature.'

She is right, of course. I tend to spend as little time as possible being single. It helps that there is always a short queue of candidates lined up, waiting to fill the vacancy. Consequently, the borderline between the end of one relationship and the beginning of the next is often blurred.

'Existential questions? What: "Who am I? Where am I going to?" How much have you had to drink?'

'I'm serious, Anna. Slow down. Spend some time with your friends. Your dog.'

'Wispa's never complained.'

At the sound of her name Wispa gets up from her bed, stretches and wobbles towards me.

'Because she loves you unconditionally.'

'That's the best kind of love.'

'There's no such thing as unconditional love, unless you're a dog.'

'Which reminds me . . .' I put down my half-full glass of Rioja. 'I need to take her out.'

Wispa reads my body language and is already by the front door.

'Catch you tomorrow, hon.'

'Try to stay single till then.'

'You interested?' I love teasing her.

'I told you, you're not my type. Too high maintenance.'

'I thought that was exactly the type of girl you went for.'

'True,' Bell sighs. 'Maybe I should try this single thing myself.'

Bell's list of disastrous flings with psycho girls is as long as a basking viper. And equally venomous.

It's a mild and humid night. It's too dark to go on the Heath, so I walk down Swain's Lane, along the cemetery. I stare at my favourite statue, an angel with big wings, looking radiant and serene in the semi-darkness of the graveyard. My iPhone pings. A message from Peter from Promax, the most effective speed-dating agency of the media world. Just kidding. I mean the glitzy media event, with the awards night that is a wet dream for all the TV promo-makers and marketing guys in the world. Back to Promax Peter. He is a Creative Director at some sports channel, charming, good-looking and with that air of keen and urgent availability so characteristic of married men with small kids. We talked, we flirted, we exchanged business cards, and here he is, texting me sexy on a Friday night. Tempting, but no. I delete the message. Wispa dashes down the dark street, as if she's seen someone she knows. She gave up chasing foxes and cats a long time ago and now the only thing that gets her going is the sight of a human friend. But the street is empty, there is no one there, and she trots back to me panting, her pink tongue lolling about happily.

Unconditional love. A feeling I don't believe in, perhaps with the exception of Wispa. But her love is also conditional: she wants my presence, walkies, her food. Well, it's as close as it'll ever get to being unconditional. Am I getting too jaded for a true, overwhelming, spellbinding emotion that would make me do things I wouldn't normally do, promise things I wouldn't normally promise? I read somewhere that parental love is unconditional, because parents feel compelled to love their children, no matter what. I probably caught a glimpse of that when, after my dad had dumped us and disappeared with some blonde floozy, my mum stood by me, fighting like a wounded lioness, so I always had everything I wanted as a child, even though money was tight. It all ended when she died of breast cancer at the age of forty, a wounded lioness till the very end, trying to look out for her cub even when she had no energy to look after herself. It was shortly after her death when I – a spoilt and angry teenager – realized that from then on I would have to earn love; it would never come free again.

Bell is right. I have to slow down and spend some quality time with my friends and my dog. Invest a little. I pat Wispa's head and walk on, hoping my resolution will last at least till Monday.

Thirty-five Days Earlier

I wake up full of energy and good intentions. Saturday mornings do that to me. Just when you don't have to get up early and rush to work, you're awake at the crack of dawn, your head buzzing with ideas. My good mood lasts through the morning coffee, a lovingly made blueberry, raspberry and banana smoothie, and a reheated croissant. It all goes downhill from there. I open the front door and find a battlefield of take-away food cartons, smeared bits of unspecified green substance, torn sanitary pads and a small spiral turd right on my doorstep. Foxes. I have a love/hate relationship with London foxes, but at this moment all I feel is pure hate.

Once that is cleared I step out onto the pavement in front of my house and feel a crunch of broken glass under my shoes. Pulling Wispa away, I look around. Yep. Just when you think you've done your penance for the day, fate dishes out something even better. The rear passenger window of my BMW has been smashed in. I go back to the house, grab my phone, lock Wispa in and come out again. I cautiously look into the car, half-expecting a homeless urchin curled up on the back seat. The car is empty, crystals of broken glass scattered everywhere. I open the front door and check the storage compartments. Nothing seems to be missing, not even the few coins that used to be handy for parking and became obsolete when most of the London boroughs introduced card and phone payments. That is strange. I take another look and then I remember. James's teddy bear! It's gone. I almost ring him to tell him his *peluche* is missing, then I remember that I dumped him the night before. Who would want to steal a teddy bear from the back of a BMW in Highgate? A desperate mother driven to distraction by her needy offspring? A spoilt brat who doesn't have enough toys to fill a landfill? I shrug my shoulders, but then a sudden thought hits me. Could it have been James? Taking back his toy because I didn't want to play with him any more? No, that's ridiculous, he's not that kind of a person. He might be too cute for his own loafers, but he's not vindictive. Oh well, it looks like the charity shop won't be getting a brand-new teddy bear after all. Phone calls to Autoglass and my car insurer seem to take forever, but by midday the matter is on its way to being fixed. My morning good cheer is well and truly gone by now.

What better to improve a foul mood than a brisk walk on the Heath with your dog? Wispa agrees it's the best idea. We walk down Merton Lane and enter the Heath by the ponds. It's a glorious afternoon. There are people milling around with their dogs, a few still silhouettes of the guys watching their fishing rods, serious joggers with greyhound expressions on their faces and a handful of birdwatchers visibly excited by something invisible in the bushes on the other side of the pond. Wispa and I quickly march up the hill, putting distance between ourselves and the crowds. At the top of the hill we turn right towards Kenwood. It's quieter and darker in the woods. I love this part of the Heath. It's never crowded and the thick bushes and old gnarly trees give it an air of seclusion and mystery. I sit on the bench dedicated to 'someone who loved this place' and close my eyes. Bell is right. I need time to process all the things that are happening in my life. It seems I've lost control over the direction I'm heading in, and I'm following a pattern of accidental twists of fate, both at work and in my private life. Opportunities, sideways moves, promotions that got me to where I am at work as Head of On-Air, Programming and Creative for a major TV company – not bad for a girl from a scabby little Essex town. But is that it, professionally? And then there is my personal life. My personal mess, as Bell calls it. The sound of a twig breaking under a boot interrupts my thoughts. I open my eyes. A guy with a shaven head and elaborate tattoos on his bare arms passes my bench and disappears into the bushes. I'm just about to close my eyes again when I see another guy, in washed-out jeans with a small rucksack on his back, following the first guy. Surely not . . . I've heard the stories of gay cruising grounds on the Heath, but I thought they were further in the woods, towards Spaniards Road. The second guy disappears into the same bushes and I'm suddenly overwhelmed by curiosity. I check on Wispa, who seems obsessed with gnawing on a big tree branch, then I get up and gingerly approach the bushes. At first I see nothing except the mass of greenery. Then I hear something. I move towards the sound. And there they are, the guy with a rucksack kneeling in front of the tattooed guy, who stands with his back to a massive old oak tree, eyes closed, a look of intense pleasure on his face. A twig cracks under my foot and I quickly move back, losing sight of the men. I turn round and face Wispa, who is watching me with her ears pricked up, tilting her head slightly as she always does when she is curious.

'You and me, kid,' I say quietly, and pat her head. 'Let's find you a proper stick.'

Saturday night and I'm not going out clubbing, I'm not meeting a man in a swanky bar, not even hooking up with friends at the Flask. I'm going to have a quiet evening at Bell's. We've been promising it to each other for months and now the time is right. I pack Wispa and a couple of bottles of wine – Shiraz for me, Viognier for Bell – into my newly glazed and valeted car and set off on my short journey through Hornsey and Finsbury Park to Stoke Newington, where Bell has a flat just off Church Street. I like Stokey, used to live there before I had a salary big enough to just about afford a move to Highgate. It's changed a lot since then, Clissold House having received a massive facelift, the park turning into a posh nappy valley, with stay-at-home mums sipping their decaf lattes, their offspring asleep in fancy prams. Church Street itself has been desperately hanging on to a few decrepit buildings and residents, being slowly pushed out by new cafes, organic grocers and a few second-hand shops dressed up as 'vintage'. I nostalgically think of the good old times at the smoky Vortex, replaced now by Nando's.

Bell opens the door with a glass of wine in her hand. Her evening started some time ago.

We finish her excellent chorizo and spinach risotto and move onto her spacious leather sofa. I'm grateful she hasn't mentioned James.

'Do you consider yourself a failure?' Bell is opening a second bottle of white for herself.

'A failure in what?' I'm not sure I want to get into this conversation.

'In everything. In life.'

'It all depends on your point of reference. What do you measure it against? Your mother's dream for her only child? Ambitious plans you had at uni? They're all pies in the sky.'

'So we're all failures by default. I personally don't have a problem with it. I practise it every day.'

Bell is not doing that badly. Having left the teaching job that was driving her insane, she retrained as a massage therapist and has a respectable group of clients who adore her. She doesn't commute to work, she works when she wants to and is her own boss.

'Oh, come on. I know a lot of people who'd swap with you right now.'

'Hey, don't take my failure away from me. It's mine.' She pours some wine for me. I watch Wispa snore blissfully at our feet.

'I think it's about being happy with what you have. Being in the present.'

'So you're happy?' I know she's edging towards the subject of James. Or the absence of him.

'I think I am.' I hesitate. 'At least I feel free.'

'You don't miss him?'

'Well, to be perfectly honest, I did miss him this morning.' I know this will annoy her, so I pause, but she doesn't take the bait. 'Someone had smashed the window in my car and I nearly rang him to ask for help. I suppose I'll have to toughen up . . .'

'I thought you'd toughened up enough during your divorce.'

'God,' I groan at the thought of my psycho ex-husband

Andrew. 'Please don't remind me of that creep. Thank goodness I don't have to go through the same with James.'

'How's work?' She changes the subject at last and tops up my glass.

'Work?' I yawn and shrug my shoulders. Wispa lifts her head and looks at me questioningly. It reminds me of the look she gave me on the Heath.

'Do lesbians go cruising?' I ask Bell, and watch her eyes go round with surprise and then amusement.

'Cruising?'

'Yeah, you know, in the bushes, I don't know, loos and stuff . . .' I'm already regretting having broached the subject.

'That's cottaging.'

'Whatever.' I shrug again. I don't want to continue this. But Bell presses on.

'Why do you ask?'

'Oh, it's nothing, it's silly.'

'What?' She nudges me and I know she won't let go until I tell her.

'I went to the Heath with Wispa this afternoon and I saw these two guys having sex in the bushes.'

Bell makes a face.

'No, it wasn't like that . . . I mean, they weren't doing it in the middle of an open field. I actually spied on them . . .'

'You did what?'

'I crept behind a bush and . . .'

'Why?'

'I don't know. I was curious, I suppose.' Embarrassed, I take a gulp of my wine. 'And then . . . I kind of got into it . . .'

'You JOINED them?!' Bell nearly knocks her glass over.

'No, no, no. No. I just . . . understood what they were about. Why they were doing it.'

'Anna, let me tell you.' Bell sounds drunk and serious at the same time. 'Lesbians don't go cruising. They don't run around the Heath looking for another dyke. WOMEN don't do it. We don't stick our minge in some glory hole and wait for a stranger to poke it.'

'Sorry!' I raise my hands. 'I was just asking.'

'And let me tell you WHY we don't do it. Because we're wired up differently to men. Because our testosterone levels are much lower. Because our needs are different.'

'Bell, I get it!'

She stops ranting and takes a sip of wine. 'Anyway,' she winks, putting her glass down, 'it's about time you climbed down from that fence you've been sitting on for as long as I've known you and join me on my side.'

'I know, Bell, I know.' I lean over and kiss her on the cheek. 'If only it were that easy.'

'But it ain't,' she says, and pours us more wine.

Thirty-four Days Earlier

The next morning I'm greeted in Bell's guest room by a hangover from hell. Wispa drags me out for a short stumble around Clissold Park. I pick up some freshly baked croissants in Church Street and by the time I'm back at Bell's she's standing in her kitchen by her coffee machine. She looks as bad as I feel. We don't talk much, which is fine. It's good to have a friend you can have a laugh with, but also be silent when you feel like it.

I drive back home around midday, knowing that it's not going to be one of those productive and soul-restoring Sundays that make you feel smug and on top of everything. It's going to be a waste of time in a can't-be-bothered kind of way. It's OK, everyone needs one of those from time to time. I call them Wispa Sundays. She loves them because she gets me, slouching around the house in a pair of old track bottoms, all to herself.

The house feels stuffy. I open the windows to air it, but it's wet and windy outside and the dampness immediately seeps into my bones. I feel tempted to turn on the heating, even though the calendar tells me not to. No one in their right mind turns the heating on at this time of year in this country. It's supposed to be summer, for God's sake, except it's not. And, as the cheerful weather people tell us, this is what we're going to get for the next ten years, if we're lucky. It could be twenty, if we're not. I decide to ignore the weather and warm up in a different way. I wrap myself in a green raincoat I picked up in a chandlery in a small coastal village while on a weekend trip to Norfolk with James and head out into the rain. It's pretty disgusting outside but I push on towards the Heath, Wispa lolloping about like a happy seal. IO6719I|AFP

I would have thought the Heath would be empty, but there are quite a few hardened walkers defying the weather. I decide to do our usual loop and Wispa and I fall into a nice marching rhythm. As I enter the woods I'm reminded of the two guys I saw yesterday. No chance of catching any of them in this weather, I think to myself. But there is someone coming from the opposite direction, down the path leading from Kenwood. It's a tall man in a grey Barbour wax jacket and as he approaches I'm struck by how handsome he is. Passing each other, we exchange a casual glance and he reminds me of the men from Dior's moody ads. Probably gay, I think to myself. I'm distracted by Wispa bundling towards me dragging a branch covered in wet moss. I wrestle it from her and throw it high in the bushes where she can't reach it. When I look round, the guy is gone.

We climb up Fitzroy Park and reach the village, both totally wet. As we pass the charity shop something in the window catches my eye. I stop suddenly, pulling on Wispa's lead. In the middle of the display, among the dusty crystals and yellow-with-age crockery, at the feet of a headless dummy in a flowery dress sits my teddy bear! I come closer to the window and stare at it. It definitely looks like James's *peluche*; not an old toy with a wonky paw and matted fur like you'd expect in a charity shop, but a brand-new, clean and immaculate plush teddy. But it can't be, mine got nicked from the car, I try to think logically. But what if . . . no, no, no, this is absurd. Why would anyone

break a car window to steal a toy and then take it promptly to a charity shop? I walk away from the window, having decided it's just a coincidence, the result of a sudden unexplained surplus of teddy bears in North London. Then a niggling thought stops me in my tracks. Could it be James, after all? No, it's impossible. This is absolutely not the kind of thing he would do. I wouldn't put it past Andrew, but thankfully he's been out of my life for years. James wouldn't do anything so creepy. Wispa pulls on the lead like crazy as we walk down our street. At least one of us is ready for dinner.

I open the front door and remember I should get my keys back from James. I pick up the phone and dial his number. He answers almost instantly.

'Anna? What a lovely surprise.'

'How are you?'

He tells me he's great, has made some new resolutions, signed on a new fitness plan.

'You know, burn that fat, build the muscle, reshape the body . . .'

'There is nothing wrong with your body!'

'Well, there's always room for improvement.' The way he says it sounds funny and we both laugh. I like his laugh.

We chat for a while longer and I feel increasingly uneasy about the true reason for my phone call. Eventually we run out of chit-chat and I have to bite the bullet.

'James . . . I know it'll sound a bit mean, but it's not really, it's just that I need . . . could you possibly drop my keys off?'

I waffle on about needing the spare set for my handyman, who'll do a bit of work in the house. I know I sound like an idiot, a mean idiot at that. But his reaction makes it instantly all right. Of course, he says, sounding as if he's to blame for

the oversight, he'll swing by
box. It's no problem at all, he assu
too profusely, and we say goodbye, w
of luck.

Revenge? What was I thinking? He's a g
I warn myself, don't even consider getting back
him. It was nice while it lasted, but now you need th
own, stay single for a while, I hear Bell's voice in my he ell
me.

'OK, girlfriend,' I say, partly to myself, partly to Wispa, and
go to the kitchen to fill her bowl.

Thirty-three Days Earlier

As soon as I arrive at work I know it's going to be a day from hell. Claire informs me my calendar has been cleared of all afternoon appointments to make room for a meeting with the President. Julian, as he likes to be called, although in my opinion Mr President would suit him much better, is coming to his London office personally. It can only mean bad news.

I ponder all the unsettling scenarios. Reorganization. Hiring freezes. Budget cuts. Lay-offs. They all imply change. I've been around the block a few times, so I'm pretty used to change. I know I can survive, even if I get the sack today. But the majority of my staff, all those supposedly free-as-a-bird creative types, producers with the resilience of a butterfly's wing, dread change. A rumour of lay-offs or even an unexpected promotion, anything that brings up fears of being unemployed, sets them off into a frenzy of panic or turns them into perpetual moaners who carry their hurt egos around like open wounds for anyone to see. Then there are the 'permalancers', who our business relies heavily upon. Freelancers who hang on to one job for months or even years, against the advice of their accountant and their own better judgement. They can be difficult and needy too, although in reality they haven't got a leg to stand on and can be got rid of with a click of a mouse. Whatever change Julian will announce this afternoon, I'm not looking forward to it. And I dread its fallout.

Gary puts his face through my open door. Damn, I forgot to shut it. My open door means anyone can pop in, in the spirit of the open camaraderie so painstakingly perpetuated by the company. Gary is my biggest promotion blunder. A fourteen-year-old boy trapped in the ageing body of a forty-year-old man, carrying his fat beer gut like an attribute of youth, Gary used to be a mediocre, but useful, senior producer until I promoted him to Creative Director. Big mistake. Now the boy thinks he's a man. He shows his temper exactly when he's not supposed to, then crumbles in tears like a baby at the sight of any challenge. Now he's on a mission to destroy Bill. Bill is an editor, one of the longest serving in the company, and he has something Gary fears most: balls. And Bill has witnessed Gary dressing down, in a particularly nasty way, a shy and rather sweet-looking permalancer named Lisa. What Gary didn't know was that Bill was going out with Lisa. So he ripped Bill's girlfriend to shreds over nothing right in front of him, in his edit suite. Bill went straight to HR. HR reacted in their own wishy-washy way. Gary was gently reprimanded. Freelance work for Lisa had immediately dried up. Bill was left fuming. And Gary had embarked on a back-stabbing mission to get rid of Bill. But as nothing happens very quickly in our company, they are both still here, hating each other's guts. I find Gary increasingly nauseating and I wish I could turn back the clock. But clocks go only one way in this place, onwards and upwards.

'You busy?' says Gary with his boyish grin that is supposed to mean 'Oh, I'm so cute.'

'I am, Gary. Sorry. Can it wait till tomorrow?'

'Sure.'

'Oh, Gary, can you shut the door?'

My glass door closes and I'm left in peace. I hide in my glass sanctuary through the morning, nipping out for a quick bite to eat in a cafe everyone avoids. It has famously bad food, but at least it's always quiet.

At five to three my work calendar pings and I make my way upstairs to the executive floor. Julian welcomes me as if I'm a long-lost relative. He is a small man, always immaculately dressed and smelling of good aftershave. He has the air of success and satisfaction about him, something that evolves over many years of huge salaries and bonuses. He asks me to sit on his comfortable leather sofa. He offers me coffee, which I accept. And then he tells me the bad news, disguised as an exciting development. It's actually a message from the Chairman, he hastens to add, relieving himself of the immediate responsibility for what he's about to announce.

'What we want to create is an efficient and streamlined organizational structure,' he says and my heart sinks. As the vision of 'accelerated growth', 'integration' and 'single operational structure' fills the office I'm already imagining a long list of redundancies, people having to reapply for their jobs, tears, grievances, employment tribunals. And then he drops an even bigger bombshell. It appears an external management consulting company has been hired to, as Julian puts it, 'manage the change'. From now on, and for the foreseeable future – the next three months to be precise – Cadenca Global will be our guardian angel. I've never heard of Cadenca Global, but Julian assures me they are the best money can buy. I don't doubt that. Spend money to save money: that sounds like a standard way of doing business in our industry. Oh, what great news. The day from hell has just turned into the beginning of a whole season from hell.

I go back to my office considering filing for voluntary redundancy myself. But of course I won't do it, the pull of the corporate gilded cage is too strong.

As soon as I'm back, Sarah puts her basset face through my door. She's a permalancer turned full-time Senior Producer, because she couldn't hack the constant insecurity and challenges of the freelance life. She's also a jolly fat girl turned miserable gastric-band dieter obsessed with her weight loss. The excess stretches of skin that used to contain fat hang loosely on her face and neck giving her the permanent expression of a sad dog.

'You all right?' she asks me in a concerned voice.

'Yes, Sarah, I'm fine. How can I help you?'

'No, no, no.' She waves her hand. 'If there's anything I can do to help,' she puts extra stress on 'I', 'please just let me know. Anything.'

'Thank you,' I say and open my laptop pointedly.

Basset Face gets the message and disappears. She knows. How on earth has she managed to get confidential information that was disclosed in Julian's office not even five minutes ago? That doesn't concern me much. She'll be the first one to go in the restructuring of the department. What worries me more is the fact that if she knows then the whole building will know by tomorrow. I need to act quickly, arrange a departmental meeting to announce the changes before the rumour mutates into some hideous, morale-destroying monster. It will be a monster to deal with anyway, but it has to come from me. I pick up the phone.

Twenty-nine Days Earlier

The next few days are a blur of meetings, planning, announcements, speculation and frayed nerves. On Tuesday Cadenca Global makes its first appearance. It arrives in the shape of five young and sharply dressed uber-androids, four male and one female. It's the female who is the scariest: cold, precise and unsmiling, she paints a frightening picture of the market realities that apparently reshape, like a pack of wolves, the media and entertainment industry. As they tear with their fangs at the old reality, new technology platforms pop up, new competition and business models emerge, gnawing at the old consumers until they are forced to change their viewing habits, shift their fat arses to a slightly different place on their sofas and start exercising different fingers, pressing different buttons. But not to worry, we're not going to lose them, Cadenca Global is at hand with its extensive media consulting experience. They'll help us adapt, simplify, break new ground and, of course, capitalize on new opportunities. I leave the conference room reassured. Reassured that life will never be the same.

By Thursday the dust begins to settle and the painful process of implementing The Change begins. Although Cadenca Global are overseeing the whole process, the dirty work has been left to us, the middle management. Some people will have to reapply for their jobs, some will have to be told there are no jobs to reapply for. Some will doggedly pursue their careers, some will crack under pressure and leave. Some will have to be pushed. The new, shiny, streamlined structure is supposed to be ready by October. An ambitious plan. But there is one good thing about the upheaval at work. It has made me almost forget about my Heath stranger. Almost . . .

At home I rely on my dog walker Nicole for taking care of Wispa. I barely have time and energy to take Wispa out for her evening walk when I get back from work. She's not happy with a short stroll around the block and makes it obvious by whimpering at night. She ignores her Kong chew toy even when I put a dollop of peanut butter in it. I'll have to make it up to her at the weekend.

By Friday I'm ready for some proper human contact. I call Michael, one of my oldest and most reliable friends. He was an art designer at a company where I was starting out as a rookie promo producer. We were both going through a rough patch with our boyfriends at the time and we hit it off straight away, comparing notes on the love front and counselling each other. I was there for him when his lover Phil died suddenly of a heart attack at the age of forty; he stood by me when I was going through the emotionally exhausting divorce from Andrew. We've been through the wars together. He sounds as if he's been waiting for my call and we arrange to meet in the evening at the Spaniards Inn, a Dickensian pub by the Heath where – and this is crucial for me – dogs are most welcome.

I stop by at home to pick up Wispa and by eight I'm turning off Spaniards Road into the pub's car park. Michael is waiting for me outside, having a cigarette. Wispa throws herself at him, overjoyed to see the old friend who always has a dog treat for her in his pocket. It's a chilly night and we're lucky to get a table inside, in the smaller of their cosy dining rooms. Quick look at the menu and I go for the sea bass, chickpeas, chorizo and cuttlefish main paired with Tripel Karmeliet, while Michael chooses gnocchi with quinoa, chestnut mushroom and truffled cream with Schiehallion Scottish lager. I melt into the relaxed atmosphere of the pub, the nerve-wracking roller coaster at work millions of miles away. Michael is telling me about his latest date, a guy he met on an Internet dating site, a working-class lad turned mature student and now a teacher at a Tower Hamlets school. 'My *Educating Rita* guy' he calls him. They met at a pub off Brick Lane and the guy spent the whole evening talking about himself, without asking Michael a single question.

'I don't think I'll be seeing him again,' says Michael and takes a sip of his Schiehallion. 'There was no chemistry between us, anyway. How are you and James doing?'

'We've split up.'

'Really?' Michael puts his glass down. 'Though I can't say I'm surprised. I was more surprised that you stayed with him for such a long time.'

I nod. 'Nearly three years.'

'It's a bit of a record for you, isn't it? But I always thought he was a little too normal for you. I don't mean boring, but too domesticated. And you, my dear, are a free spirit. You love adventure, challenge, you can't be tied down by cosy domesticity. Here's to audacious Anna.'

He raises his glass and we both take a sip of our beers.

'I actually quite liked him,' he continues. 'A nice lad, cute, intelligent, kind. Maybe a tad too nice. I've always thought he could be gay.'

'Gay? He was the straightest guy I've ever met.'

Michael smiles. 'Even the straightest guys can have their gay side. Take those dads with lovely wives and a nice brood, who still go to the Heath for their little kicks. Well, not so much these days with the Internet and everything, but it's still going on.'

Our food arrives and it is delicious.

'Kicks on the Heath. I saw a bit of that last weekend.'

'Really? Where?'

'Near the West Field Gate to Kenwood.'

'That's unusual. It used to be West Heath in my day.'

'Your day? Don't tell me you used to do it.'

'Oh, it was a long time ago, before I met Phil. I was quite a stud then.'

'I can't imagine you prowling the Heath like a meerkat with a hard-on.'

Michael laughs. 'I was young, oversexed and quite lonely, I suppose. Imagine a naive Scottish boy in a big city.'

'Surely you met some nice fellow students at Saint Martins?'

'Yes, but I wasn't looking for a picnic with my friends. I wanted the anonymity, the rush of adrenaline, a certain element of danger.'

'Were you ever in danger?'

'No . . .' Michael hesitates. 'I don't think so.' He looks as if he wants to add something, then he changes his mind. 'How about some dessert?'

We decide to share a brandy bread and butter pudding with buttermilk ice cream. I'll burn it off during a quick jog with Wispa tonight and Michael doesn't have to worry about his figure.

Twenty-eight Days Earlier

Saturday morning and I'm wide awake at 7 a.m. There's no point in trying to sleep longer, it'll only give me a headache. I get up and put my jogging gear on. Wispa is overjoyed.

On our way to the Heath we pass by the charity shop and I notice the teddy bear has gone from the window. I hope it's found a good home. I jog down Fitzroy Park, Wispa following me off the leash, her pink tongue lolling happily.

We enter the Heath and I'm so overwhelmed by its beauty I have to stop. The morning mist is hanging over the pond, the sun touching the tops of trees, painting everything in warm light. Wispa is half-heartedly chasing a coot and I shout at her to stop. There is a heron standing on a fallen branch on the side of the Bird Pond, looking regal and still. Everything is perfect.

We trot slowly up the hill and I feel high on endorphins, appreciating the moment, appreciating my life, the closest to being happy I ever get. I turn right at the top of the hill, towards Kenwood. And there he is, jogging towards me. The Dior Man. His muscular legs move rhythmically, his T-shirt is wet with sweat. He is absolutely gorgeous. His blond hair shines with moisture, turning into little curls, his lips full and sensuous. The delicate stubble on his face is darker than his hair, giving him a slightly mischievous look. But it's the gentleness of his features, the boyish perfection combined with the grown-up strength of masculinity that I find most attractive in him. I falter in my step, slow down and bend over as if caught by a sudden side stitch.

'You OK?' I hear his voice, but he doesn't slow down.

'Yeah,' I say hoarsely, unable to say anything else.

He jogs on and disappears. My legs feel weak. I have to sit down, right there, on the ground. I take deep breaths and slowly regain composure. What the hell was it? Have I suffered a stroke? Am I getting an early menopause? I ask myself these silly questions, although I know the answer perfectly well. I've been knocked off my feet by the sight of a complete stranger, who didn't even break his stride to look on me. This is the second time I've seen him at exactly the same spot. Is it coincidence? I get up and start walking. I don't feel like jogging any more. Wispa follows me closely, as if sensing my confusion. Of course it was a coincidence. People are creatures of habit. Just as I choose to do the same loop on the Heath over and over again, so does he, obviously. It's a public park, joggers come here every day. I probably bump into the same people all the time without even realizing it. I've noticed him because he is extraordinarily handsome; he probably hasn't noticed me. He just saw some cranky jogger with a stitch in her side. End of story.

But it's not the end of the story, because I can't stop thinking about it. Can't stop thinking about him, his wet T-shirt snug against his pecs. This is insane. It's only been a week since I broke off with James, far too early to start going man-crazy. I stumble home, unable to move any faster. Wispa keeps running forward, then coming back, checking on me, worried by my slow pace. Yes, I know, it's unlike me. I can't understand it myself. What's going on?

Twenty-seven Days Earlier

The rest of Saturday disappears in a hazy fog of inertia and red wine. Bell wants to see me and I make up some silly excuses, a stomach bug and a migraine. You should never give more than one excuse if you don't want to be caught out lying. I know she knows I'm lying, but I don't care. I just want to be left alone.

And then it's Sunday morning and I'm wide awake at 7 a.m., bright-eyed and bushy-tailed, not a sign of a hangover, despite all the wine I drank last night. I throw on my jogging gear and bounce out of the door, Wispa nipping at my heels. I storm down Fitzroy Park, Wispa barely keeping up with me.

The Heath looks different to yesterday. It's foggy and overcast; dark clouds hang over Parliament Hill, threatening rain. The colours, so vibrant yesterday, are muted and pale. Even the birds look miserable. I steam up along the grey meadow, Wispa panting beside me. We stop at the top to catch our breath and then we enter the woods. My eyes have to adjust to the semi-darkness, only then I realize I'm wearing sunglasses, ridiculous in this weather. I take them off and hook them on the V-neck of my T-shirt. I trot further into the woods. There's no one here today. I pick up the pace again, determined to burn that anxious feeling that drives me forward, the thump-thump-thump of my heart in my ears. Faster, faster.

And suddenly there he is, right in front of me, the same chiselled features, blue eyes, a wet T-shirt tight on his chest. We bump into each other and he catches me before I fall. Wispa barks at him, I shout at her and she runs off with her tail between her legs. I push him against a tree and look into his eyes. There's something in them, a question or a need, which I choose to interpret as lust, because I want to. I slide my hand into his shorts and grab him, swollen and heavy. I squeeze and pump, my breath catching in my throat, my face against his wet T-shirt, the smell of washing powder and sweat overwhelming me. I feel my own excitement, barely control-lable, and I tug at him harder. His breath quickens and he puts his hands on my shoulders, an unexpected gesture of tenderness. His grip begins to tighten and then he suddenly pushes me away. I stumble backwards like a drunk, trip on a broken tree branch, nearly fall, find myself suddenly alone. No, not alone. An elderly couple in matching green anoraks are staring at me, bewildered.

'You all right, dear?' asks the woman, worry in her eyes.

'Yes,' I nod, trying to smile sheepishly. 'I just slipped . . . I'm fine.'

They stare at me a bit longer, then shuffle off, two identical, dwarf-like figures disappearing in the mist. Wispa comes back to me, her head low, watching me suspiciously. When I reach out to touch her, she jumps away.

'It's OK, baby, come here.' She approaches me cautiously and I pat her head. 'Good girl.'

I don't remember getting back home. I take a hot shower, wrap myself in a thick towelling robe and sit down in the kitchen with a mug of steaming coffee in my hands. What have I done? From snippets of feelings and flashes of images, a coherent thought begins to emerge. I've sexually assaulted a man. I almost laugh. Is there even a precedent for such a thing? I'm sure there is – the mythical images of harpies drawing men into their grasp come to my head. Wow, no need to be so dramatic. OK, I pounced on him, but he wanted it, too. I had the hard evidence in my hand. A wave of embarrassment runs over me, making me hot and sweaty. What if he called the police? Would I get arrested? What would be my excuse? That I fancied him and it somehow gave me the right to assault him? Does it make it OK because I'm a woman? I feel I'm entering a minefield of double standards. I grab my Mac and google 'sexual assault'. Wikipedia provides an instant definition: *'Sexual assault is any involuntary sexual act in which a person is threatened, coerced, or forced to engage against their will, or any sexual touching of a person who has not consented. This includes rape, groping, forced kissing . . .'* I close the Mac and sit motionless for a long time. The definition I've just read did not specify the gender of the assailant and the assaulted. Whichever way I look at it, it appears I have committed a statutory sexual offence. But somehow, deep down, I don't feel guilty. And this is bothering me even more than my transgression.

Twenty-six Days Earlier

I'm woken up by the urgent ringing of the alarm clock. It's Monday morning. I swing my legs out of bed, ready to face the day, then I remember yesterday. The memory makes me squirm. I need to think it through rationally before I'm able to function properly, not to mention dealing with the upheaval at work. This is a supremely bad moment to take time off, but I can't even bear the thought of going into the office right now, unhinged, my nerves and weaknesses exposed. I need a day, no, at least a few hours to collect myself, get ready, before I become the harbinger of the corporate cull. I leave a message for Claire, asking her to cancel my morning appointments and let everyone know I'll be in after lunch. Wispa, who's forgiven me for giving her a fright yesterday, has guessed I'm staying home and brings me her chewy toy to show appreciation. I go through our routine of taking it from her and then giving it back. Her tail is doing circles like a helicopter's rotor. I hug her and kiss her brown ear. 'Mummy will be fine,' I whisper to her, 'she just needs to sort something out in her head.'

But . . . the place I always go to whenever I have a problem to think through or a decision to make is the Heath. Do I dare to go there now? Yes, I decide. It's like going back to the scene of the crime, getting back on your bike once you've fallen off and hurt your knee. I need to go back there. Except I'm not the victim here, I'm the perpetrator. Why do I feel so fragile then? I throw on my jogging pants and a T-shirt and grab Wispa's leash.

The Heath welcomes us like an old friend, patient and forgiving, perhaps not having all the answers but asking the right questions. I follow my usual route, forcing myself to go back to the crime scene, as I now think of the place. It's quiet but there are people around, joggers mostly, a haggard-looking dog walker with six unruly dogs on separate leads, all pulling in different directions, and a man pushing a wheelchair with an old woman in it wearing Uggs on her swollen legs.

As I turn off the main path into the woods I'm struck by how quiet my footsteps become, from the noisy crunching of pebbles to the barely audible pat-pat-pat of my feet on the soft dirt path. My heart begins to pound faster and I know it's not because I've exerted myself too much. I'm approaching The Spot. I glance at my feet and see a used condom, trodden into the dirt by walkers' boots. How ironic, I think, forensic evidence, but not of my crime. I slow down and look around. There's no one here. I recognize the tree I pushed the man against, approach it, put my hand on the coarse bark. Why did I do it? Is this what midlife crisis is about? Indulging your every spon-taneous whim? Wanting to live dangerously, experience every extreme emotion before I'm dead? I do recognize the urgency, the anxiety I've carried within me since my mum died. We have so little time. I'll be the age when she died soon. What if the same gene sits dormant inside me, ready to pounce, the BRCA1/2 mutation that makes the bravest of women rush into surgery, mutilate their bodies in the hope that nothing will be left for the gene to attack? But does it give me the right to drag strangers into my private battle with time?

And what about him? Was he shocked or had he anticipated it? Did he want me? Perhaps he's gay and doesn't want sexual advances from a woman? I remember the moment he put his hands on my shoulders. I interpreted it as affection. But maybe he wanted to push me down onto my knees, expecting a blowjob? Another wave of embarrassment washes over me. I spot my sunglasses, lying in the dirt by the tree. Must have lost them yesterday and didn't even notice. I pick them up. One temple hangs down pathetically off its hinge, the lenses are scratched and dirty. No big deal, I didn't like them anyway. No big deal, I repeat to myself. It would be great if it was the answer to all my questions. But it isn't.

It's after 1 p.m. when I get to the office. I'm struck by the heavy, still air inside, as if the air-con is on the blink. Then I realize the mood of the place has changed from positive corporate joviality to apathetic gloom. Nobody cares any more. But I'm wrong. Claire comes into my office with her iPad and a grin on her face. She shows me her Facebook page and scrolls to a status update from Sarah. The first casualty of the cull strikes back, even before she's been officially made redundant. I skim through the long anti-corporate rant Basset Face has posted on her page. It's mostly about her, about all those years of loyal service she'd put into the company only to be thrown away, discarded like an old rag. All that talent wasted. All the skills, the expertise, the charm, unappreciated. She's completely lost it and the update will be her own undoing. Ah, the beauty of social media. One problem less for me.

The process of restructuring has started in earnest and I spend the rest of the afternoon in meetings. It's turning into a long and ugly summer. Telling people that they are no longer needed is a thankless task. I dread the intensity of it, the shock, the tears, followed by despondency. The cracks are already beginning to emerge within the management itself, unofficial cliques forming spontaneously. But the comfort the coteries seem to offer is just an illusion. Everyone is interested in saving their own position only, by whatever means necessary. I wonder if it's worth the fight, but then what would I do if I were to lose my job? Being Head of On-Air in a broadcast company doesn't really equip you for survival in the real world. Well, I could always become a consultant, a synonym for being superfluous and unemployable. To my surprise and disappointment I realize I'm missing James. He'd talk me through it, help me see the whole picture . . . Stop. What has happened to the self-sufficient, tough bitch Anna? I'm going to get through it on my own.

Twenty-three Days Earlier

I manage to dodge Bell's phone calls for a few days. I know she'd instantly sniff out that there is something strange going on in my life and I don't want to have to lie to her by omission. Being busy at work has its uses. But she is not easily put off by the sound of the answerphone and by Thursday I call her back. We arrange to meet for a quick bite at Dim T, a cheap and cheerful dim sum place in Charlotte Street. When I arrive she's already there, sipping hot sake. It's not going to be such a quick bite, after all.

I immediately launch into a predictable work moan. Actually, there's a lot to tell and she listens sympathetically. She lets me talk through three baskets of dim sum, which we share. When the fourth basket arrives she goes straight to the point.

'Are you seeing someone new?'

I look at her, pretending astonishment.

'Someone new? When would I have time for that?'

She just stares at me without a word. I finish off the sake and wave to the waitress for more. Bell is still staring at me.

'You've met someone.' It's a statement, not a question.

I sigh. She knows me too well.

'I'm not "seeing" anyone.' I make the inverted commas sign in the air.

'What's going on then?'

A new carafe of sake arrives and I fuss around it, pouring some for both of us, giving myself time to think what to say.

'I haven't technically met anyone, either.' It comes out lame.

'Oh God,' she says. 'Sounds like your rebound behaviour.'

She's always given me a hard time over this.

'It doesn't and it's not, Bell.' I try to sound authoritative, which is quite hard after so much sake. 'OK, I've met this guy, he is absolutely gorgeous, but it's not going to lead anywhere.'

'Where did you meet? What's his name?'

'You're worse than the Stasi.' I take another sip of sake.

'Because I care about you?'

She's upset now. I reach out and touch her hand.

'I'm sorry, I didn't mean it.'

'I know.' She pats my hand. 'Come on, spill.'

'There's nothing to spill, really. We've bumped into each other a couple of times on the Heath. I don't know who he is. I don't know his name. I only know he's gorgeous. End of story.'

'Or the beginning of one?'

'Nah. It's not going to happen, Bell, I told you.' I'm fed up with her interrogation and she knows it. 'Let's talk about you.'

She sighs and pours more sake.

'Not much to report. Well, that's not true, actually. I did meet someone on TangoWire. She's quite cute, makes me laugh, we ended up chatting through the night.'

'So what's the problem?'

'She lives in Moscow.'

'Oh . . . Her English good?'

'Moscow, Idaho.'

'Oh, another one from the other side of the pond.' Bell's penchant for American girls has caused her much heartache, not to mention the expense of long-distance air travel. I keep reminding her that 'I love you' means 'Have a good day' over there and not 'I want to live with you till I die'. But she doesn't listen.

'Yes, but she seems genuinely nice.'

'What do you do for a living in Moscow, Idaho?'

'She actually works at the uni.'

'They have a university there?'

'They do, quite a big one, apparently. She's a lecturer in anthropology.'

'So you did manage to have some proper conversation, besides your lesbian sex banter?'

'Oh, come on, it's a dating site, not a porn chat room.' She seems quite pissed off.

'I'm kidding, Bell.' I raise my hands in mock apology.

She smiles and we both finish the last of our sake in one gulp.

'More?' She points at the empty carafe.

'I'd love to, but I have a Friday at work to go through.' I look at the time on my iPhone. 'I have to get going.'

We part in front of the restaurant, Bell off to catch the number 73 bus from Oxford Street, while I hail a cab. I used to feel guilty about taking black cabs in London, but the value of my comfort has gone up proportionally to my wage packet.

Twenty-two Days Earlier

Friday used to be a light-hearted day at work, carrying the promise of a weekend filled with lovely laziness for singles or frantic catching up on family life for people with children. The light-hearted atmosphere has been destroyed successfully by the recent announcements. I drive to work with a heavy heart and arrive to find the car park filled with balloons. More balloons in the lift. And in the office. A laminated sheet on my desk explains everything. Today is Doughnut Day, a combined initiative of HR and Happy Workplace, which will lead to the Office Bake-Off next Friday. D-Day seems a rather unfortunate name, bringing to mind the high number of casualties in Normandy, perhaps a cruel joke by HR, who are now working on the number of casualties in our corporate cull. Oh well, happy D-Day, I think as I grab two greasy dough balls from an ornamental basket in the kitchen.

Back in my office, I look through the lists of staff in my departments. It's going to be a tough one. The editors are already unhappy with the looming change in the working hours. Some of them have been starting work late and finishing late, out of sync with the working hours of the producers, who need editors. The sound guys are up in arms because their ten-hour shifts will be scrapped, forcing them to go back to the regular five-day working week. The production team has been driven to distraction by the new tape-less delivery system that seems to grind to a halt every day, hours of digital output vanishing into computerized limbo. Oh, bring back the good old times of physical tape, the Digi-Beta, or even the clunky Beta-SP, a real object in your hand that could be delivered and be done with, that's the mantra of any producer over the age of thirty. That brings me to the producers, a profoundly insecure bunch, always complaining about something, sometimes as trivial as their desks being moved half an inch in the wrong direction. Any challenge, no matter how small, and off they go, pouting and whimpering like a kid with a grazed knee. And soon they will have to face the biggest challenge of their careers: having to justify their own existence. I look through the list: Gary, he'll do fine, a consummate corporate player; Caroline, a solid workhorse, she'll even deliver for the Bake-Off next Friday; Sarah, she's practically gone already; Kevin, lazy but talented, he may actually survive; Karen, big and noisy, always going on about herself, the jury's out; JJ, whose brain is fried by so much pot, he probably won't even see it coming; Sam, young and naive, may crack under pressure; Mina, a technical whizz who could leave anytime and would be snapped up immediately by someone who'd pay her much more; Dan, a stuttering graphics genius who should be writing a blog from Nepal instead of sitting at his desk; Linda, a vacuous and nasty bitch who'll stay, because nasty bitches always stay . . . Claire interrupts my reverie. The shoot next week. Do I want to be involved? Not really. But it's going to be at Pinewood Studios and the big shots are flying in especially from the States. In that case I'll be involved. My self-preservation instinct, developed painstakingly over the years, kicks in. I busy myself with looking through scripts and approving the crew for the shoot with Stephan, my favourite production manager. I'll have to make sure he doesn't become one of the casualties of the corporate cull.

Twenty-one Days Earlier

Saturday at last and I'm up at the crack of dawn, as usual. I throw my running clothes on while Wispa is watching me suspiciously from her bed. It's too early even for her. I have to coax her with a dog biscuit and off we go, down Fitzroy Park.

The Heath is empty and quiet, except for the birds who make their morning racket. Soft fog is hovering above the lake, a thin haze that makes everything look Photoshopped. I huff and puff up the hill, my breath visible in the air. Wispa is following me lazily. I get into the rhythm that works like meditation, putting me in the running trance, a hypnotic state of floating on endorphins, my body purring like a perfect machine. I reach the top of the hill and follow my usual route into the woods.

I'm just about to turn and look for Wispa when someone pushes me roughly from behind. I stumble forward, regain my balance and nearly run into a tree, my outstretched arms cushioning the impact. He's right behind me, I can smell him as he pushes me against the tree. The Dior Man, I'm sure of it – the mixture of sweat and freshly washed clothes makes my head swim. His hands are under my shirt, on my breasts; he fondles them briefly, then one of his hands slides down my belly, slick with sweat, into my jogging pants. I'm already wet when he touches me, his fingers probing urgently. I can feel his hard cock against my back. He slides my pants down and enters me roughly from behind. I stifle a cry. My face hits the tree and I can feel the sharp bark biting into my cheek as he fucks me, selfishly and relentlessly. I come just before he does, sticky wetness, his and mine, running down my thighs. I gasp as he withdraws and then he's gone.

I lean against the tree, unable to stand on my own. I slowly pull my pants up, then turn and slide down, my back against the tree trunk. I don't know how long I sit there, semi-conscious and spent. Someone jogs past me and I make an effort to get up, to look normal. Then I remember. Wispa. I stumble among the trees, looking for her, calling her name. She's gone. I trot back to the top of the hill but she's not there. I retrace my steps back to the woods, then continue towards Kenwood, calling her all the time. 'Have you seen my dog, a chocolate Labrador?' I ask a familiar-looking elderly couple in matching green anoraks, but they just stare at me suspiciously and shake their heads. Eventually I spot her at the bottom of the meadow, a brown speck in the green grass. I call her again, but she doesn't move. I run towards her, then slow down to a trot because I don't want to scare her any more. She is looking at me with big, round eyes. I call her and hold out my hand towards her. She slowly comes to me, her ears flat against her head, her tail between her legs. I pat her gently and kiss her head. 'Forgive me,' I whisper to her. We walk back, two wounded soldiers returning from a battlefield.

At home I go straight to the bathroom and turn the power shower on. I look at myself in the mirror. My face is dirty and I have a huge abrasion on my cheek, fresh blood congealing where the skin has been rubbed off. This will be fun to explain.

I dab the graze with some antiseptic and it stings like hell. I get into the shower and stand under the hot water, losing track of time. When the skin on my fingertips begins to crinkle I get out and rub myself with a fresh towel. My skin is pink and dry, but I feel dirty. Dirty, dirty girl.

The weekend slips through my fingers like sand. I dodge Bell's phone calls. I ignore Michael's messages. I sneak out to Tesco in the village and buy some ready-made pizzas, then spend most of the time watching a box set of *Game of Thrones*. Epic fantasy, that's exactly what I need to escape the reality I myself have created.

By Sunday evening I'm restless, with images of the Heath encounter relentlessly coming back to me. How do I feel about it? Dirty, a bit disgusted and very sexy. The memory of the Dior Man fucking me against that tree turns me on. I can exactly recall the smell, the sounds, the extreme eroticism of the situation. I masturbate right there in my sitting room, on my pristine Heal's sofa, some ludicrous *Game of Thrones* sex scene flickering on the flat screen of my TV.

As I snooze with the TV sound turned down, an unexpected thought starts buzzing around in my head like a persistent wasp. It makes me instantly awake. It *was* the Dior Man, wasn't it? Of course it was him, I recognized his smell, his touch, I'm sure. And if it wasn't? If it wasn't him, then was I raped? No, it was consensual, I wanted him. But . . . I wanted the Dior Man, not some stranger. I catch myself making the assumption that somehow the Dior Man is not a stranger. He is a stranger, but a stranger I know. A stranger I know: the oxymoron sounds like the title of a bad thriller. No, this is crazy. It was him, and that's the end of it. I have to stop thinking about it.

Wispa keeps avoiding me; she lies on her bed with her back turned pointedly towards me. She's pissed off with me, I know, but somehow I don't care as much as I would normally. I don't even feel like taking her out for a walk; she'll have to make do with short trips to the garden.

I dread Monday, having to deal with the Americans at work, having to deal with any people. And, of course, there's the nasty scab on my face and there will be questions. I decide to invent a spectacular fall while jogging, involving a crazy sausage dog and a fallen tree. Claire won't buy it, but even in her wildest dream she wouldn't guess how I really got it.

Nineteen Days Earlier

And then it's Monday morning and I drag myself out of bed, force down some black coffee and drive to work, the Monday-morning traffic making me want to scream. The scab itches on my cheek under the layers of Clinique foundation, concealer and powder. It's still as obtrusive as a rotten brushstroke on a masterpiece. Masterpiece being my face this morning, after a prolonged make-up session at home.

'Ouch,' says Claire, looking at my cheek when I walk into the office. She's wise enough not to ask questions.

'Too much wine,' I volunteer and instantly hate myself for it. Why volunteer a lie if she's not even asking?

She nods with understanding and goes back to her typing. She's good.

The morning drags on with the first meeting with the Americans. They are mildly amused by my story of the crazy sausage dog that ran into my feet and made me fall flat on my face, catching a fallen tree trunk with my cheek. They are impressed I go jogging every day and suggest I sue the owner of the dog, bless their litigious American hearts. As the meeting spills into the lunch break, I begin to feel unwell. I plough through the afternoon presentation, trying to ignore alarming twinges in my body. By the final PowerPoint slide my lower abdomen feels really strange. I excuse myself from the meeting and call the Marie Stopes Clinic in Fitzrovia. They can fit me in tomorrow at 9 a.m. Damn, the shoot at Pinewood. The sensible part of me tells me I should really be there. But the same sensible part tells me to see a doctor. A missed opportunity to collect some brownie points, but it can't be helped, I decide. The Americans will have to fend for themselves tomorrow morning.

Eighteen Days Earlier

'I can't really see anything unusual, but let's do a smear just in case,' says the gynaecologist, an older Indian woman with a patient face and delicate hands. 'The pain you've described has been most likely caused by a working cyst on your ovary. In most cases the cysts are harmless and disappear on their own. But if the pain persists, do come back to see me.'

Once I'm fully clothed and back on a chair by her desk she asks me kindly, 'Is there anything else?'

I'm grateful for the way in.

'There is, actually. I've had unprotected sex with a stranger.'

'And when was that, my child?'

She doesn't make a judgement, she's not shocked, she just asks a question. I don't mind her calling me 'my child', it actually makes me feel a little tearful. She listens patiently and then suggests I go to the Sexual Health Centre at St Bart's. I can book an appointment online or just drop in. And they can do all the tests straight away.

The Centre is bright, efficient and full of women like me. I'm surprised and I don't quite know why. Surely I haven't been expecting a bunch of seedy-looking slappers with matted hair and no teeth? I'm seen quite quickly by a young female doctor. I have a feeling I may have seen her somewhere before, but I can't place her. She's friendly and professional and she doesn't beat around the bush.

'Any chance of unwanted pregnancy?'

'No, I'm on the Pill.'

She nods and marks something on the form.

'We'll need to test you for STIs, primarily chlamydia, gonorrhoea, trichomoniasis, herpes . . .'

'HIV?'

'Well, it's a bit early for a test. But if you're really concerned you could take PEPSE, that's post-exposure prophylaxis, a four-week course of HIV medication you can take after unprotected sex to reduce the chance of becoming HIV positive.' She looks at her notes. 'You're just within the seventy-two hours' time limit. Otherwise you should come back for a test. It can show positive as early as two weeks after infection, but HIV infection cannot be excluded until twelve weeks after exposure.'

I feel very hot and a bit faint. I decide to opt out of PEPSE, but make a note in my iPhone to come back for a blood test in twelve weeks. She asks if I've been vaccinated against Hep A and B, then takes a blood sample and sends me off to the toilet to do a swab. Quick, efficient, matter-of-fact. When I return, she smiles at the top of my head. I wonder if she does it to avoid the sight of the scab on my cheek.

'I'd like you to wait in the waiting area for the results of the immediate tests. If we think you need treatment for anything, we will give it to you before you go. The other results will be texted to you as soon as we have them.'

She closes her file and shows me to the door. I go back to the waiting room and sit down among other patients, avoiding eye contact with everybody.

If I survive this, I think, I'm going to be a nun for the rest of my life.

By the time I get to work it's far too late to drive out to Pinewood. Too bad, especially as, Claire tells me, a legendary producer from the US is there, overseeing the shoot. No brownie points and no autograph for me this time. But there is plenty of chaos produced by Cadenca Global to keep me busy for the rest of the day.

I get home late, totally exhausted. I normally enjoy work, the corporate hustle and bustle, enriched with human emotions, ambitions and jealousies. But the last two weeks have been unbearable, the heavy weight of the looming restructure taking all life and colour out of daily routines. Throw in a crazy Hampstead Heath encounter and my whole world seems out of kilter, an unsafe and unpleasant place. Would having James around help? I pick up the phone, then put it down. No, I decide, I have no space for teddy bears, however sweet, in my life.

I don't feel like going for the evening walk with Wispa. She's disappointed when I let her out to the back garden, but she'll have to live with it for tonight. I only hope she had a good walk with Nicole earlier in the day. I take a long bath, then dig an old tub of ice cream out of the freezer. It's going to be one of those nights. I'm just settling on the sofa when my phone rings. A number I don't recognize. Probably someone offering me a free upgrade or a new mobile. I ignore it, but a few minutes later it rings again. The upgrade people normally wait at least a day before they call back. I answer it.

'Oh, hi.' A male voice, hesitant, polite. 'Are you the owner of a chocolate Labrador named Wispa?'

Oh shit, Wispa. I rush to the back door and open it. She's not in the garden.

'Yes,' I say breathlessly to the phone. 'Did something happen to her?'

'No, she's fine.' The voice sounds reassuring now. 'She's here with me, I found her wandering Highgate Hill, looking a bit distressed. Found your phone number on her name tag.'

A wave of relief washes over me. The guy offers to drop her off and I give him my address. He rings my doorbell five minutes later, Wispa happily wagging her tail by his side. I hesitate, not knowing whether I should invite him in, but he makes it easy for me, saying he is on his way to pick up his daughter from a piano lesson and he's already running late.

'I'm so grateful. I have no idea how she managed to escape from the garden. It's never happened before.'

'Dogs and children,' he says with a smile and I notice he's quite handsome. He has dark, curly hair, pale skin and strikingly green eyes with long, dark lashes. 'We could spend hours swapping tales of joy and woe. Actually,' he hesitates for a second, 'why don't you pop round for a drink sometime? You and your partner, I mean,' he adds awkwardly. 'My wife and I would be delighted. We live just round the corner.'

I say yes, it would be a pleasure, and we agree to arrange a date by phone as we already have each other's phone numbers, thanks to Wispa's tag. His name is Tom, by the way, Tom Collins, like the cocktail. His dad loved gin and his mum lemonade, he tells me with a grin. I close the door and have a serious chat with Wispa. Of course it's far too late to tell her off for running away, she wouldn't be able to connect the events and draw a conclusion; she's a dog, after all, not a child. And it's my fault for leaving her out in the garden for too long. But how did she manage to escape? I find a torch in the cupboard under the stairs and venture out into the dark garden. In the shaky beam of the torch the walls and the fence look fine. I'll have another look in the morning. I decide to give Wispa a rawhide bone as a peace offering and settle with her in front of the TV. I don't know what I would do if she got lost.

Seventeen Days Earlier

The results are back and I don't have chlamydia, gonorrhoea, herpes or any of the other STDs with long and scary names. The only test I'll still have to do in three months is the HIV, but I suddenly feel purged and elated. I want to celebrate, to tell the world, but 'I'm STD-free' doesn't really have the right celebratory ring to it. I call Michael instead and invite him to dinner 'somewhere really nice'. My treat. He's free and delighted to accept. By fluke I get a table at Ottolenghi in Islington because someone has just cancelled tonight's reservation. It's an 8.30 slot, so I'll have time to give Wispa a proper walk before I go out tonight. I feel lucky, not only because I've managed to get in on a whim to Ottolenghi.

Over a growing number of beautiful small dishes on our table I tell Michael about the stress at work. He listens sympathetically, nibbling on roasted aubergine with feta yoghurt and seared yellow fin tuna with soy and ginger sauce. I never have an opportunity to reciprocate his good listening, as he never complains about his job. He runs his own web design company, and I'm sure he'd have plenty to moan about if he chose to, but he never does. Our grilled quail with smoked chilli chocolate sauce arrives and I have to stop my saga of corporate woe. The food is simply too good to taint with everyday misery.

'Sometimes I think I should just quit and start my own business, I don't know, garden landscaping or selling hand-knitted teddy bears on the Internet, anything but TV and media.'

'No, hon, you should sit tight and wait until they make you redundant. And then hire a good redundancy lawyer and make them double their offer.'

'Sounds like a good plan.' I scoop a bite of black-peppered tofu with saffron dashi onto my fork.

'I'm serious, darling. Nobody just quits in television. You always manoeuvre yourself into the most lucrative position to be pushed from.'

'Did you get pushed?' I have never asked him why he left his full-time job and started his own business.

'Of course I did, although it may have looked quite innocent to the naked eye.'

'Did you make some money out of it?'

'Not enough, darling, not enough.' Michael takes a sip of his wine. 'But there are other compensations, you know. Like being able to take a stroll in the park in the middle of the day, when everyone else is at work, for instance. Well, not everyone.' He has a mischievous grin on his face now.

'You didn't!' I exclaim a bit too loud for the intimate space of the restaurant and get some curious glances.

'Yes, I did.'

'You met someone,' I whisper, the leftover bits of our delicious dinner suddenly forgotten.

'He met me, to be precise.'

'Enough riddles, hon, I want the whole story.'

'Well . . . I was sitting in a beautiful spot, reading the new Ian McEwan book—'

'Where?'

'Richmond, darling.'

'What were you doing in Richmond? It's miles away from your house.'

Michael looks at me with mock reproach. 'Do you want to hear what happened or not?'

'I do, sorry.'

'So I'm sitting there under a tree with Ian McEwan, when suddenly this rather gorgeous man appears out of nowhere and asks me if he can sit next to me, as apparently I hog the best spot in the whole park. Considering that the park is nearly four square miles, it's quite an achievement to stumble upon the best spot without even trying, so I let him know I'm happy to share my precious spot with him. He unfolds his blanket, chatting rather pleasantly all the time, drawing me away from Ian and into a conversation with him.'

A waitress clears our table and offers some dessert. I quickly choose a coffee pecan financier with maple cream for us to share, keen to hear the rest of Michael's story.

'He offers to share his blanket with me as the ground is getting a bit chilly. I move to his blanket and . . . we cuddle a bit.'

'Cuddle?!' I'm too loud again.

'Yes, darling, cuddle. Light petting, really, nothing more.'

Our dessert arrives and it silences us. We savour the nutty texture, slightly crisp on the top and edges, soft and moist inside, luxuriating in the maple cream. When it's all gone, I nudge Michael to continue his story.

'So you "cuddled" . . .' I make inverted commas in the air.

'Believe it or not, we did.' He's slightly annoyed by me teasing him. 'Not all gay men have the urge to jump into the bushes with the first stranger that comes along. And to be honest, once

I start talking to someone and he turns out nice, interesting, engaging, once I get to know him a bit, I don't really feel like a quick handjob. I actually prefer warmth and intimacy to the thrill of the unknown.' Michael pauses. 'Perhaps I'm getting old . . .'

He looks sad and I feel a bit guilty about teasing him earlier.

'I do miss what I had with Phil. The companionship, camaraderie, love. I miss having a partner, Anna.'

'I'm sorry.' I reach out and touch his hand. I see his eyes glaze with tears, then he straightens up, waves at the waitress and orders two espressos. He knows we both like to finish our dinners with a small injection of caffeine.

'So, at the end we exchange business cards – imagine doing that in the dark in the middle of Richmond Park – and go our separate ways.'

'Will you see him again?'

'I don't know. But I do know I'm ready for another relationship.'

As I drive back home along Holloway Road I think about Michael and what he said. About the threshold of familiarity which, once crossed, makes it impossible to engage in anonymous, impulsive sex. Michael is looking for a relationship, someone he can trust, be with on a daily basis. What am I looking for? I have pushed away a man who wanted to start a family with me, and I don't mean just teddy bears. James did talk about having kids occasionally and perhaps that was the trigger that made me want to distance myself from him, to run away. Do I want a family? Do I want kids? As hard as I search for an answer within myself, I can't find it. I simply don't know.

When I get home Wispa greets me with a pure joy that compensates for the lack of any real human emotion in my life. Although it's late, she wangles another walk out of me. I need to walk off the espresso anyway.

We bounce down Swain's Lane, our energy disturbing the stillness of the cemetery statues. Wispa leads happily, her tail wagging. The silence is suddenly interrupted by the buzzing of my phone. I forgot I left it on silent. I look at the screen. It's Bell. There are a number of unanswered calls from her, which I didn't hear. It's late for her, so it must be something important.

'What's up, babe?'

'Why aren't you at home? I've been ringing your landline for hours. Where are you?' She's really wound up.

'I had dinner with Michael. And now I'm walking Wispa.'

'Now? It's midnight!'

'What's wrong, Bell?'

'I've been worried about you.'

'Why?'

'Because I couldn't get hold of you.' She sounds almost hysterical.

'I'm fine. What's going on, Bell? Do you want me to come over?'

'No, no, no.' I can hear her take a couple of deep breaths. 'It's fine. It's just . . . this woman has been attacked on the Heath, and I got so worried, because of you and your jogs with Wispa at all sorts of hours, and then I couldn't get hold of you . . .'

'Slow down. What happened?'

'There's been a rape on the Heath.' I feel a cold chill run through my body. 'I heard it on the news.'

'That's awful, Bell. When did it happen?'

'Sometime today, I think, I'm not sure. I was so worried when you didn't answer your phone.'

'Oh, sweetie, I'm so sorry. I didn't hear it ring. I'm fine. I'm walking home now. And I'll text you when I get there.'

'OK.' She sounds calmer now. 'Go straight home and lock the door.'

'I will, I promise.'

I call Wispa and walk back, suddenly aware of the impenetrable darkness on both sides of the road. When I get home and lock the door, I realize how tense I've been. I text Bell and open my laptop. I find the news almost straight away.

Camden police are appealing for witnesses and information following a sexual assault on Hampstead Heath this morning. The victim, a thirty-two-year-old woman, was attacked while she was jogging in the area of Parliament Hill sometime between 06.45 a.m. and 07.30 a.m. The suspect is believed to have followed the woman from Holly Lodge Estate, before pushing her to the ground and assaulting her. He then fled in the direction of Gospel Oak.

The suspect is described as being a male of Mediterranean appearance, 5ft 8–5ft 10, wearing a dark T-shirt and light-grey tracksuit bottoms. Anyone with information is requested to contact DI Brown of Camden CID on . . .

I close my laptop and sit motionlessly in the darkness of my sitting room. Poor woman. I'm paralysed with fear just imagining what she must've gone through. A frightening thought occurs to me. Bell is right. It could've been me. Suddenly I'm covered in cold sweat. What if it *was* me? My weekend doubt hits me again and it's even more alarming than the first time. What if what I considered a consensual encounter was some kind of a testing ground for a rapist? Is it possible at all that the Dior Man is the rapist? Have I, with my reckless behaviour, created a monster? He liked the taste of it with me and now he can't stop and attacks other women? I open the laptop again and frantically look for more information about the attack. The victim, although they don't reveal her identity, could've been me. Young, probably professional, jogging in the park before her commute to work. But the attacker . . . It definitely wasn't the Dior Man, unless he'd completely changed his appearance. And his dress sense . . . light-grey tracksuit bottoms, yuk, I bet he wouldn't be seen dead in a pair of those. My own flippancy shocks me. But somehow it helps me to shake off the awful feeling of suspicion and guilt. It's not him.

Fifteen Days Earlier

It's been nearly a week since I last jogged on the Heath. I have a legitimate excuse – it's been a hellish week at work. I get to the office early and work late every day, barely staying on top of the massive tsunami of change that is slowly gathering momentum under the watchful eye of Cadenca Global. The Friday Bake-Off, cheerfully orchestrated by HR and Happy Workplace, is a distraction no one wants and no one needs. The few cakes, baked by some mad souls who still have spare time and energy to be wasted in the kitchen, sit on the table in the main conference room, barely nibbled on. There will be no Bake-Off winners this Friday, because everyone is a loser right now. A new structure is being put in place, new job descriptions drawn up and approved, and the painstaking process of elimination is just about to begin. For some reason I'm reminded of a Borg cube from *Star Trek*, with all the superfluous drones being ejected into space, their place immediately filled by the newly assimilated useful entities. Resistance is futile, that's for sure. I have to do my job, while trying to prepare the most advantageous exit strategy for myself. Bell, a devoted Trekkie who infected me with a passion for the indestructible TV series, would be proud of me.

Bell – I need to see her, to apologize once again for giving her such a fright when I didn't answer my phone on the day of the Hampstead rape. I've been scouring the Internet for any more news of the assault, but there is none. I wonder if the woman is OK, whether there is an investigation into the incident and who is running it. I also think that I can't stay away from the Heath forever. I miss it.

I arrange to meet Bell in YumYum in Stoke Newington, the best Thai restaurant outside South-East Asia, some Stokie locals say. True, the food is rather good and the atmosphere appropriately exotic. When I arrive, Bell is already there, sitting barefoot Asian style on the floor by a low table. I plonk myself down opposite her, grateful she's already ordered passion fruit mojitos for both of us.

'Just caught the end of happy hour,' she says proudly.

'Well done, you should've ordered two each.'

'Things that bad at work?'

I make a face and take a big gulp of my mojito. It tastes divine.

'Look, I'm sorry I overreacted the other day about the Heath thing. For one crazy moment I thought it might be you . . .' Bell shakes her head.

'No, don't be silly, it should be me apologizing for not answering your calls. I do appreciate you were worried about me.'

'Well, that's what good friends are for.' She clinks my glass. 'You haven't bumped into your Heath guy lately?'

'Nah, haven't been out jogging for a week. I can feel the flab already building up.' I pat my stomach, hoping she'll drop the subject. Luckily a waitress appears to take our order.

'How is your Moscow girl?'

'Good, really good.' Bell beams at me happily. Oh God, I think, she's fallen for it again. And, as if on cue, she says what I've been dreading to hear. 'Actually, I've been thinking I might go and see her.'

'In Idaho?'

'No, we've been talking about meeting up in Vancouver. It's only a stone's throw for her and I've always wanted to go there.'

'Vancouver sounds lovely,' I say, carefully avoiding mentioning her virtual girlfriend.

'Vancouver is lovely,' she says, sounding hurt. 'But I'm talking to my best friend, not TripAdvisor. You haven't even asked me what her name is.'

'What is her name?' I don't want yet another argument on the subject of Bell's girlfriends.

'It doesn't matter. You think it's all nonsense, don't you?'

'No, Bell, I don't. I'm happy for you. I just don't want you to get hurt again. You don't even know her.'

'But I do. I've spent more hours chatting to her in a week than an average couple spends talking to each other in a year. That's what long-distance relationships are about. Talking and listening. When was the last time you really listened to one of your boyfriends?'

Careful, I think, let's not get provoked into a full-blown row. The waitress saves the day again, bringing our food. We tuck in to our Thai green curry with king prawns and lemongrass chicken, savouring the subtle combination of spices, sweetness and salt, our girlfriend/boyfriend tiff forgotten for the rest of the evening. I know the subject will surface again, but I'm relieved it's not going to happen tonight. And I'm glad Bell has let the subject of 'the Heath guy' drop so easily.

But I can't stop thinking about it. Having dropped Bell off at her place, I drive home, allowing myself to form the question I've been avoiding for a week. Could the Dior Man, despite my conviction to the contrary, based mostly on the colour of his track bottoms, be the rapist? Could he be the man who attacked a young woman who was jogging on the Heath one unlucky morning? Was it him? Should I be going to the police, I ask myself, as I crawl in traffic along ever-congested Green Lanes, watching men standing in front of Turkish kebab shops. No, it can't be him. He doesn't look Mediterranean and, according to the police description, the rapist is medium height. The Dior Man is taller. But how can I be so sure he's innocent? I know nothing about him.

It can't be him because he's not a rapist. We had rough sex in a public place, but it wasn't rape. It was instigated by me, after all. Could I have flicked some unknown, violent switch inside his psyche? I feel I'm going round in circles, asking myself the same questions, again and again. And always arriving at the same conclusion: it's not him. It can't be him. I don't want it to be him.

There is nowhere left to park in my street, the usual Friday-night car-owner nightmare. I drive round the block looking for a space. Nothing. I make another loop, poised like a panther to pounce on a freshly freed parking space. Still nothing. I have a choice of either driving out further, towards Highgate Hill, or doing another kerb-crawling circle. Perhaps when people start leaving the pubs something will become free. I stop in the middle of the street, undecided.

A sudden knock on my window makes me jump. I see a man leaning in, smiling. He's saying something I don't understand. My heart is pounding and my foot moves instinctively towards the accelerator. Then I look at the man again and recognize him. It's the guy who found Wispa. Tim Something. I buzz down the window.

'Hi, I'm so sorry I startled you,' he says with a sheepish grin. 'It's Tom, I found your dog the other night.'

'Of course! Hi, Tom, sorry, I was miles away . . .' I feel silly for overreacting.

'No, it's my fault, I shouldn't have knocked on your window like that.' He actually looks cute in his embarrassment.

'Let's forget about it,' I laugh. 'No harm done.'

'I was just doing my late-night Tesco run.' He raises his hand with a pint of milk in it. 'We always seem to run out of milk in the middle of the night.'

'I know the feeling.' I nod with understanding although I don't. I never run out of milk because I never have it.

'Actually, we're having a bit of a get-together tomorrow night, just a few friends from the neighbourhood, nothing fancy . . . would you like to join us? I know it's last minute . . .'

Why not, I think. It's not like I have a better offer for the Saturday night.

'I'd love to. But . . . can I bring Wispa with me?'

'Wispa?' He seems confused.

'My dog.'

'Oh yes, of course, do bring her, the kids will be thrilled. Seven thirtyish? We're just round the corner.'

He gives me the address, we exchange goodnights and he walks off carrying the milk like a trophy. Funny man. I wonder what his wife is like. Miraculously, a car right in front of me pulls out, leaving a prime parking space just waiting for me. Good karma, I think, I must have done something right today. The good karma feeling continues as I take off my make-up later on and notice the scab on my face has faded considerably. Healing like a dog, my grandma used to say.

Fourteen Days Earlier

It's true, their house is literally round the corner from mine. Wispa seems to know the way and she's first by their front door, her tail wagging. I ring the bell and Tom opens the door. He looks more handsome than I remember, his curly black hair pushed back with some gel, a dark shadow of stubble on his chin. He seems genuinely pleased to see me as I push a bottle of Blanquette de Limoux into his hands. Wispa's already inside – I can hear kids' voices cooing over her. He leads me to the sitting room, a huge space with French windows overlooking the garden. There are a few people already there: an older couple I've seen around in the High Street, a slim young man with long hair and the lost look of someone who's done too many drugs, a tall woman with strikingly red lips and a couple of kids, a boy and a girl, fussing over Wispa, who's gladly soaking up all the attention. Tom introduces everybody and it turns out we are all neighbours. The conversation is about tree pollarding, the latest craze to have been plaguing our neighbourhood.

'It's barbaric and it should be banned,' says the woman with red lips, whose name is Fiona.

'It's the wrong time of the year for it anyway, it should be done between November and February, not now,' booms David, the older guy. His wife and the young guy remain silent. I feel they are expecting me to chip in on the subject of pollarding. I'm frantically trying to think of something to say when Tom's voice saves me.

'Anna, I'd like you to meet my wife, Samantha.'

I turn, relieved I don't have to suffer the pollarding discussion any more, take one look at Samantha and freeze in horror. I shake her hand and she smiles and says something. Shit. Shit. Shit. It's the nice doctor from the Sexual Health Centre at St Bart's. I'm mortified. She doesn't show any sign of recognizing me and I muster all my wits to follow what she's saying. It's about Wispa and she tells me how much her children would love to have a dog but how impossible it would be to keep one. I know she's already placed me on her clinic couch and I'm grateful to her for giving me time to recover. I slowly regain my composure and we happily banter about dogs and children for a while. Then she moves on to tend to other guests and I'm left on my own, shaken and ashamed. I excuse myself and find my way to the loo. I lock the door and stare at myself in the mirror. What does she think of me? Is she going to tell her husband? 'Oh, that nice lady who you helped with her dog the other night is a sex addict who shags strangers on the Heath.' She actually wouldn't know it happened on the Heath, but I add it for dramatic effect. Of course she's not going to tell her husband, doctor–patient privilege and all that, but I'm not sure if it doesn't apply only to crime dramas. I bet in reality doctors gossip about their patients all the time. Maybe she's telling all her guests about me right now: 'Anna is an interesting case, a nymphomaniac, but you'll be pleased to know she's currently free of STDs.' I have to stop this nonsense, pull myself together and go back to the party. I splash some cold water on my wrists, take a deep breath and unlock the bathroom door. When I get back to the sitting room, everyone is busy greeting new guests, Francesca and Simon, an attractive couple who instantly charm the whole party. I'm relieved they've taken all the limelight. It turns out Simon is a bit of a celebrity, a business genius who has made millions in advertising. Francesca and Simon have a house on The Bishops Avenue, David tells me in a hushed, reverent voice. Oh, real millionaires, I think, and take another good look at them. They present themselves rather well, I have to admit, a mixture of extreme confidence and charm giving them the well-pampered, glamorous air of people from another dimension. Simon regales everyone with a tale about Michael Birch, the co-founder of the social networking website Bebo, who sold it in 2008 to AOL for 850 million dollars and bought it back recently for just 1 million.

'This is what I call a bargain,' Simon says, as if it was something one could pick up in Oxfam. 'And he actually tweeted everyone about it.' He's clearly amused by the story and everyone chuckles in unison.

I empty my glass of Prosecco and quickly pour myself another one. Thank God for tweeting millionaires, but I still can't stop feeling awful about the secret I now share with Samantha. Thankfully, Simon has moved on to Rupert Murdoch and tells everyone with glee how he forked out over 500 million pounds for MySpace in 2005 only to get totally creamed by Facebook and sell it six years later for the measly sum of 35 million. Everyone finds it hilarious.

'And then there was Friends Reunited, of course . . .' continues Simon.

I've had enough of social networking investment fiascos and I go to the kitchen in search of nibbles. I find Alden, the spaced-out young man, feeding Wispa big chunks of roast chicken. He's quite apologetic when he sees me, but I let him off for overfeeding my dog, making him laugh with the story of Wispa's monstrous appetite. He turns out to be quite sweet and isn't stoned at all. He's an aspiring film director, freelancing as a director's assistant, a harsh reality job that most aspiring directors have to do to survive. He met Tom and Samantha on the Greek island of Skopelos, only to discover that they were neighbours in Highgate. Samantha is a doctor (don't I know it!) and Tom has a dental practice in Soho. They've been really nice to him, looking after his cats when he's away on shoots and feeding him when he's around. Alden's girlfriend sings in a band and is away touring quite a lot, but I must come to her next gig at XOYO in Shoreditch. He'll get some freebie tickets for me. Then he asks about my work and actually listens when I tell him about the recent upheaval. I'd normally find him quite attractive, a charming little boy locked in the lean, almost ascetic body of a young man, but I realize I'm completely switched off to the charms of other men at the moment. Despite my evident obsession with the Dior Man I actually quite enjoy talking to Alden. We both feel reluctant to go back to the sitting room, but eventually we decide it would be impolite to stay in the kitchen any longer. I'm suddenly keen to join the rest, as I'm struck by the thought that Samantha will have noticed Alden and I are missing and probably thinks we're shagging on the kitchen table. It's paranoia, I know, but in every paranoid thought there must be a grain of truth.

Thirteen Days Earlier

It's Sunday morning, but I wake up with a sense of purpose. It's my Garden Sunday, one of the rare occasions when I put a bit of time and energy into the jungle at the back of my house. I know very little about gardening and I choose not to do it on my own. I have Pia, the Danish gardener extraordinaire, come to help me once a month. I know it's not enough for my overgrown garden, but it's better than nothing. Even with one day every month Pia manages to do wonders with all the plants and bushes, the names of which I don't even know. Garden Sunday is also a day all my friends know I'm at home and they can pop in any time, providing they bring a bottle of Prosecco with them.

Pia arrives at 10 a.m. on the dot with a precise plan of action in her head. I'm sent off with a shopping list to the garden centre in Ally Pally and when I come back the work's already started. I feel a bit superfluous standing over Pia's shoulder, so I make myself useful by brewing some fresh coffee for both of us. Pia, before she became a professional gardener, used to run her own garage. She knows as much about cars as she knows about plants; she's one of those women who's perceived as an immediate threat by men because she encroaches on their field of expertise. She's not a lesbian, although she'd make a fabulous one – or so I'm told by Bell, who never misses an opportunity to see Pia and I bet will turn up at some point today. She's rather petite, with a mane of curly red hair and Pre-Raphaelite looks. You wouldn't think she'd have enough strength to pull a single weed out, but I've seen her handle a sixty-litre bag of compost as if it were a packet of crisps.

Wispa adores Pia and she's busy helping her, digging holes wherever Pia puts her tools down. Over mugs of steaming coffee I tell Pia about Wispa's escape the other night.

'How did she do it?' Pia's looking at the fence.

'Actually, I have no idea.' I'm annoyed I haven't thought about it earlier.

'Let's find it and fix it, so she won't run away again.'

We go along the garden fence, looking for a missing panel or a hole she may have dug. Everything looks intact.

'Could she have jumped over?' asks Pia.

'Just look at her, she wouldn't be able to jump over two bricks stacked on top of each other, and I mean Lego bricks.' I know I'm unfair to my little puppy.

'So how did she do it?'

We take another good look at the fence, the back wall, the overgrown shed.

'There's no way she could've done it,' says Pia categorically. Those Danes, they don't beat around the bush.

'But she did escape and Tom caught her in the main street.'

'Well, maybe you should ask Tom, then.' Pia puts her empty mug down and picks up her edging shears. As far as she's concerned, there is no way Wispa could have escaped from the garden, so there is no problem. But it gets me thinking. How on earth did my fat little sausage manage to get out of a garden surrounded by a solid fence and adjoining gardens, and end up in the street? A doorbell interrupts my puzzling over the issue.

It's Sue, my old friend, a production manager known, because of her extraordinary organizational skills, as *Sue*-perwoman. Her work stories are always outrageous and, indeed, she doesn't disappoint this time either, launching straight away into the story of her recent shoot in Beirut. Apparently the cameraman, a burly gay guy named Hank, was obsessed with grinder.

'A power tool?'

'Not a grinder, Grnder,' she corrects me. 'A geosocial networking application.'

'What the hell is that?'

'It's an application you get on your phone and it lets you locate other gay men within close proximity – from the nearest to the farthest away.'

I suddenly feel totally technologically challenged, like one of those old ladies who refuse to learn how to use the Internet because, as they claim, 'it would waste their time'.

'How do you keep up with all this apps shit?'

'I don't. I just keep an eye on other people. Talking of which . . . I think I saw James the other day.'

'My James?' Ooops, an unfortunate slip of the tongue. 'You mean my ex?'

'Well, I hope he's your ex, because he had a rather dishy blonde on his arm . . .'

'Really? He's dating someone?' I realize I'm not upset; on the contrary, I'm rather relieved I don't have to feel guilty about dumping him any more. 'Good for him.'

We're interrupted by the doorbell. It's Michael, followed by Alden, whom I invited yesterday on the spur of the moment. I haven't mentioned my Garden Sunday to Tom and Samantha. I'm still getting used to the idea of someone knowing something so intimate about me, without even being close to me. My doorbell rings again and I decide it's time to open the first bottle of Prosecco.

Twelve Days Earlier

Monday morning and I think I'm ready to go back to the Heath. Wispa watches me in disbelief when I put my jogging gear on. Eventually she gets up from her bed, stretches herself and goes to wait for me by the front door. I open the door and can't believe my eyes. There is a bouquet of red roses lying on my doorstep. No wrapping paper, no card, just beautiful, long-stemmed, lush flowers. All fifteen of them. I go back in, find a suitable crystal vase and put them in water. I leave the vase on the kitchen table, thinking I'll find a better place for it when I get home in the evening.

Both Wispa and I are a bit rusty and it takes us a while to get into our stride. We're turning off into Fitzroy Park when another jogger overtakes me, slows down and turns towards me. It's Tom. Wispa greets him like a long-lost friend. What a coincidence.

'Do you mind if I join you?'

'Not at all. Although we might be a bit too slow for you. I haven't jogged for a week and I can feel it. We both can.' I look at Wispa, who is panting happily. Tom laughs and I notice how white and straight his teeth are. Then I remember he's a dentist.

'I really enjoyed your little get-together, thanks for inviting me over.'

'It was a pleasure to have you. Both Sam and I are very excited to have a new friend in the village.'

Somehow I can't imagine Samantha being excited about having me in close proximity to her house and husband, but I let it pass.

We enter the Heath and it's clear Tom is planning to follow me along the whole route. I find myself annoyed by it. As nice as he is, I somehow don't fancy his company. I feel quite possessive about my loop, as if he's encroaching on my own, private territory. When we get to the top of the hill I turn left instead of the usual right and trot towards Parliament Hill instead of Kenwood. I feel his presence somehow would ruin the intimacy of my usual route. I want it all to myself and I don't want him there. Just in case I bumped into the Dior Man? I question my motives, but whatever they are I feel irritated by him. He doggedly follows me, seemingly oblivious to my change of mood. Even worse, he catches up with me and wants to chat.

'Have you heard about the poor girl who got attacked? It must have been somewhere here.' He waves in the direction of Parliament Hill.

'Yes, I heard, how awful.' I pretend I'm out of breath to cut the conversation short. But he continues.

'And it happened in the morning, when there were plenty of people around, joggers like you and me . . .'

He's not going to get another word out of me. He waits for me to respond then adds, 'Terrible. They should have more wardens patrolling the area.'

I nod in agreement and huff and puff theatrically to get him to shut up. But he doesn't.

'If you ever need a running mate, just to feel safer, do give me a shout. Sam doesn't really jog, she's more of a gym girl.

I'd be happy to be your jogging escort . . .' He laughs and I grunt noncommittally.

He gets the message and we jog back in silence. When we say goodbye at the top of Fitzroy Park a thought occurs to me: is he the sender of the mystery roses? Nah, I reject the idea, he would've mentioned it by now. The guy is a talker, he wouldn't be able to keep schtum about it for so long.

I realize I'm really pissed off with him. I feel as if he's intruded into my private sanctuary. At the same time I know it's completely unreasonable to feel this way, it was just the natural gesture of a friendly neighbour. He's a nice man, I tell myself, don't behave as if he's taken your favourite toy. I try to reason with myself, but I feel my bad mood has settled in for the day. Even the sight of the beautiful flowers on my kitchen table doesn't manage to lift my mood.

But as I drive to work my thoughts go back to the anonymous gift. Were they meant for me? Most likely, as I found them on my doorstep. It couldn't have been a wrong address blooper by Interflora because clearly they had been delivered by hand by an individual person. That leaves two questions: who are they from and what do they mean? A quick check on my iPad while I'm stuck in traffic: fifteen roses apparently mean 'I'm sorry'. Who is sorry and what for?

The roses are forgotten as soon as I get to work. Some arse-hole has parked his banger in my parking space and the security guys take ages to sort out an alternative place for my car. As soon as I settle in my office, Karen sticks her head round the door.

'Can I have a quick word?'

'Sure.' I need this like a broken heel on my stiletto. 'Come on in.'

She carefully closes the door and settles in one of the chairs on the opposite side of my desk.

'How can I help you, Karen?'

'It's about JJ.' She's on the verge of tears. 'He stalks me.'

I look at her in disbelief. JJ? The guy who is so stoned most of the time he doesn't know a trailer from a camper van?

'He stalks you. How?'

'He keeps calling me all the time on my mobile.'

'What does he say?'

'Nothing. It's just these terrifying silent calls, from a withheld number.'

'How do you know it's him?'

'Oh, I know . . .' She wipes a tear away. 'It's the way he stares at me all the time in the office.'

As far as I know, JJ stares mostly into space. Perhaps Karen gets into his line of vision accidentally.

'Are you sure?'

'Yes, I am.' She lets out a sob. That's all I need now.

'What would you like me to do?'

'I don't know,' she wails back.

'OK, Karen, let me tell you what we'll do.' I speak softly, as if to a small child. 'First of all, you block all withheld number calls to your number. I'm sure your mobile provider offers the service and it's instantaneous and quite cheap. If this doesn't help, I'll get HR to talk to you and offer some advice. Does that sound OK to you?'

'Yes,' she says, dabbing her eyes with a crumpled tissue. 'Thank you.'

'You're welcome.' I smile warmly and check the time on my iPhone. She gets the message, lifts her large frame off the chair and backs towards the door. When she's out of the room I let out an exasperated sigh. All I need in the middle of this mess is a bunch of bickering kids.

I get home late, open a bottle of Argentinian Malbec and heat up an M&S ready meal. As I wait for the microwave to ping I look at the roses sitting in the vase on the kitchen table. I'd love to know who they are from, but I have other things to think about now. In between today's meetings and emails at work I realized I've developed an addiction to my Heath experiences. My reaction to Tom's friendly imposition this morning has convinced me there is a problem that I need to address. The truth is, I can't stop thinking about the Dior Man. I'm quite positive he has nothing to do with the rape on the Heath. I refuse to add the assault to the equation. There are enough conflicting elements in it already, without complicating it any further. The facts, as I see them, are 1) I love running on the Heath, it's a place that restores my mind and soul, and I will not give it up; 2) I'm addicted to the Dior Man and he is connected to the Heath; 3) The scenario I myself have created can't go on in its present form.

Halfway through the bottle of Malbec I have a solution. I need to de-cloak the Dior Man, demystify the situation, break the obsession created by the fact I don't know who he is. I need to speak to him, get to know him. Once he stops being a stranger, the sexual frisson will dissipate and the whole thing will fizzle out, sink into oblivion. I go to bed with a clear plan.

Eleven Days Earlier

I'm awake at the crack of dawn, throw my running clothes on and am out of the house by 7 a.m. I quietly negotiate with Wispa, begging her not to bark, and pray I don't bump into Tom this morning. That would ruin everything. We run down Fitzroy Park, exhilarated by the clarity of the day. The air is fresh, the birds are chirping and trilling, their different songs complementing each other in the trees. I reach the Heath without even breaking sweat. And off we go up the hill, then right, following my usual route. I don't even know if I'll see the Dior Man this morning, but I have the whole speech ready in my mind.

We run noiselessly through the dark woods and suddenly there he is, right in front of me, running from the opposite direction. I stop and he slows down. Wispa barks sharply and I say it's OK and tell her to wait. It's strange to hear my voice. He's stopped and is looking at me, a question and a challenge in his eyes. I feel my speech evaporating as I look at him. I desperately try to recall the words, but they are all gone. There are no words left in my mind, no thoughts, just a primal instinct that drives me forward as I approach him, brush against his arm as I go past him and get off the path, into a dense thicket that opens up into a tiny clearing, a small patch of grass and moss, where bluebells probably grow in the spring. I pause for a second and then I hear him following me. I go deeper into the clearing, then stop and turn. He's right behind me, watching me, motionless. He's so close I can see the droplets of sweat on his forehead. I reach out and touch his chest, feeling his heartbeat under my hand. I slowly slide his T-shirt up, over his arms and head, and he doesn't protest. His chest, almost hairless, shines with sweat. With my hand I follow the delicate line of soft golden hair down from his belly button to the top of his running shorts, grotesquely stretched by his erection, then grab the waistband elastic and pull them down. He stands in front of me, naked but for his running shoes, beautiful and motionless like a Greek statue. I drop to my knees and take his cock in my mouth, my hands on his small, muscular buttocks. His masculine smell hits me as I savour its texture, hard and smooth, feeling the saltiness of sweat on my tongue. I pick up my pace and dig my fingernails into the skin of his buttocks. He lets out a loud moan and pushes me off him. I fall on my back and he's right on top of me, tearing off my T-shirt, pulling my pants down. He enters me roughly and I'm ready for him, pulling him in, ploughing the skin on his back with my fingernails. His face hovers above mine, his pupils dilated, his mouth wet, but our lips don't touch, there's no space for the softness of a kiss in our embrace. We fuck greedily and hard, and I can feel my mouth going numb and cold, the rest of my body on fire. I come first with a cry I try to stifle but can't; he's a few seconds behind. He rolls off me and we both lie on the cool, damp moss, panting, unable to move. Then he slowly gets up and gathers his clothes and I keep my eyes shut, silently praying, please don't speak, don't say a word, don't break the magic of the moment. When I open my eyes, he's gone. I feel cold and there's a sharp stick digging into my thigh. I stand up shakily and put my clothes on, run my fingers through my tangled hair, getting bits of moss out of them. I push my way through the bushes onto the path and see Wispa, lying in the middle of it, her hazel eyes following me attentively.

'Good girl,' I say to her, patting her head. 'You're such a good girl.' I'm grateful to her that she hasn't run away. I walk back home slowly with my dog by my heel, quiet and content, refusing to let the demons I've unleashed into my thoughts.

The work meeting in Soho drags itself on well into the lunch break and by the time I'm back in my car driving to the office it's nearly 2 p.m. It's been a busy morning and I haven't had time to think about the Dior Man. Just as well. I need to consciously block the flashes of memory as I find them too distracting to go about work. As I enter the flow of Marylebone Road I turn on the air-con and the radio in the car. It picks up the pre-set for BBC London 94.5 and I listen to Robert Elms going on enthusiastically about some derelict building in East London. I like the man, not only because he dislikes the Beatles almost as much as I do. If I recall correctly he said they are 'either childlike and simple or leaden and pompous' and they shouldn't be above criticism. I couldn't agree more. Then the 2 p.m. news comes on and I nearly run into the car in front when I hear the first news item. There's been another rape on the Heath. I turn up the volume and listen, frozen in disbelief. A woman has been assaulted and badly beaten sometime this morning. She's in a critical condition in hospital. DCI Jones of Camden CID comes on.

'At present we are not linking the two recent incidents on the Heath,' she says, 'but we are appealing to witnesses to come forward. Something which may seem unimportant on its own may be crucial to the investigation so please do come forward no matter how insignificant you think the information might be.' She adds that the police presence in the area has been increased and anyone who sees anyone acting suspiciously should call the police on 999.

I tune out the rest of the news and try to think calmly about what I've just heard. There's been another rape and there are no witnesses. The woman is in hospital, probably too traumatized to describe the attacker. And there are no suspects. Otherwise they would have given a description, some sort of indication who might have done it. DCI Jones said they are not linking the two incidents. Perhaps she doesn't want to create panic with the notion of a serial rapist. But why should two different rapists be better than a serial one? Whatever she says, something tells me both rapes have been done by the same man. And he's getting more violent.

I grab my phone and text Bell while I'm waiting at the traffic lights, looking out for cameras that might catch me breaking the law. I know she'll be worried and I have to let her know I'm OK. She texts me back almost straight away, thanking me for checking in. Good old Bell. I get a warm feeling thinking that there is someone who cares whether I'm fine. I remember the moment, many years ago, when I realized that being single means there is no one who gives a damn whether you are OK or not. You might just as well drop dead and no one would notice. Friends tend to flock around you when you're successful and happy, but when something goes wrong, forget it, you are on your own. I sometimes get annoyed with Bell for clucking about me like a mother hen, but I know she is the closest to a family I'll ever get.

As I enter the flyover and gather speed, my thoughts go back to the Heath. I was there this morning, probably more or less at the same time another woman got badly hurt. I cast back in my memory to the hazy moments after my encounter with the Dior Man, but I'm pretty sure I haven't seen or heard anything that may help the police. And I'm absolutely positive the Dior Man has nothing to do with the rape. In other words – I justify my own cowardice – there is no reason for me to contact the police. What would I say to them, anyway?

It's been a long day at work and by the time I get home I'm exhausted. I'm just about to unlock my front door when my mobile rings. It's Bell. I talk to her while saying hi to Wispa and putting my Sainsbury's bag on the kitchen counter.

'I've now booked my tickets to Vancouver to see Candice,' says Bell.

'Oh, great.' I pour myself a glass of Malbec and go to lie down on the sitting-room sofa. 'When?'

'On Thursday.'

'Wow, that's soon.'

'I know, but I found a really cheap last-minute flight with some charter company, and I thought, why not? Candice can take some time off, so we'll have a long weekend together.'

'Hope you'll have a great time.' It's a long way to go for a weekend. I think back to a couple of disastrous trips to America Bell made to meet her Internet girlfriends.

'I will. This time it's for real, Anna.'

'I hope so, babe, you really deserve it.'

'I know, I'm so excited. And a bit scared.'

'It will be fine,' I reassure her, although I'm not entirely convinced Bell's Internet quest for intercontinental love is the best way forward. But *à chacun son goût*, as the French say. Who am I to disagree?

Once I finish talking to her, I remain on the sofa thinking of my own tastes, and what Bell would have to say about them. I haven't got the guts to tell her about the Dior Man, because I know she'd be horrified. Not because she'd find it shocking – she's done plenty of shocking things herself – but because she'd think I'm putting myself in danger. I catch myself thinking about it in the present tense and it worries me a bit. Perhaps I should start going to counselling.

Wispa barks suddenly and I hear a man's voice in my house. I jump up, grabbing my phone, ready to dial 999. Wispa's bark changes its pitch and becomes friendlier. I venture out of the sitting room into the hallway. My front door is wide open and there's a young man standing in the doorway, swaying slightly. It's Alden.

'Anna!' He waves a bottle of Lidl's-own Putinoff vodka at me. 'Sorry to barge in like this . . .' He slurs his words as he steps into my hallway.

'How did you get in?'

'How . . .' he says, looking around as if he's lost something. 'I believe the door was open.'

Shit, I must've left it open, distracted by Bell's phone call. I go past Alden to shut it. He reeks of booze.

'Anna,' he tries to catch my arm and kiss me, 'Anna, Anna, Anna, lovely Anna.'

'Alden, you're pissed.' I gently push him away.

'I know.' He sinks down to the floor and starts crying.

Great, that's all I need, a drunk kid crying on my hallway floor.

'What's wrong?' I ask him as I go to the kitchen, pour a glass of water from the tap and come back to the hallway.

'Tina's left me,' he wails, a big snot hanging from his nose. I remember Tina is his girlfriend, the musician. 'She's fucking that wanker from the band.'

He takes a swig of vodka and when I offer him water he pushes my hand away clumsily. The glass slides out of my hand and shatters on the floor. There's water everywhere, but Alden doesn't even notice. He takes another swig, then closes his eyes. Two minutes later he's snoring. And I think he may have pissed himself, although I'm hoping it's just water. I collect the largest pieces of broken glass and go back to the kitchen.

I have to get rid of him. I have absolutely no intention of babysitting a drunken kid going through heartbreak. I pick up my mobile and dial Tom's number. He answers immediately and I explain the situation. He says he's on his way and there's a knock on my door five minutes later.

'Tom.' I open the door for him. 'Thank you so much for coming to the rescue. I really don't know what to do with him.'

Tom smiles his perfect-teeth smile and instantly the situation seems to be under control. Maybe I do need a man in my life, after all. Should I call James, see how he's doing? Nah . . .

'Don't worry, Anna, we'll sort it in no time.' Tom looks down at Alden, who's curled up on my floor, sound asleep.

'His girlfriend's left him, apparently.'

'Quite some time ago. He's been deluding himself he can get her back. Poor kid.'

'Oh, I thought she dumped him today.'

'No, it's been going on for a while.' Tom looks at Alden,

who is snoring peacefully. 'He just needs to sleep it off. I've got keys to his flat – the kids go there to water his cat and feed his plants when he's away on shoots.' I laugh at his feeble joke because I'm grateful. He lifts Alden off the floor, holding him under his arms. Alden's head lolls back, but then he opens his eyes and mumbles something.

'It's OK, mate, we'll get you home,' says Tom, leading him to the door. I thank him profusely as I watch him guide Alden down the front steps. He flashes another perfect smile at me and they are gone.

Ten Days Earlier

No Heath for me this morning, I have a splitting headache and don't feel well. Normally this wouldn't deter me from running, but the thought of some psycho lurking in the bushes waiting for a woman to pounce on taints my image of the Heath. I know the feeling will pass, but at the moment the Heath has lost its attraction. Even the Dior Man isn't going to tempt me out there.

At work the restructuring shit is hitting the fan with the full force of corporate ruthlessness. We, and by 'we' I mean the higher echelons responsible for The Change I reluctantly include myself in, are hitting the first snag in a long line of structural obstacles. We, the selected few, gather in a small conference room on the top floor and are addressed by Anthea, the harassed-looking head of HR. Strangely enough, the representatives of Cadenca Global are absent. The reason for the snag, she explains in a boring monotone, is the anti-nepotism policy actively promoted by our company. Why should this highly principled – at least in theory – policy be a problem? Because The Change is going to shake the very foundations of our corporate structure, cause a massive reshuffle, an avalanche of shifts, promotions and demotions; and this may lead to 'unwitting nepotism' where couples who previously had nothing to do with each other professionally are put into the position of boss/subordinate. Thank God I have never been inclined to have an office romance, I think to myself, discreetly checking my iPhone for emails and messages. There is a voicemail from my Filipina cleaner Sherie Lou; she comes to the house once a week and today is her day. I'll listen to her message later. As our company does not prohibit inter-office dating, Anthea drones on, we should consider restrictions on both assignments and communications about job performance in the case of existing couples as a precautionary measure. I have nothing to add as a discussion breaks out on the subject of the increased risk of litigation.

As soon as the meeting is over I'm back at my office, answering emails that seem to multiply like rabbits on speed. There is another message from Sherie Lou. I access my voice-mail. She sounds upset and goes on in a chaotic way about broken glass in my house. I can't quite work out what she means, so I call her.

'I broke a glass in the hallway last night, but I thought I'd picked up all the pieces. I don't want Wispa to cut her paw.'

'No, no, Anna, I mean the kitchen. I found the flower vase all broken, in pieces on the floor. And plenty of water and roses scattered everywhere. I don't want you to think I broke it, I found it like this.'

Now I get it.

'Don't worry, Sherie Lou. Did you manage to clean it all up?'

'Yes, yes, no danger for Wispa.'

'Thank you. I wonder how it happened?'

'I have no idea. Maybe Wispa or a draught when I opened the front door? I'm sorry, Anna, but I didn't do it.'

'That's fine, Sherie Lou, don't worry about it. As long as you've managed to pick all the pieces up.'

She assures me all is well in the kitchen, I thank her again and put the phone down. Bless her heart, she gets so worried when something gets broken or damaged on her watch.

I get home to an immaculately clean house, as is always the case after Sherie Lou's visit. The kitchen is spotless, all signs of the broken vase cleared away. The roses stand on the kitchen table in a silver champagne bucket. Good thinking, Sherie Lou. Prompted by a touch of OCD, I reposition the bucket so it's right in the middle of the table. With all the water and flowers in it, it's heavy. Too heavy to be blown off the table by a bit of a draught. A shiver of unease runs through me. What could've happened here? I wish I'd left my Mac open with Witness running before I set off for work this morning. Michael installed it on my laptop, mainly to track Wispa's behaviour when I'm not at home. The software changes your laptop into a spy camera, triggered by movement and recording thirty seconds of action every time. It simultaneously sends an alert to your iPhone. Unfortunately, I hardly ever use it, maybe because I know exactly what Wispa is up to when I'm not around. She's asleep and snoring. I find an open bottle of Malbec, pour myself a glass and go to the sofa in the sitting room.

The mystery roses, they were an emotionally charged gift I still feel slightly uneasy about. Who were they from? James? I haven't heard from him since he dropped my keys off right after our last phone conversation. He's probably busy seducing the blonde Sue saw him with. There are a couple of other guys who would be capable of such a dramatic gesture, including my psycho ex-husband. Thankfully, I haven't heard from him for years. Maybe Tom after all? I put my wine glass down. The charming dentist with the million-dollar smile. He did seem a bit keen during our morning jog the day the roses got delivered, but maybe he was just trying to be friendly. Anyway, he wouldn't be making such romantic gestures right on his doorstep, under the nose of his wife. That reminds me of the lovely Samantha, the keeper of my shameful secret. I groan and put my face in my hands. Since I went to see her at the hospital I've had another encounter in the park, and I'm not even considering going back to the clinic for more tests. I'd completely forgotten about my HIV test. Another ten weeks to go. How could I have grown so desensitized in such a short time? I know I'm playing Russian roulette with my health by keeping up the encounters with the Dior Man. The Dior Man . . . could he be the mysterious sender of the roses? He doesn't know where I live. But he could've followed me from the park. No, it would completely destroy what those encounters are about. What are they about? I'm not sure myself, it's all gut instinct, some primal urge that doesn't translate into words. I jump when my phone rings. It's Bell.

'Just saying goodbye, hon. Off to catch my plane at the crack of dawn.'

'Bon voyage, babe. Do you need a lift to the airport?'

'No, thanks, it's far too early to drag you out of bed. I've booked a cab.'

'Hope you'll have a fabulous time. And hope Candice is nice.'

'Hope so too. I'll keep you posted. No need to water my plants, I'll be back on Tuesday. Oh, by the way, did you get your keys back from James?' There she goes, in her mother hen mode again.

'Yes, I did, actually.'

'Good girl.' She ignores the note of annoyance in my voice. 'And promise me one thing.'

'What?'

'Stay away from the Heath until I'm back.'

'Bell . . .'

'I'm serious, Anna. Don't go there this weekend. Jog around Waterlow Park if you must. Promise.'

'OK, I promise,' I say half-heartedly. I'm not sure I'll stick to my word.

I put the phone down and pour myself more wine. Something Bell has said makes me feel uneasy. The keys. James has given me his set back, but he could've easily made a spare. A chilling scenario builds in my head. James comes in, for some reason, this morning. Wispa knows him and doesn't lift a paw when he arrives. James sees the flowers. Gets jealous and angry. Knocks the vase over. Leaves before Sherie Lou arrives . . . Whoa, stop right there. Am I getting just a teeny-weeny bit jealous that James is dating someone else? Am I developing a dog in the manger syndrome? Would I actually want him to come over and break some glass just to show that he still cares? The problem is, James is not the jealous type. He would never create such a scene. And I'm getting paranoid. But the vase incident has unnerved me and, just to put my mind at ease, I decide to change the locks. To save myself the hassle of getting spare keys for all the locks, I decide that changing just the main mortice will do. I get up, go to the front door and put the chain on.

Nine Days Earlier

Thursday, a day I occasionally work from home, just to catch up on emails without interruptions. Emails, they do make our lives easier, but aren't they a sneaky time-thief? They have been gathering in my inbox since the beginning of The Change with a frightening speed, multiplying faster than bacteria in a warm fridge. I need to D&D them urgently, deal and delete. I ring Claire and let her know I'll be working from home. Then I call the local locksmiths and arrange for a visit. I'm in luck, they can send out a locksmith with a new lock almost straight away. By the time I've brewed my coffee he's ringing the doorbell. He doesn't ask me why I want to change a perfectly good lock, just sets to work with a knowing nod.

I'm bringing a mug of coffee out for the locksmith when someone calls my name through the open front door. It's Tom, looking businesslike in dark trousers and a white shirt, clearly on his way to work.

'Hi, got a bit worried when I saw all this . . .' He gestures at the locksmith's tools on my front steps. 'It wasn't Alden making a nuisance of himself again?'

'Oh no, just replacing an old lock that hasn't been working for some time,' I lie to him. 'Nothing to worry about.'

'Good.' He flashes his gorgeous smile at me. 'Oh, by the

way, it's my daughter's birthday this weekend and we're having a small party – actually two parties, kids at eleven a.m. and grown-ups at seven p.m. on Saturday. It would be lovely to see you.'

'Thank you, that's sweet, I'd love to come, but I'm going away to visit friends in Norfolk this weekend,' I lie to him again. I don't think I'm up to facing Samantha just yet.

'No worries, next time. I've got to rush, I'm running late today.' He waves goodbye and marches off down the street.

I don't think I'm imagining it, but I'm sure he fancies me. Or am I just thinking that to make myself feel better? Anyway, I must say I'm slowly warming to the idea of neighbourly friendships. They certainly make living in the urban jungle less lonely. But they do take away the anonymity of a big city, which is something I value a lot, having grown up in a small, nosy town. You can't have everything, I think, as the locksmith calls me to the door and hands me five brand-new keys.

'Have you ever considered enhancing the security of your home?' he asks me.

'I have, but I've never got around to actually doing anything about it, to be honest.'

He launches into a lecture about the dangerous world we live in and how his firm offers free security surveys for homes.

'It's like looking at your home through the eyes of a burglar,' he explains and goes on listing all kinds of extra protection they offer: window locks, patio-door locks, door bolts, grilles and alarm systems.

'It's definitely something you should consider, being a woman alone in a big house like this,' he concludes.

I'm annoyed by his 'woman alone' comment. I tell him I'll consider my options, pay him for the new lock and close the door. I go to the study, log on through the remote access to my work account and start the tedious process of sifting through my emails. If only people stopped hitting the 'Reply All' button so readily! I'm deleting millions of emails that should've been addressed to one person only (not me) and another million that should not have been written at all. I read somewhere, probably in an email, that thirty per cent of people's time at work is spent reading and writing emails. Bring back pen and paper and pneumatic mail! I'm just about to go to the kitchen to make myself another coffee when I hear a strange sound at the front door. Wispa rushes to the hallway, but doesn't bark. The noise stops, then repeats itself. Someone is trying to get into the house. My heart is pounding as I grab my phone. I select 999 and with my thumb on dial I peek out from the study down the hallway. Wispa is standing by the front door wagging her tail. Through the small stained-glass window in the door I can see someone dressed in pink. Somehow this unlikely-for-a-burglar colour reassures me and I step into the hallway, shouting out a tentative 'hello'.

'Hello,' answers a female voice.

Of course, it's Nicole, my dog walker. I open the door for her, feeling like an idiot.

'Nicole, I'd forgotten you were coming.'

'Anna! Nice to see you. Sorry, I didn't know you were home, I would've rung the bell. I couldn't open the lock . . .'

'Oh, I'm so sorry, I've just changed it, that's why your key wouldn't work. It actually wasn't even locked.' I laugh sheepishly. 'Let me get you a new key.' I rummage on the hallway shelf for the set the locksmith has given me.

'You all right?' asks Nicole.

'Yes, thanks, just have tons of emails to catch up on, so decided to work from home.' I know she's asking me how I am because I'm behaving strangely and because I've changed the lock. 'I was just about to make myself some coffee. Would you like one?' I'm giving her the new key.

'No, hon, thanks, I'd better go, I have another three dogs to pick up. Do you want me to take Wispa?'

'Actually, why not? I wouldn't be able to take her out for a while with all the work,' I lie. Wispa looks at me accusingly when Nicole puts a leash on her.

'OK, I'll drop her off in a couple of hours.'

'Thanks, Nicole. Be careful out there, will you?'

Nicole throws me a curious glance.

'I always am, Anna. Cheerio!'

I shut the door behind them and put the chain on, then take it off, remembering that Nicole will be dropping Wispa off. I'm wound up about something, but I don't know what it is.

I'm usually quite disciplined about working from home and get much more done than in the office. But today it's as easy as drawing blood from a stone. I sit in my study, looking out through the window, staring at my lush garden, and I know I should be feeling extremely lucky that I am where I am, with a beautiful house, great job – despite the on-going shit-storm – and all the trappings of an affluent life. Of course, I do have a hideous mortgage to repay, thankfully ticking over nicely on a very low interest rate, and I am a prisoner in the golden cage of a big corporation, but I can live with it. What is bothering me, then? Am I getting broody? Nah, I've never wanted to have children and being on the wrong side of thirty-five hasn't changed how I feel about it. My friends with kids say the biological clock will wake me up sooner or later, but I haven't heard it ringing yet. I need to clear my head and I fall back on the only way I know how to do it: I have to go for a run. I remember what I've promised Bell and decide to head to Waterlow Park. Just as well – I don't want to stumble upon Nicole with the dogs on the Heath, it would only confuse Wispa.

I trot down the High Street, stop briefly to peek at the bookshop's window, then enter the park through the gate next to Channing School for Girls. As I pass the tennis courts on my right I slow down and look back for Wispa, only to remember she's with Nicole on the Heath.

Waterlow Park is small, but it always takes my breath away when I get to the top of the hill and look at the rich meadows sprawling down its gentle slopes, the elegant trees, the windy alleyways and the magnificent view of the London skyline below. Today there is a group of happy pensioners, amateur watercolour enthusiasts, scattered on the lawn, busily recreating the view. I can feel my body and soul sing as I pass them and run down the alley towards the ponds. The singing stops when I see a pale-skinned and almost-naked silhouette lying in the grass, right by my path. Alden. He seems to be blissfully asleep in the sun, but when I pass him he raises his head and shades his eyes with his arm.

'Anna!'

Damn. I slow down and turn towards him with a forced smile. I really don't fancy any company right now.

'Alden.'

He's on his feet now, his tan Bermuda shorts riding down his flat stomach, revealing a tuft of dark hair above his belt. Normally I'd enjoy this slightly narcissistic display of a cute male body, but now it just annoys me.

'Anna, I'm so sorry about the other night. I really don't know what came over me. I saw your front door open and . . .' He waves his arm and gives me his charming puppy-like look.

'No worries, Alden, glad you're OK now.'

'Oh, yes.' He brushes his face with his hand. 'It was just a little tiff with Tina, all well now. You OK?'

'Yes, I'm fine, just getting my endorphin rush.'

'Oh, I get mine from eating hot chillies and sex.' He winks.

'Lucky you.' I can't help but laugh.

'You off work?'

'Working from home,' I say with a pang of guilty conscience.

'I can see that. Me too.' He keeps his face comically straight and I must say he is cute.

'How's your film?'

'Still trying to get funding for it. It's really tough these days. Even the freelance jobs have dried up. But I have a lodger now, so at least the bills get paid.'

'I'll give you a shout if I hear of any DA jobs opening.'

'That would be awesome, cheers, Anna.'

He waves at me and lies back down in the grass. Strange boy, I think as I continue jogging. There is something weird about him, going on about his girlfriend. Didn't Tom say they'd split up some time ago? Why is he acting as if they are still together? He's either in complete denial about the whole thing or they've got together again, unbeknown to Tom.

I do a loop round the park then head for the gate out to Swain's Lane. When I'm at the gate I slow down and look back, a habit of waiting for Wispa, who's usually dragging her paws a bit when we run together. Of course she's not there, I remember, but when I look back I catch a glimpse of a runner who looks familiar. I stop and turn, but by then the runner has veered off into a side alley and disappeared behind the bushes. This is not good, my suspicious mind is beginning to play tricks on me.

I get back home and hop under the shower, taking time to

check my breasts for any suspicious lumps, a self-check I do regularly since I discovered a benign cyst in my breast a few years ago. I emerge from the bathroom feeling reassured, clean and energized. I'm ready to do some work. I'm just settling in with a cup of coffee in the study when the front door opens and I hear the pitter-patter of Wispa's paws. She comes straight to me, her tail wagging.

'Anna?' I hear Nicole's voice.

'Yes?' I put down my coffee and go out to the hallway.

Nicole is standing by the open door, looking pale, clearly distraught.

'Nicole, you OK?' I go to her, pull her gently inside and shut the door. 'Come through to the kitchen. What happened?'

'There was another rape on the Heath this morning. The whole area's been cordoned off. There's police everywhere.'

Nicole sinks heavily down onto a kitchen chair.

'Another rape?' I can't believe what I'm hearing.

She starts sobbing uncontrollably. I put my arm round her and wait for her to collect herself. Then I get up and pour her a glass of water. She takes a sip and wipes her face with her hands. Belatedly, I offer her some tissues. She blows her nose noisily and clears her throat.

'I don't know the details, but the other dog walkers were saying he's done some horrible things to her . . .' Her chin begins to quiver again.

'Have they caught anyone?'

'I don't think so.'

We both fall silent, digesting the terrifying news.

'They were saying she was a jogger. But someone said she was a dog walker and they're still trying to catch her dogs . . . Oh, Anna, I don't know if I ever dare to go back there again

. . . My favourite place in the whole world, my sanctuary, my livelihood . . .'

'I'm sure they'll catch him.' I know how feeble it sounds but I don't know what else to say. I turn the kettle on and prepare two mugs. Tea, the universal British remedy. With our steaming mugs we move to the sitting room where I switch on the TV and search for the BBC News channel. They are talking about golf, but there is a red crawler at the bottom of the screen flashing the headline BREAKING NEWS and LATEST. We wait impatiently as it crawls along: 'G20 finance ministers back an action plan drawn up by the OECD to crack down on tax avoidance by multinationals,' followed by 'Israel to free Palestinian prisoners.' And there it is: 'Police are appealing for witnesses and information following a serious sexual assault on London's Hampstead Heath.' That's it. I know there'll be more on the Internet and Twitter, but I don't want to further upset Nicole. I switch the TV off.

'Look, Anna, I think I'm going to take some time off and go to my parents in Milton Keynes. I'm sorry, I really don't want to leave you in the lurch, but I don't think I'll be dog-walking for a while . . .'

'I totally understand. Absolutely, go to your parents, that's a great idea.'

'I'd better go then and call them.' She puts her mug down and gets up from the sofa. 'Oh, nearly forgot, your keys.' She hands me my front-door keys.

'Thanks, Nicole.' I close the front door behind her and put the chain on. Then I go to the study and sit down in front of my laptop. There isn't much about it in the news yet, just a short item:

Police are appealing for witnesses and information following a serious sexual assault
of a woman on London's Hampstead Heath.
Officers were called to Cohen's Fields area
of the Heath at 7.00 a.m. this morning after
the victim was discovered by a passer-by.
Detective Chief Inspector Vic Jones is asking
the public to stay away from the area . . .

It's followed by the usual phrase about contacting the police.

But Twitter is buzzing with information. The police are now linking all three attacks. I wonder if that means his previous victim has been able to give a description of him. Apparently this woman was a jogger. She was attacked on the path not far from Kenwood Nursery and dragged into the bushes. There is one tweet that is particularly horrific, if it can get any more horrific than it is already. She was found unconscious, with her knickers stuffed in her mouth.

For a long while I just sit at my desk, feeling cold and numb. How could this be possible? One of the most peaceful places in London has just been tainted with yet another brutal, grotesque act of violence. I feel as if someone has deliberately taken away one of the things I value most, a place I connect with freedom, well-being, spontaneity. And what about the victim, presumably a young woman, running one minute, full of life, brutalized and left for dead the next. Will they catch the attacker? Will the Heath ever be able to recover? My thoughts go back to the Dior Man. It's not him, it's not him, it's not him, I keep repeating to myself. Then why do I feel somehow responsible for unleashing all the violence? Here we go again . . . Perhaps I should have myself checked for OCD and do something about the inflated sense of responsibility. My mobile rings and I let it go straight to my voicemail. But its shrill sound brings me back to reality. I need to deal with some practicalities. I won't be able to find a replacement dog walker at such short notice and Bell, who is usually my emergency Wispa-sitter, is away. That reminds me, I have to email her, just in case the Heath news filters through to Vancouver, although I doubt it. It's not the Stock Exchange or the Royal Family after all. I email Claire and let her know I have a stomach bug and am taking Friday off. I know I shouldn't be doing this, especially not with everything that's going on, but I simply can't face work just now. Claire replies almost instantaneously, wishing me a quick recovery and updating me on the news. I'll be very sorry if she ever decides to leave her job, I don't know what I'd do without her. I compose a short email to Bell, just to let her know I'm alive, and then I curl up on the sofa in the sitting room and fall asleep.

I wake up to Wispa snoring on the floor by the sofa. My back is stiff from being curled up in one position for too long. I look at my iPhone and realize I've slept for two hours. It always happens when I'm stressed, it's my body's way of switching off to let the mind rest. There are five voicemails on my phone. Two from work (Gary and Sarah – both can safely be ignored), two from Michael and one from my friend Kate in Norfolk. I call back Michael straight away.

'I was a bit worried about you. This Heath thing, how awful . . .'

'Terrible. I must say, it's shaken me badly.'

'No kidding. I couldn't believe it when I heard it on the news . . . What are you doing tonight?'

'Me? Nothing.' I really don't fancy any social activities.

'That's perfect, darling. I'm coming over with a bottle of wine. And I won't take no for an answer. Shall I bring some food as well?'

'I'm sure I can rustle something up.' I smile at his way of being bossy.

'Lovely. Have to rush now, see you in a couple of hours.'

I put the phone down and realize I'm really glad he's coming. I was dreading an evening on my own.

I grab Wispa's leash and we walk to the High Street's grocer where I pick up some mushrooms, broccoli, beef tomatoes, rocket, a couple of ripe avocados and gloriously fragrant fresh basil. It's going to be a pasta night. I throw in a punnet of huge yellow raspberries, get a tub of ice cream at Tesco and the dinner is sorted. It's not going to be Ottolenghi, but simple flavours with a nice bottle of wine can be equally satisfying. I decide to take a larger loop going back home and enter Waterlow Park for the second time in a day. It looks different in the sunset: with the longer shadows and reddish light it feels more dramatic, mysterious. Wispa trots off with her nose to the ground and I sit down on a bench, absorbing the view. It's hard to imagine anything bad happening in such a peaceful place. I think of the Heath and the horrendous drama that played out over there this morning. Such an evil act changes the energy of the whole place, makes it cold and unfriendly, with danger lurking in every shadow. Will I ever dare to go back there? Will I trust it again? I call Wispa, who is sniffing around a rubbish bin, collect my shopping bags and climb the path towards home.

Before I start cooking I go to my study and check the BBC

news on my laptop. There's a bit more about the Heath rape. The victim has been identified as a twenty-eight-year-old woman who lives locally. There is a short video of Detective Chief Inspector Vic Jones addressing the public. She's a tall woman with short curly hair and a kind face.

'This was an appalling and violent attack by an individual with a propensity for violence towards women,' she says and somehow I trust her that she'll do everything to catch the rapist. 'I am grateful to a number of witnesses who have already come forward and appeal for anyone else with information to contact us. We would particularly like to hear from any other women who live in this area who may have been assaulted on the Heath.

'I can understand why you may not have come forward, but if this has happened to you then you may have a vital piece of information that can help us stop him.'

The video clip ends and I sit staring at the laptop, digesting what she's said. She's linking the rape attacks, although she hasn't said it directly. Any piece of information can help them stop him. Stop him, I repeat in my head. It means she thinks he'll do it again. I play the clip once more and this time it feels as if she's talking to me. *You may have a vital piece of information.* Do I? Is it relevant? Is it up to me to decide? And do I have a moral obligation to go to the police with the Dior Man story? I vacillate, unable to make up my mind.

I'm in the kitchen chopping the vegetables for the sauce when Michael rings the doorbell. As he walks in, dressed in a stylish linen summer suit, he complains about the disappearance of the lovely wine shop in the High Street.

'This is the best I could do.' He produces a bottle of McGuigan Shiraz out of a Tesco bag.

'It'll do nicely,' I tell him as I go back to making the sauce and he opens the bottle and pours us some wine. He peeks over my shoulder and I can feel he's dying to take over.

'Do we have some chillies, darling?'

I tell him he can find everything there is in the fridge and sit down at the kitchen table with my glass of wine. I get up again when Michael demands an apron, pointing to his light linen trousers and immaculate shirt. I find him one, a present from my friends in Australia, and he puts it on. Sipping my wine, I watch him whizzing around my kitchen, wrapped in an Australian flag, and I feel warm and cared for. He's busy putting fusilli into a pan of boiling water when my doorbell rings again.

It's Tom, in his running clothes. I look at him, surprised.

'I thought I'd just stop by to say hi. What a terrible tragedy on the Heath . . .'

'Yes, absolutely awful,' I answer, not sure what he wants.

'Makes you not want to go there for a while. But if you ever feel like venturing out that way again and—' He stops when he sees Michael in his apron, coming out of the kitchen, a glass of wine in his hand. 'Oh, I'm sorry, I didn't realize you had guests.'

'No worries, Tom, this is Michael; Michael, this is my neighbour Tom.'

'Coming in for a glass of wine?' asks Michael as a way of introducing himself.

'Oh no, that's very kind but I have to get back home – it's the kids' bedtime.' He flashes his bright smile at us and is gone.

Michael looks at me, raising his eyebrows.

'No, no, no, definitely not,' I say, shaking my head. 'He's really just a neighbour, nothing more.'

'That's nice. Very neighbourly.' He gives me a look. 'And very good-looking.'

He disappears into the kitchen and I follow him. The pasta sauce smells divine.

Michael helps me clear the table and load the dishwasher. We hold on to our ice-cream bowls, not sure if we want some more dessert. I go to the wine rack in the hallway, pull out a bottle of Châteauneuf-du-Pape, get a corkscrew from the kitchen and put it in front of Michael, stretched in an armchair in the sitting room.

'Michael, I have a confession to make.'

'It must be serious,' he says, looking at the wine bottle. 'But in the absence of the Pope, I'm prepared to listen, my child.'

He opens the bottle, sniffs the cork and, satisfied, pours the wine into clean glasses. I sit on the sofa facing him and take a deep breath.

'I have been having sex with a stranger on the Heath.'

He puts his glass down and stares at me in silence. I feel a hot wave of embarrassment rising from my neck onto my face, something I haven't felt since I was a teenager.

'And now I don't know if I should go to the police about it,' I blurt out. 'Oh, Michael, what a mess . . .'

He raises his hand to calm me down.

'OK. Start from the beginning.'

'Remember the conversation we had at the Spaniards Inn?' He nods slowly. 'I wasn't just curious about your experiences . . . I was actually trying to understand my own feelings.'

He nods again, waiting for me to continue, and picks up his glass.

'I'd bumped into this guy on the Heath. There's something about him, I don't know, something straight out of *The Great Gatsby*, some kind of elegant decadence . . .' I stop, knowing that what I say sounds silly, as if I'm trying to dress something quite basic and dirty into some lofty guise. 'OK, I fancied the pants off him, literally, and it just happened.'

'What makes you want to go to the police?'

'I don't know . . .'

'Do you have any reason to believe it's him?'

'No,' I shake my head. 'I honestly don't.'

'So why would you want to report it?'

I'm already regretting telling Michael about it because he's making me face the truth. But I have to plough on now.

'I saw this policewoman on the news. She said that anyone who's had a similar experience on the Heath should come forward.'

'Similar to what? Getting raped?'

'No,' I whisper.

Michael puts his glass down.

'Anna, has he raped you?'

I've never seen him so serious.

'No, of course not.' My laugh comes out a bit lame. 'He's never done anything I didn't want him to do.'

'Are you telling me the truth?'

'Yes, yes, I am.' I look him in the eye. 'I swear. He hasn't hurt me in any way, everything we did was totally consensual. I instigated the whole thing and it's . . . developed.'

'Are you still seeing him?'

'No.'

Michael visibly relaxes.

'What you've been doing is quite dangerous.'

'I know. But I'm fine. It's just that whole thing on the Heath today has unhinged me and somehow I've felt compelled to do something about it . . .'

'Was it unprotected?'

'Yes, but I've had myself checked.'

'Good.' Michael smiles and pours some more wine for both of us. 'Anna, the Heath harlot. Who would've thought?'

We laugh, a release of tension we both need. We chat for a while about Bell's Vancouver adventure, my work, Michael's holiday plans. Suddenly it's almost midnight and I call a cab for him. Once he's left I lock the front door and put the chain on. I feel much lighter, as if a great burden has been taken off my shoulders. I'm glad I've told him, even though, I realize now, he hasn't given me any advice regarding going to the police.

Eight Days Earlier

I'm woken up by the persistent ringing of my doorbell. Wispa is barking her head off and I have to shout at her to be quiet, which she does, reluctantly. I grab a nightgown that's hanging on the back of the bedroom door and run down the stairs, combing my hair with my fingers.

'Hello?' I say as I unlock the door, leaving the chain on.

'Hello,' says a woman's voice I don't recognize.

Through the crack in the door I see a pale face and it takes me a moment to put a name to it. Samantha, Tom's wife, the lovely doctor. I undo the chain and open the door wide.

'I'm sorry to bother you so early, but I wanted to catch you before you go out to work.' She takes in my nightgown and falls silent.

'I'm actually off sick. How can I help you?' I'm not sure if I should invite her in.

'I was wondering if I could have a word with you.'

'Sure.' I gesture for her to come in. What's it about, I think frantically, hoping they haven't made a mistake with my tests. 'Let's go to the kitchen.'

I lead the way, then ask her if she would like a cup of coffee. She shakes her head and sits at the kitchen table. Just to keep my hands busy I put a cartridge in the coffee machine and press the button. She waits for me until my cup is ready and I sit at the table, facing her.

'It's about Tom.'

'Tom? Has something happened to him?' I say, feeling relief that she hasn't mentioned my test results.

'No, he's fine.' She looks away. 'I've come here to ask you to leave him alone.'

'I'm sorry?' I'm not sure I heard her right.

'I know you've been out jogging with him.'

I just stare at her, not knowing how to react. Let's try to be civilized about it, I think to myself.

'Look, Samantha, yes, I've jogged with him on the Heath once, because he joined me en route, and I called him once to ask for help with Alden who turned up drunk on my doorstep one night. Oh, and I've been to your house, for your party. This is the extent of my knowing him. I can assure you there is absolutely nothing going on between me and your husband.'

'I know,' she says and she looks like she's about to cry.

'Look,' I get up from my chair, 'let me make you some coffee. Or would you prefer a cup of tea?'

'Coffee would be fine, black, thank you.'

What the hell is this all about, I think as I wait for her cup to fill. Do I have a complete nutter in my kitchen? I put the coffee in front of her and she takes a sip.

'I'm so sorry, Anna, I really don't mean to upset you . . . or offend you . . .' She seems a bit more composed now.

I sit down with my coffee, facing her. I don't even know if I'm angry with her any more.

'What do you want me to do?' I say at last.

She sighs.

'Obviously, it's not going to be easy, because we're neighbours

. . . Tom's always had a soft spot for beautiful women, a harmless, almost childish fascination I've learnt to live with. But with you . . . basically, if you could try to avoid him . . . not encourage him . . .'

'I've never encouraged him in any way.'

Suddenly I've had enough of her. I get up from the table. 'I'll do my best. But now I'd like you to leave.'

She gets up, not looking at me.

'I understand. I'm so sorry . . .'

I open the front door for her and she leaves, hunched and frail-looking. What a weird woman, I think. Has working at a sexual health clinic somehow impaired her way of seeing the world? Or does she really think I'm a total harlot?

This is all too much, I think as I go back to the kitchen and let Wispa out into the garden. My life has suddenly transformed itself into a dark farce and I'm not laughing. I feel suffocated by the walls of my own house, by the village, by the whole city. I need to get out. I pick up my phone and call Kate, who left a message for me yesterday.

'Kate, it's Anna. You know I've been threatening to visit you for ages, so . . . what are you doing this weekend?'

'Not much, do you want to come over?'

'Yes, please.'

'Great, just text me when you're on the way, so I know what time you'll arrive.'

An hour later the car is packed and Wispa is sitting in the back on her travel bed, wagging her tail excitedly. She loves our trips. I negotiate a bit of traffic on the North Circular and soon we're heading up the M11 towards the gentle fields of Norfolk. Seeing the open space right past the M25 makes my heart sing. There is something comforting and reassuring in the amount of land that hasn't yet been turned into a concrete jungle. I get off the M11 onto the A11 and then I'm on the A1065 towards Brandon, Swaffham and Fakenham, my favourite stretch of the road. I stop briefly at a pub on the way to let Wispa out and grab a stodgy, half-baked baguette filled with grated cheese that doesn't resemble any cheese I know. Then we're off again, both looking forward to our seaside adventure.

Kate sold her London flat a few years ago and bought a charming cottage overlooking the sea in the picturesque village of Burnham Overy Staithe. She used to own a successful broadcast recruitment agency, got burnt out at the age of forty-three, sold her agency to the highest bidder and moved to Norfolk, to practise her two newly discovered hobbies: photography and gardening. The latter has developed beyond the hobby status as her allotment has grown from an amateur two-veg patch to a blossoming organic enterprise selling fresh herbs, salad garnishes and edible flowers to a nearby Michelin-star restaurant. I tease Kate that she'd left London to retire and relax, but she's never worked as hard as she works now. She laughs and says it's an entirely different kind of 'hard', the nurturing and fulfilling kind she'd never experienced running her agency. And it's true: she's never seemed as happy and healthy as she is now.

We arrive in good time and Kate, tall, tanned and handsome, welcomes us outside her cottage. I've always envied her Mediterranean complexion, her black hair framing her face in lovely curls and her striking green eyes. Since she's been in Norfolk she's developed the healthy countryside glow of someone who spends a lot of time outdoors.

Wispa is going berserk, running up and down Kate's garden, quite an uncharacteristic expression of joy for the overweight old puppy that she is. But she loves Kate and loves to be here, especially if there's a walk on the dunes and a swim in the sea in store for her. I unpack the car and bring Wispa's bed and bowls to Kate's kitchen, which is lined with beautiful stoneware tiles.

Kate suggests we go out straight away to catch the afternoon sun and we get into her vintage Range Rover and drive the short distance to Holkham Beach, the most beautiful expanse of sand I have ever seen. We walk along a wooden boardwalk erected amidst the pine trees above the sand dunes and arrive at the salt marshes and the tidal foreshore. I have to stop and take in the view, which always fills me with awe. We pass a flock of serious-looking birdwatchers in camouflage gear and walk towards the sea, which seems miles away. Even though it's a warm day, the stretch of sand is almost empty, dotted here and there with a few silhouettes of walkers. We turn left and walk along the dunes, our bare feet luxuriating in the fine sand. Wispa makes circles around us, her chocolate snout covered in sand.

'So, what are you running away from this time?' asks Kate. She knows me well enough for me not to protest. As we stroll on, I tell her about my split-up with James, the assaults on the Heath and the mind-boggling visit from Tom's wife. What I don't mention are my encounters with the Dior Man. She doesn't say a thing, but I know she listens to my every word, a consummate listener with years of practice.

'Wow,' she says when I've finished. 'It's quite a surreal story.'

'I know. Even as I was telling you, I doubted it'd actually happened.'

'It is quite weird of her to come to you. Why would she mind her husband jogging with a neighbour from time to time?'

'I don't know.' I shrug my shoulders, then change my mind

and tell Kate what had occurred to me when I was driving here. 'Maybe she suspects he's the Heath rapist?'

'But if she knew he was a rapist, would she be protecting him? I'd go straight to the police.'

'Well, the lengths women go to stand by their men . . .'

Kate laughs. I think of her ex-partner Robert, a TV executive accused of molesting a teenage intern when she still ran her agency in London. She'd never said a bad word about him, but divorced him almost immediately and moved to Norfolk shortly after. I don't know if there's anyone in her life now; she certainly hasn't mentioned any men since she's left London.

A couple of riders pass us, their horses frothing with excitement. I watch with envy as they gallop away, free and exhilarated. We walk on a bit further, then turn off and take the path through the pine woods back to the car park. Back at the cottage, Kate makes me sit down in the garden with a book while she prepares dinner. As usual, it's a work of art, entirely vegetarian and consisting of produce only from her allotment. I savour her nettle soup with sour cream and a few wild garlic leaves, followed by freshly dug potatoes and houmous made from different varieties of beans, accompanied by salad adorned with pansies. After dinner, pleasantly relaxed by Kate's elderflower and wild rocket wine, we sit in the garden watching the creek-side harbour, bustling with bird life in the dusk.

Seven Days Earlier

Next morning I'm up before Kate, buzzing with anticipation of my favourite morning run. Wispa is waiting for me by the door, and we sneak out quietly, cross the harbour car park and climb the coastal defence bank alongside Overy Creek. There is no one here yet, except for the cows that watch us lazily as we trot along the high bank. It looks like the tide is at its highest, the currents flowing fast between the mudbanks. I remember Kate telling me that apparently this is where Nelson learnt how to sail as a boy. I fill my lungs with sea air and feel the pure joy of being surrounded by natural beauty. We run all the way to the boardwalk at the foot of a high dune, then turn and start running back. A swift breeze that was pushing us forward when we ran towards the sea hits me in the face and makes my body work harder. The windmill at the centre of the village is beckoning us now and I'm thinking of Kate's breakfast. It's only by the harbour car park that we encounter the first humans of the morning, an elderly couple walking their Jack Russell, Pocket, who makes instant friends with Wispa.

I enter Kate's kitchen and the glorious smell of fried bacon and freshly brewed coffee welcomes me. A quick shower and I'm sitting at the kitchen table, tucking into Kate's scrambled eggs with mushrooms and bacon. The coffee, smooth and almost sweet, with a delicate cocoa aftertaste, is from the Monmouth Coffee Shop in Covent Garden, which Kate visits whenever she is in London. Once the breakfast is over, we move to the sun-drenched bench outside the kitchen door.

'I think I could get used to this gentle decadence,' I say and Kate laughs.

'Don't tell me you're ready to retire.'

'Well, television is an ageist business.'

It's true, the creative hubris, so characteristic of young, talented and hungry 'media people' is very quickly replaced by the need to settle down and make some serious money. By the age of forty most producers are either burnt-out, frustrated failures who hang on to their jobs for as long as they can, or they've moved on, swapped their low-crotch jeans and woolly hats for suits and white shirts. And for all those who hang on comes a moment when their phone stops ringing, their work email account is empty and their accountant tells them they should drop the idea of having their own production company. From the point of view of big corporations it's simple economics: it's much more cost-effective to employ inexperienced but cheap kids than to have to fork out for mature producers who know what they are doing, but are expensive. The quality of their work is a secondary issue.

'Maybe I should find myself a self-sustainable hobby and just quit the whole TV thing . . .'

'You're far too young and ambitious for that,' says Kate, although I'm not sure she is right. 'Talking of hobbies, I want to show you something.'

We go to her study, a quaint room on the first floor with a huge double-glazed window facing the harbour. There is a massive oak desk by the window, with a twenty-seven-inch ultra-thin iMac in the middle of it. She touches the mouse to wake it up and the screen comes alive with the most beautiful close-up of a beanstalk.

'This is my new project: photographing my garden as it goes through all the seasonal transformations.'

We look through the stunning collection of macro-shots, revealing unexpected details of fruit and flowers. The quality of the photographs is impressive.

'You should publish a book.'

'I'm thinking of it.' Kate closes the macro folder and clicks on a jpeg icon on the screen. It opens up to reveal a huge photograph of the harbour and the marsh bank along Overy Creek.

'And this is you this morning.'

I can see myself now, the grey silhouette of a runner with the brown speck of Wispa's fur beside me, right in the middle of the frame.

'What's this?' I lean towards the screen.

At the very bottom of the picture, almost by the harbour, there is the shape of a man, wearing a black hooded fleece and jogging pants. He is just standing there, looking at the stretch of bank I'm on, his back to the camera.

'Another runner?'

'I didn't see anyone there, except for this old couple with a dog.'

'Maybe he went another way.'

'There isn't any other way,' I say quietly, paranoia seeping in. There is something familiar about the man's silhouette.

'Well, he must've changed his mind.' Kate gets up and stretches herself. 'Do you want more coffee? Then I'll take a quick shower and we'll decide what we want to do today.'

'Great,' I say, hiding my anxiety. We go back to the kitchen and Kate brews a fresh pot.

When she's gone to the bathroom I sneak back to her study and move the mouse of her iMac to wake it up. It's locked and the box in the middle of the screen asks for a password. Damn, I really wanted to see that picture again.

We decide to drive up to Blakeney, have a walk on the coastal path and then pick up some fish for lunch at the Cley Smokehouse. I try to hide the anxiety caused by Kate's photograph, but I know she knows something isn't right.

Back at her cottage Kate prepares a beautiful food spread on the table in her garden. As we dig into the smoked crevettes, dressed crab and kiln-roasted salmon from Cley, she pours some of her wine for us and looks at me.

'Tell me what's really bothering you.'

'If only I knew myself . . .' I wipe my fingers on a linen napkin.

'Just give it a try.'

She's not going to be fobbed off.

'Seeing that man in the photograph this morning really unsettled me.'

She nods and waits for me to go on.

'I don't know, I get this weird sensation of someone's presence hovering around me. And it's not friendly, benevolent, like knowing that a friend thinks of you. It's dark and menacing. Sometimes I feel I'm being observed, that my every step is being noted and judged. That's why I freaked out a bit when I saw your photograph.'

'But you do realize it's very unlikely it was someone you know?'

'Yes, I do . . .'

We sit in silence for a while, watching the butterflies chasing each other in Kate's garden.

'Since those rapes on the Heath, weird things have started to happen to me, or maybe I just started noticing them.' I pause, thinking of the best way of telling Kate as much as I can without mentioning the Dior Man. I realize I'm ashamed to tell her about him, not because I worry she might judge me, but because it would reveal something about me I don't even want to know myself.

'For instance?'

'For instance, someone had left a bouquet of red roses on my doorstep the other day. No card, no sender, just flowers. Then the vase with the roses magically flies off the kitchen table and smashes on the floor, spooking my cleaner.'

'Could be Wispa?' At the sound of her name Wispa pricks up her ears and looks at Kate.

'No, I doubt it. She's never damaged anything in the house.'

'It may seem unsettling, but there might be a perfectly innocent explanation for it. You're obviously worried and stressed and that makes everything get slightly out of proportion.'

She takes a sip of her wine and continues.

'It's good you've come here. When you go back, try to look at the whole situation with fresh eyes, without the emotional baggage. If it still feels wrong, call the police.'

'You're right,' I say and just talking to her makes me feel

better. But the dark cloud that has been obscuring my judgement remains: I haven't told her I'm convinced all the weird
things that keep happening to me are somehow connected to
the rapes on the Heath.

Six Days Earlier

I drive back to London after a leisurely Sunday breakfast at Kate's and another walk on Holkham Beach. Kate has been right, after all: the short holiday has helped me to shake off the oppressive atmosphere of the last few days. I feel refreshed and refocused. The good mood lasts until I stop to enter Tottenham Hale's monstrous gyratory, hear a crash and my car jerks forward. Great. Someone's just rear-ended my pristine BMW. I reluctantly get out of the car, keys in hand. Sitting on my rear bumper is another BMW X5, an exact replica of my car, down to the colour and the design of the alloy wheels. Its driver's door opens and a tall black guy in a dark suit gets out. Wispa starts barking and I shout at her to stop, getting ready for a verbal fight. But the guy approaches me with his hands raised in an apologetic gesture and a smile.

'I'm so sorry, it's my fault entirely. Hope you're OK?' he says and I can't quite believe what I'm hearing.

'Yes, I think I'm fine.' All the fight has gone out of me in a flash.

'I can't apologize enough,' he says, getting a card out of his wallet. 'Here are my details.'

The cars behind us begin to honk; we're blocking the entry to a major junction.

I take his card and he continues, 'Would you care to give me your phone number, so we can sort it out as soon as possible? My name is Ray, by the way, Ray Chandler.'

No way, I think to myself, shaking his hand, this guy is too good to be true.

'I'd like to take a few pictures of this.' I take out my phone. I can see there isn't much damage, just a dent on the bumper.

'Sure, by all means,' he says while I snap a few shots. 'I'd like to take care of it without involving my insurance company, if you don't mind. A mate of mine runs a great car body workshop in Tottenham – he'll fix it straight away and I'll cover the cost.'

Everything he says sounds dodgy, but I like his smile and his charming manner and, against my better judgement, I trust him. So I give him my phone number, he promises to ring tomorrow morning, we get back into our cars and drive off.

What's going on with you, Anna, I think, where's your street-wise attitude, your fighting spirit? The truth is, I don't feel like fighting and I enjoyed the whole encounter in some perverse way. It helped that the guy was charming and handsome, his laughing eyes and sensuous mouth not lost on me, even in the middle of Tottenham Hale gyratory.

I get to my house and unlock the front door with slight trepidation. But it seems fine, no sign of an intruder, everything is exactly as I've left it. I catch up on work emails and start getting ready for a busy Monday, then I remember that Nicole's gone and there's no one to take Wispa for her walk tomorrow. I go on Gumtree and do a quick search for Hampstead dog walkers. All the usual culprits come up, students who want to house-sit and look after your animals for a small sum, professional dog-walking companies who stress their 'individual touch' and a few disturbing ads, 'practically raised by dogs' and 'your dog's mistress'. There's one ad that looks promising – 'I am a student and an experienced dog walker looking for work in the Hampstead area' – but the guy's name is Tom and I quickly move on. Looking for a reliable dog walker in London is a tough business. And having one is expensive. On the off-chance I text Nicole, but she's still at her parents and doesn't know when she'll be back. Eventually I fall back on my 'emergency babysitter' as he calls himself, Michael. He'll be happy to take Wispa out for a spin, but I'll have to drop off the keys to my house for him on my way to work. Problem solved, at least for a day. I take Wispa for her evening walk and we stop in front of the High Street newsagent, looking through the ads. Just as I thought, it's still the best local noticeboard and there are a couple of names and numbers I take a photo of with my iPhone. I'll check them out tomorrow, if I have time.

Five Days Earlier

Having dropped my keys off at Michael's I arrive at work early, but not early enough to beat Claire to it. She gives me five minutes to settle in my office and then pounces on me with all the outstanding issues of the last week. It's going to be a busy day.

At lunchtime Claire offers to get a sandwich for me from the canteen and I'm just unwrapping it at my desk when my mobile rings.

'Hi, it's Raymond Chandler,' says a deep male voice and for a moment I think it's a prank call. Next I'll be getting a call from Humphrey Bogart. 'We had a collision in Tottenham Hale yesterday.'

Ah, Mr Charming, I think as it all comes back to me.

'Yes, Ray, of course.'

'I just wanted to find out when would be a convenient moment for you to drop off your car at the garage. I'm afraid you'll have to leave it with them for a couple of days. I'm so sorry to cause you all this inconvenience.'

'It's all right, Ray, these things happen.' I look at my diary. On Wednesday and Thursday I have meetings in Soho, so I won't need my car. 'I could drop it off tomorrow evening?'

'That's great.'

He gives me the name and address of the place and we arrange I'll be there before 6 p.m. tomorrow when the garage closes. While I'm eating my sandwich I Google the name of the garage he's given me. It turns out they have their own website and it does look legitimate. Then I look up the two dog walkers' phone numbers from the newsagent in Highgate and give them a call. The first one doesn't answer but the second one sounds promising: an Italian woman with a lovely lilting accent who lives locally, works from home and takes a few dogs for a walk every day to subsidize her income. We arrange that she'll pop in tonight 'to see if Wispa likes her' as she puts it. Relieved that things are beginning to come together, I get on with work uninterrupted for most of the afternoon. At 5 p.m. I get a text from Michael:

Had a long walk on the Heath. Princess tired and happy. Bumped into your admirer on the way back. Xxx

I ring him straight away.

'My admirer?'

'Hello, my darling, and you're welcome, looking after your pooch was a pleasure.'

'I'm sorry, Michael, of course, thank you. I'm really grateful, I know I can always count on you.'

'No need to exaggerate,' Michael laughs. 'Yes, your neighbourly admirer, what's his name, Tom?'

A wave of anxiety comes over me.

'Where did you see him? Did he approach you?'

'Anna, darling, relax, I bumped into him in front of your house when I was coming back with Wispa, it was all very innocuous.' He pauses and his tone changes. 'Is he your Heath stranger?'

'No! No, he absolutely is not.' I catch myself raising my voice.

'OK . . .' he says hesitantly.

'He really isn't, believe me.' I don't feel like telling him about Tom's mad wife.

'Oh well, just to warn you, he probably thinks I'm your boyfriend.'

'What do you mean?'

'He saw this gorgeous guy at your place cooking for you the other night, right? And now he sees him walking your dog . . .'

I can't help but laugh at Michael's reasoning. I thank him again, tell him I'm seeing a prospective dog walker tonight and will let him know how it goes.

It actually wouldn't be such a bad thing if Tom thought Michael was my boyfriend, I think as we end the conversation.

I continue working a bit longer, then dash home to meet the new dog walker. In my mind I've already given her the job.

Chiara rings my doorbell at 7.30 p.m. on the dot, as arranged. She has gorgeous red hair and a freckled, open face. Her hand-shake is strong; so is her Italian accent. I like her straight away. Wispa seems to like her too; she runs to greet her with her toy bone between her teeth. She only gives her favourite toy to the chosen few and I'm impressed by the immediate effect Chiara has on her. Chiara spends a few minutes playing with Wispa, then we settle at the kitchen table and she shows me her infor-mation leaflet, insurance and references, all neatly laminated. It turns out she's cheaper than Nicole. We chat about dogs for a while, then our conversation drifts towards the Heath and the most recent attack. There hasn't been much about it on the news since it happened; we both hope the police will catch the culprit soon and restore tranquillity to the Heath. In the meantime, Chiara tells me, she carries a pepper spray when she walks the dogs there. She gets the job, of course, I give her the house keys and we arrange that she'll pick Wispa up every day at around 1 p.m. till the end of the week. She mentions she'll be away next week for a few days, but I say it's fine, we'll worry about it then. I'm happy I've found such a good person so quickly and to have the dog-walking problem sorted, at least for this week.

Four Days Earlier

The next day is a blur of memos and meetings. I don't get as much done as I'd hoped and I stress about having to leave early to drop the car off at the garage. Bloody nuisance, I think, all I need on a day like this is having to schlep all the way to some obscure part of Tottenham. The last meeting of the day drags on and I know I'll miss the closing time of 6 p.m. As soon as I leave the meeting I text Ray to let him know I'll be late and he texts me back, saying no worries, they'll wait for me. Thankfully, the traffic is light and I get to the garage, with the help of my GPS, only ten minutes after closing time. The first thing I see on its forecourt is my car, that is, Ray's car which looks exactly like mine, except for the damage to the front bumper. As I park, Ray comes out of the office and I'm struck by how handsome he is. Another guy follows him, equally good-looking, long-legged and broad-shouldered, and with the same charming smile. When we shake hands, I'm beginning to suspect they might be brothers. We inspect the damage and Daniel, Ray's lookalike, tells me the car will be ready by Thursday evening. I leave my car keys with him, hoping it's not some elaborate set-up to steal my car, and ask him for the number of a local cab company. Ray won't hear of it, and insists he'll drive me home.

'This is the least I can do. In fact,' he pauses as if a wonderful thought has suddenly occurred to him, 'please allow me to buy you a drink as a way of apology. I know the whole thing's inconvenienced you a lot.'

I must say, his smile is irresistible. I've had a tough day at work and I need to have some fun, I decide, and say yes. Somehow I know an evening with Ray will be fun. Soon we're on our way to Hackney's best-kept secret, the Nightjar.

'In fact, it's not a secret any more,' Ray tells me, 'it's officially the third best bar in the world, according to *Drinks International*'s annual list. People from all over the world flock to it now.'

'And your good mate owns it,' I say.

'How did you know?' he laughs, the deep-chested laugh of someone who enjoys life. It's contagious and I find myself laughing, too.

Indeed, Nightjar doesn't disappoint. And Ray's company is a delightful combination of wit, charm and subtle flirting. After a Shrubbler, a Jungle Bird and a London Mule, accompanied by excellent tapas, the conversation flows with wonderful ease.

'So, Ray, tell me, what do you do for a living?'

'If I told you, you wouldn't believe me.'

'You're a drug dealer.' It slips out before I think.

He laughs, not offended by my terrible joke. 'And I have a car to match it. So do you, as a matter of fact. You dealing as well?'

I apologize for my silly remark.

'OK, I won't keep you guessing.' He pauses for effect. 'I'm a hairdresser.'

'Wow,' I say lamely as I try to hide my surprise. This is not what I've been expecting. He laughs, seeing my reaction.

'I have my own salon.'

He tells me about his humble beginnings twenty years ago when he took over a newsagent shop in then run-down Islington and gradually built up his business, eventually buying a shop next door to expand it. Now the salon is thriving and last year he released his own exclusive haircare range. As I listen to him I can see his pride and passion about his job, and I'm impressed. It turns out Ray speaks fluent French, which he picked up in Paris as a teenager. And this is where he cut his stylist's teeth, or should I say scissors, working as an apprentice in the best Parisian salons.

'But I'm not exactly Raymond Bessone,' he says with a mock French accent and goes on to explain when I don't get the joke, 'Bessone was a big guy in the sixties, had his salon in London, totally OTT, complete with champagne fountains, Diana Dors hairdos and an awful faux French accent.'

Mr Bessone aside, his true inspiration is Oribe, yet another name I've never heard of.

'I'll tell you about him some other time,' says Ray, 'because now I want to hear all about you.'

Reluctantly at first, I tell him about my career in television, starting with the early years as a junior producer at a local TV station. His interest in what I say is so genuine that I get into my story, weaving in some juicy anecdotes from the past. When I look at my watch it is nearly 11 p.m. and I jump up suddenly, thinking of Wispa.

'I'm so sorry, Ray, I have to go and walk my dog, otherwise she'll shred the whole house.'

Wispa would never shred anything, but I add it for effect because I don't want to appear dog crazy. He understands, of course, and it turns out he has a Miniature Schnauzer called Roller.

Ray stops the car in front of my house, gets out and walks me to the door.

'Thank you for the lovely evening.'

'No, thank you,' he says, 'I really enjoyed it. Perhaps we can repeat it some time.'

He leans over and kisses me gently on the cheek. What a true gentleman. The moment breaks when Wispa starts barking and scratching the door from the inside and I have to let her out. As an overexcited Wispa greets us with her toy bone in her mouth I watch Ray play-acting a tug of war with her. A man who is so sweet to my dog must be a good man, I decide. The way to a woman's heart is through her chocolate Labrador, obviously. Eventually he drives off in his black BMW and I realize I haven't thought about the Dior Man even once this evening. Thank you, Ray.

Two Days Earlier

Two days of meetings with production facilities in town are a complete waste of time, made even more frustrating by the knowledge that the backlog of work in the office is growing. But I'm just following Cadenca Global's orders, or rather a 'solution' proposed by our architect of change, as they like to be called. The solution in this case is outsourcing of production, hence my trek around the Soho production facilities. But being in Soho has its pluses and when Bell texts me on Thursday morning that she's back and bursting to tell me her Vancouver story, I suggest we meet at our usual chinwag place, Dim T in Charlotte Street. My meeting finishes early and I sit for a while in Soho Square, watching the media types bustling around, busy on their phones, oblivious to their surroundings. I used to be one of them, I think, but not any more. Yes, I'm still part of the media crowd, but more and more I find myself on the outside, looking in, aware that there is life beyond the corporate bubble. Midlife crisis? Apparently it hits women around the age of forty-four, so I still have a good few years to go, but I scan my life for obvious signs of it. Splashing out on an expensive car. Tick. Taking vitamin supplements. Tick. Buying organic. Tick. Considering going on a spa holiday. Tick. Having at least three direct debits for charitable causes. Tick. Looking up old boyfriends on Facebook. Occasional tick. Having sex with a stranger on the Heath. I hesitate, then put an imaginary question mark next to it. I stroll along Rathbone Place and arrive at Dim T before Bell. Turning up for appointments early. Tick.

Bell walks in five minutes later and I know straight away her trip to Vancouver wasn't a waste of time. She has the glow of someone who's had a great holiday and lots of sex. We order our usual dim sum and sake.

'Well?' I say to Bell, who's just sitting in front of me, grinning. She reaches into her bag and puts a maple-leaf-shaped bottle on the table.

'Canadian maple syrup, for you,' she says.

'That's very sweet.' I study the hideous thing with faked interest.

'Yes, very.'

I look at her and we both burst out laughing.

'Well, it was fantastic.' She waits for the waitress to deliver our sake carafe and cups. 'From the moment I landed till the moment I took off.'

'Would you care to elaborate?'

Oh yes, she would. She tells me about Candice, who is very much like herself, into healthy, active lifestyle, running, surfing, cycling. She's athletic, smart and gorgeous. And she's amazing in bed.

'Four orgasms in an hour. Each,' she says and I'm impressed.

'So, when are you going to Moscow, Idaho?'

'No,' Bell grins at me, 'she's coming over here. In a couple of weeks.'

'Wow, it's serious then.'

'I think it is.'

We drink to that and delve into our first basket of dim sum. Bell shows me some pictures of Candice on her iPhone and I must admit she is very pretty, in the all-American way. Big smile, blue eyes in a tanned face, slim, muscular body.

'And no strings attached?' I ask. 'No ex-husband, children, psycho-girlfriend stalking her?'

'Nope. She'd been single for quite a while. Honestly, Anna, I can't believe my luck.'

'She's the lucky one.'

Bell beams at me and I'm glad she's happy.

'Anything exciting happened here while I was gone?'

I tell her about the attack on the Heath, my new dog walker and the trip to Norfolk to see Kate.

'And I've met someone,' I throw in casually.

She puts her chopsticks down, waiting for me to continue.

'He's quite handsome, charming . . . and he's a hairdresser.' A giggle I've been suppressing comes out and Bell, after a moment of surprised silence, joins in.

'He has his own salon in Islington. And he's definitely straight –' I briefly hesitate – 'I think. We only met once and nothing happened, but I like him. He's so . . . different, so refreshing . . .'

'Well,' Bell raises her sake cup, 'if having a boyfriend who can do your hair is good enough for the Australian ex-prime minister, it should be good enough for my Anna, too.' We drink a toast, one of many this evening.

'Is he married? Any children?'

'You know, I have no idea. It hasn't even occurred to me to ask him . . . Wow, I'm becoming a little bit socially challenged.'

'Self-centred, more like.'

I know it's probably true, but it doesn't even sound like a

criticism when it comes from Bell. It's more of an objective statement and she's usually right.

Bell and I part in front of Dim T and, as usual, she goes off to catch the 73 and I hail a cab. I realize I've forgotten to pick up my car, which was supposed to be ready by this evening. There's been no message from Daniel or Ray, so I assume there's been a delay and make a mental note to ring the garage tomorrow morning. But as I get out of the cab in my street I notice my car, parked in its usual spot right in front of my house. I take a good look at it and the rear bumper looks like new. Then I notice something on the windscreen. It's a single red rose stuck behind the wiper. What a sweet man. When I open the front door to my house I find my car keys on the floor. He must've put them through my letter box. Not only sweet, but thoughtful.

One Day Earlier

As soon as I come into the office Claire tells me I've been summoned to the executive floor. I'm to go to Julian's office straight away. I have no time to speculate on what kind of disaster awaits me. As Julian welcomes me, the smell of his aftershave envelops me like a cloud. He leads me to his leather sofa and offers me coffee, which I gratefully accept. He tells me how much he values me as his 'right hand' as he calls me, and I begin to suspect the worst. He's getting rid of me, I think, and my heart rate increases. Bad news like this usually strikes when you least expect it. I impatiently listen to him praising me, waiting for the inevitable 'but' and 'regretfully'. But the bad news never comes. In fact, Julian wants to enlist my help, or, to put it plainly, wants me to become his scout.

There is a global company meeting next week in Paris, a meeting he can't, for personal reasons he doesn't go into, attend. He wants me to go there and be not only his envoy, but his eyes and ears. I am to present his speech and answer all the questions that may arise, presenting 'his vision', as he calls it. At the same time he wants me to flush out his opponents, read their minds and report back to him. For the rest of the day he explains his vision to me, based on diversification of the supply base. It sounds like a scenario for the takeover of the world, done by tiny steps on a local level. Needs and objectives of stakeholders are being mentioned, creativity and the people are not. The fluffy packaging that will appeal to the minions will come later. I begin to get glimpses of the real Julian, a steely-cold man with the empathy of a Borg, emerging from behind the jovial and caring facade of Mr President.

The day in Julian's office is a sobering and formidable experience. It's making me realize I live in cloud cuckoo land, a naive place I've created for myself through my complete lack of knowledge and understanding of the real corporate world. How on earth did I get to the position I'm at? The only consolation is the hope that I'm not the only puppet whose strings are being pulled by the invisible hands of the corporate gods above.

Walking me out of his office, my hand warmly nestling in his, he tells me that his assistant Laura has already made all the travel arrangements for me. I'm catching the 07.01 Eurostar on Monday and coming back on Wednesday morning at 08.43, to arrive in time for an 11 a.m. update meeting with Julian. I shall be staying in Paris at Hotel Plaza Athénée, which he makes sound like his personal favourite.

'Go out of the door and turn left and you're on the Champs-Élysées, turn right and there's the Eiffel Tower.'

It transpires that this is where the meeting will take place. Oh, he adds as I walk into the lift, Laura has also taken care of my other work arrangements and my appointments diary has been cleared till Wednesday afternoon.

I go back to my office and take a few minutes to gather my thoughts. There's no way of escaping it, my make or break time has arrived. I pick up the phone and ring Chiara to arrange dog care for Wispa. Bad news, she's going to Italy on Sunday and won't be back until next Saturday. I'll have to beg Bell for help and, if she can't do it, drive Wispa to Norfolk and leave her with Kate. I call Bell and she answers on the first ring, still high from jet lag.

I explain the situation, crossing my fingers she won't say no. I really don't feel like driving to Norfolk this weekend.

'That's no problem, hon,' she says to my relief. 'In fact, it'll work out rather well. I've found this wonderful Polish handyman and I want him to do a bit of decorating before Candice arrives. He'll be painting the whole flat from Monday, so I might as well move to yours instead of sitting in the stink of emulsion. When are you back?'

'On Wednesday, but you can stay at mine as long as you want.'

'No, it's fine, I think he'll be done by Wednesday.'

I put down the phone, grateful to Bell for providing such an easy solution. I'm also impressed by her sudden burst of home improvements. She's been talking about decorating her place for years. It's amazing what a new relationship can do to you. I pick up my phone again and call Ray. I texted him last night thanking him for delivering my car and for the rose, but he hasn't texted back. The call goes to his voicemail and I leave him a message, thanking him once more and saying that I hope we'll see each other again. As soon as I disconnect I kick myself for sounding too keen. But it's too late to erase the message. Oh well, I'll just have to live with it – hopefully he won't use it against me. I leave work late, drive home, take Wispa for a short spin round the block and go straight to bed. I have a lot of brainwork to do this weekend.

The Day

Saturday disappears in a flurry of work. I go through all the documents Julian has given me, marking the passages that are particularly complicated, memorizing the main points, listing all the potential pitfalls. I'm not convinced by his vision, but who am I to disagree? I'll have to be convinced enough by Tuesday, when the most important session takes place, to try to bait the company sharks with it. I stop working only to take Wispa for a walk. It's a hot day, 'a mini heatwave' as the papers call it, caused by an unusually hot stream of air coming from Spain. Wispa seems to be limping badly, which may be caused by the heat, but worries me. I check her paw and there's nothing obviously wrong with it, no cuts or thorns, no broken toenails. I hope it's nothing serious, otherwise I'll have to ask Bell to take her to the vet on Monday, a kerfuffle I'd rather spare her.

By the time I've gone through everything, it's late in the evening. My head is throbbing with all the information; I feel cranky and restless. I need to go for a run. Wispa looks at me putting my running gear on and limps back to her bed. It's clear she doesn't want to come with me. She must be in a lot of pain to miss her evening run. I stop at the front door, go back and rummage in the hallway cupboard, looking for a pepper spray I brought from the States a few years ago. I'm not sure it's still working, but I tuck it into the pocket of my shorts, just in case.

Dusk is settling on the Heath, making trees and grass lose their colour. The shapes become blurred and unreal, all detail suddenly gone. The sky is dimming its brightness and the first stars and planets appear above the horizon. There is a handful of people about, mostly carrying their blankets and baskets in the direction of a few cars still parked in Merton Lane. I run up the hill at full speed and realize how unfit I've become lately. I can hear my heart pounding in my head, my breath quick and shallow. Once I reach the top I slow down. I don't turn right into the woods because it's too dark there already. I run down across the meadow, which is still getting enough light from the sky, then turn sharply left, making a loop. I reach the main path again and decide to cross it and continue in the direction of the Ladies' Pond. I hear footsteps behind me, regular and strong, another runner making the best of the twilight hour. I run across the South Meadow at a steady pace. The sound of footsteps is still behind me. There's no one else left on the Heath now. I try not to panic, thinking that whoever it is will change their direction soon. But the sound of trainers pounding the ground persists, going exactly at my speed, not trying to overtake me and not slowing down. I quickly glance back and see the dark silhouette of a man, about twenty paces behind me. I think of stopping and letting him pass me, but fear is pushing me forward, my muscles locked in the mechanical movement of my limbs. I try to breathe steadily, not to break my rhythm, not to show that I'm afraid. I turn right onto a path and he does the same. I check my pepper spray, still tucked safely in the pocket of my shorts. At least I have something to defend myself with, if he attacks me. But for now my flight or fight response is limited to flight. The Ladies' Pond, I think, maybe one of the guards is still there. I change direction and run towards the back gate of the pond. I pick up speed, hoping I'll shake him off, and for a moment I think I'm winning, his footsteps no longer audible behind me. I see the wrought-iron fence, the sign that says WOMEN ONLY, MEN NOT ALLOWED BEYOND THIS POINT, and for a split second I hope it'll stop him, but I know it won't. I reach the gate and it's locked, a huge chain and padlock in place. I think I hear the footsteps behind me again and I grab the top of the gate and leap over it, half-climbing, half-vaulting. I'm on the narrow, overgrown path that runs behind the toilets and the guards' house. I slip in the mud, then keep running, reach the main path and turn left towards the swimmers' platform. I enter the square of concrete in front of the bathrooms and look hopefully at the guards' house. The door is locked and it's dark, there is no one here. I turn to keep running and there he is, standing on the path, blocking my escape route. I take a step back, my heart pounding, my hand on the spray. He moves forward, coming out of the shadow of the building into the moonlight, and I recognize him. It's the Dior Man. My fear gives way to relief, to be instantly replaced by more fear. What is he doing here? How come he always manages to find me on the Heath? What does he want this time?

He takes a step forward and I instinctively move back towards the edge of the pond. I can always jump into the water and swim round to the meadow, try to get out on the other side, I think frantically, trying to anticipate his next move. I slide the pepper spray out from my shorts' pocket and hold it hidden in my hand. If it doesn't work, I can still hit him with it, it's better than trying to fight with bare hands. Slowly, he raises his arms and pulls his sweat-drenched T-shirt off. I watch him as he drops the T-shirt on the ground, unsure what to do, my heart thumping. His wet bare chest shines in the moonlight. Then he moves his arms down and unbuttons his shorts. His shorts drop to the ground and he bends over to take off his running shoes. I watch him as he straightens up and stands before me, completely naked, unashamed and beautiful in the blue light of the full moon. He takes a step towards me and I gasp, my fear mixed with awe. And then he is in full motion, running towards me, and I cry out, teetering on the edge of the concrete platform. He passes me, his beautiful body stretches above the water and he's in, swimming with large strokes out towards the middle of the pond.

My fear suddenly replaced by lust, I drop the pepper spray to the ground and rip my clothes off, oblivious to everything, my body screaming for him. Naked, I dive in, bracing myself for a cold shock, but the water is surprisingly warm. I resurface and look around, trying to locate him. Ducks, scared by the disturbance, flap their wings by the shore, but he's nowhere to be seen. I try to find the bottom of the pond with my feet, but it's too deep, so I stay on the surface, paddling with my arms. The commotion dies down and it becomes very quiet. I float on the water, inhaling the fresh, watermelon smell of the pond. The moonlight shimmers on the surface, framed by the impenetrable darkness of the bushes surrounding it.

And then he's right behind me. I feel his hands on my breasts, his cold body next to mine, his erect penis nudging my back. He grabs my waist and turns me round to face him and my legs float up, embracing him. He feels solid, anchored, as if he's standing on something on the bottom of the pond, his back against the swimming platform. Still holding my waist, he guides me onto him. My heart racing, I want to laugh and cry at the same time, the sensation so strong it overwhelms me. We begin to move rhythmically and the water moves gently around us, holding us afloat, caressing our bodies. Our rhythm changes, it's faster now, more erratic, and I tighten my legs round his waist, digging my fingernails deep into his skin. And then I come and I know I've never come like this before, the orgasm so complete and overpowering I feel paralysed. All I'm able to do is to hold on to him in order not to drown. He comes right after me and lets out a moan, the first sound he's uttered tonight. We remain motionless in the water and everything around us becomes still, an occasional cry of a bird breaking the silence.

The Day After

I don't quite know how I got back last night, all I remember is standing under a stream of hot water at home, a mixture of mud and bits of water plants at the bottom of the shower. I must've gone to bed straight after that and slept like a log till Wispa woke me up this morning, demanding her walk. Her leg is better, thankfully, she's not limping any more, one thing less to worry about for Bell when she stays here next week.

I'm having my morning coffee at the kitchen table, thinking about yesterday. Flashes of images and feelings I had last night have given way to more rational thoughts. I am unsettled by my encounter with the Dior Man, but not because it was sex with a stranger in a public place. Of course I'd be naive not to acknowledge that there might be a connection between him and the Heath attacks, but somehow this part of the experience, the danger and the taboo nature of it, doesn't bother me now. Yes, it was furtive and illicit, but it was also sexy as hell, probably one of the most satisfying sexual experiences of my entire life. What worries me is that it felt different last night, it wasn't a rough and selfish fuck like I'd experienced with the Dior Man before. There was a new emotional intensity to it, new tenderness, a hint of affection. The Dior Man didn't seem like a stranger any more, my body recognized a certain familiarity in him and responded to it with an urgency that took me by surprise. Yes, he did give me a fright, chasing me across the park, but wasn't it part of the game we had invented together? I have to face the truth: I'm falling for him. I caught myself, as I lay in bed this morning, wondering who he is. I no longer want him to remain anonymous. I want to know his name, hear his voice, see him smile. I want him to know my name. Why does it worry me, I think, as I refill my coffee cup? Because I know I can't let it go on any longer. Without me noticing it, a casual experience has morphed into an addiction. I can't let it go on because it will lead to my own undoing. I feel a sense of loss, disappointment, regret, but I know I have to break the spell now, before it's too late.

Bell calls me to arrange the time she'll arrive at my place tonight. I tell her to come for dinner and then I start packing. Luckily all my uber-business-bitch clothes have just been dry-cleaned, so there isn't much to think about. I check the weather in Paris and it's more or less the same as London, just a couple of degrees warmer, which makes it even easier. By the time Bell arrives I'm packed and ready to go. Laura, Julian's efficient guardian angel, has booked my cab for the ungodly time of 5.45 a.m., so I'll need to go to bed early. I relax for the evening, listening to Bell's Vancouver stories.

Two Days Later

The cab takes me along Euston Road towards St Pancras. We pass by the uninspiring new building of the British Library and then the grand facade of the St Pancras Renaissance Hotel, one of the most romantic and stylish buildings in London. The architectural brilliance of the hotel contrasts with the Victorian functionality of the train station, but somehow the two facades work well together.

'Thank goodness they've finished renovating it at last,' I say to the cab driver and he turns out to be an expert on everything London, telling me the story of George Gilbert Scott's architectural masterpiece.

'They had to close the Midland Grand fifty-nine years after it opened in 1876. And you know why? Because it had only eight bathrooms for three hundred rooms. Imagine dealing with that, if you're in a bit of a hurry. They only invented the toilet six years after it was finished, so the hotel was, pardon my French, in deep shit from the start.' But he reassures me the bathrooms are plentiful there now, all marble and glass, raving about the new place as if he owned it himself.

I check in at the entry gate with my iPhone and have enough time to grab a quick coffee and a croissant in the Business Lounge. The train boards on time and soon I'm in my Club 2 seat, spreading the *Guardian*. A train journey puts me straight away in a holiday mood and although this is far from being a holiday trip, I can't resist indulging in the leisurely activity of reading a newspaper from start to finish. But the news in the paper quickly spoils my holiday mood. A woman politician received a deluge of hostile tweets, including threats to rape and kill her, simply because she tweeted something the trolls didn't like. I find a series of articles on Twitter abuse of women by cyberbullies and the devastating effect it can have on the victims. A psychologist explains the term 'disinhibition', the anonymity of the web that tempts people to behave in a way they wouldn't face-to-face. I'm not on Twitter, but the articles make me think of my recent experiences. Would a visit from Tom's wife classify as some form of stalking? Could her request to leave her husband alone classify as the normal behaviour of a worried wife, or was it excessive jealousy, straight from the *Jeremy Kyle Show*? Then I remember that Samantha is privy to my secret, one that may make me look reckless or predatory in her eyes. Then another possible version of events occurs to me: perhaps she's told Tom about my visit to the clinic and now she's worried he'll develop an interest in me as a result of her indiscretion?

The clinking of the breakfast trolley interrupts my chain of thoughts and I have my second coffee and croissant of the day. As we enter the tunnel I amuse myself by watching my fellow passengers. They are mostly British businessmen, going to Paris for the day, catching up on their emails and polishing spreadsheets on their laptops. I'm sure the morning train from Paris is full of their French counterparts. The man sitting opposite me, whose incessant phone calls in French have been mercifully interrupted by our entry to the tunnel, stares at my legs appreciatively. But there is something so insistent about his look that it makes me uncomfortable. It's not a compliment any more, it's an intrusion. But we are in the civilized and safe environment of the Eurostar and I ignore it, closing my eyes and instantly falling asleep. I wake up just in time to see the stunning skyline of Paris on my left, and then we enter graffiti-covered suburbia and the train manager announces first in French, then in English that still sounds like French, that we'll be arriving in Gare du Nord in a few minutes.

The noise and smell of the station hit me as soon as I leave the train. There is a handful of people waiting for passengers at the exit from the platform. A few young guys mill around looking for punters for their Moto Taxis. I spot my driver holding up a card with my name. He grabs my suitcase and leads me to the car. He sets off, fast and efficient, and I enjoy the ride along the straight, wide boulevards with their cafes and shops, the Haussmann buildings flanking them gracefully. Soon we're in the heart of Paris, on tree-lined Avenue Montaigne, the driver is passing on my suitcase to the hotel porter and I'm welcomed inside like a long-lost friend. My deluxe room at the Plaza Athénée is an Art Deco-style extravagance overlooking Avenue Montaigne. It's so huge you could get lost on the way to the bathroom.

I have a business lunch with other participants of the meeting in the courtyard restaurant. I know most of them from various company gatherings I've attended over the years. The loud Americans, laid-back Scandinavians, precise Germans, hyperactive Italians, irritable French and solemn Slavs. In the afternoon I manage to negotiate a couple of hours to myself and head to Institute Dior for a massage. The irony of my choice doesn't escape me. A full hour of bliss and then the official dinner at the overindulgent Alain Ducasse Michelin-starred restaurant, which lasts past midnight. I think I'm doing a good job preparing the ground for the presentation of Julian's vision tomorrow morning. I get back to my room, check the time, and as it's one hour behind in the UK I decide it's not too late to ring Bell. Her voicemail kicks in and I leave her a message, asking how she's settled in my house and how Wispa's paw is. I tell her briefly about the extravagant hotel I'm staying at, promising the whole story when I get back.

Three Days Later

The meeting, which starts at 9 a.m. sharp, is a nerve-wracking affair. I'm no stranger to being a speaker at that level, but being someone else's envoy is a different matter. Part of me suspects some hidden agenda on Julian's part, some Machiavellian twist I'm not aware of, and it's making me nervous. But my presentation goes well and the response to Julian's vision is positive on the whole. I'm relieved once my solo performance is over and I'm able to take the back seat. Others take over and the subject of restructuring resurfaces at the top of the agenda. It seems it causes similar problems in most of the EMEA countries. Acronyms abound as we learn that restructuring is proceeding well in all the other regions. After the French-wine-fuelled lunch the meeting rambles on for a couple more hours and wraps up well before dinner. To clear my head I decide to go to my favourite part of Paris, Montmartre. I quickly change into casual clothes and leave the hotel.

The hotel taxi drops me off, at my request, at the bottom of the hill, on Boulevard de Clichy, where the tourist village meets the real world with all its bars, peep shows and kebab shops. I walk up the hill towards the Sacré-Coeur and the serene beauty of the basilica standing out against the clear sky moves me, despite its commercial packaging. I ignore the hordes of Maghreb boys trying to sell me key rings in the shape of the Eiffel Tower, sets of postcards and garish T-shirts, and climb the steps up. Once I reach the basilica I turn round and the stunning panorama of Paris spreads before me like a gigantic tourist poster. The view feels familiar and yet it surprises me with its richness and intricacy every time I come to this city. For a while I watch a young guy cheered by the crowds as he climbs a lamp post and does death-defying stunts with a football, and then I move towards the Place du Tertre. The real starving artists moved on from here a long time ago because they couldn't afford it any more and now the place is filled with commercial portrait sketchers and caricaturists who woo tourists with their pieces of prêt-à-porter art. I can't resist an overpriced crêpe with chestnut filling and then escape the crowds and start walking down a set of steep steps. As I stop and stare at the beautiful roofs in the early evening light, something, or someone, catches my eye at the bottom of the steps. It's the silhouette of a man, partially obscured by a big acacia bush, who looks just like the man I saw on Kate's photo in Norfolk. His back is turned to me, but he seems familiar. The broad shoulders I know, the dark curls escaping a navy baseball cap. What is he doing here? I rush down the steps, just as he starts walking away. I nearly trip and fall, the steps suddenly seem steep and precarious, and by the time I reach the bottom, he's disappeared round the corner. I sprint to the street junction and see him again, the navy baseball cap bobbing in the distance. I run, ignoring the reproachful stares of passers-by, and before he reaches the next corner I'm right behind him. I grab his shoulder.

'Hey!' I shout, perhaps a bit too loud.

He turns and I see a handsome Arabic guy staring at me

with a mixture of surprise and apprehension in his eyes. I don't know him.

'*Je suis désolée de vous déranger,*' I mumble in my school French, 'I'm so sorry . . .'

The guy's face lights up in a smile.

'No problem, mademoiselle, what is it that you want?' His English is better than my French.

'No, nothing, it's a mistake . . . I made a mistake . . . I thought you were someone else . . .'

'You are looking for someone? Are you lost?'

'No, no, I'm fine, I thought you were a friend . . .'

'I could be your friend.' He flashes another charming smile.

'No, thank you!' I say, perhaps too abruptly, and waffle on, not to offend him. 'I mean, you are very nice, but I have to go – I'm meeting my husband, you see.'

'Ah, your husband . . .' He seems genuinely disappointed.

'Yes, my husband, he's waiting for me.'

'OK,' he says, raising his arms in a surrender gesture. 'Maybe next time?'

'Yes, next time . . .'

'It's shame. *Bon bah, salut, ma jolie.*' He turns away, shaking his head.

As he walks away, I take in his baseball cap with a glitter skull logo, hip-hop jeans and electric green and orange Nike trainers. I feel mortified. Am I going insane? Accosting some strange guy in a foreign city? What am I doing?

I look around and realize I'm lost. It's much quieter and dirtier here than in Montmartre, the smell of urine wafting from the pavement. I know vaguely I should be heading east. I pass a few brasseries, buzzing with local life, some ethnic restaurants that look shut, a handful of shops filled with bric-a-brac. And then the vibe changes and I'm in a Maghreb village, with groups of Arab men standing on street corners, talking loudly, as if arguing. It's Barbès–Rochechouart and something tells me I shouldn't be walking here on my own at this hour, but I persist, my sense of danger anaesthetized by the adrenaline from my earlier encounter. I cross the main street, looking for the Métro sign or a free taxi, but can't see any. I turn off into what seems like a street leading to somewhere and continue, trying to look confident and walking purposefully. Suddenly a group of teenagers surrounds me, having a fight, pushing and shoving each other. One of them staggers and bumps into me, the others crowd round, I feel a tug and they run off as quickly as they appeared. My small travel bag, which I carried on a strap on my shoulder, is gone. I stand in the middle of the pavement, pushed by people squeezing by, trying to understand what has happened. I've been robbed. It's never happened to me before. I try to remember what was in my bag. My iPhone, my sunglasses and my wallet. Luckily, I have a habit of keeping a selection of wallets, designated for different currencies. This was my Euros wallet, with no cards or IDs inside. My proper UK wallet with all my cards is locked, together with my passport, in the hotel safe. The thieves made off with about a hundred Euros, no big deal. My hotel card key is in the back pocket of my jeans. But the real problem is the loss of my iPhone. Although I have all the contacts backed up on my Mac, it's the hassle of having to report it stolen, then getting it blocked and replaced that I dread. It also means I'll be phoneless until I get back to the UK tomorrow. I return to the main street, looking for a taxi, and quickly realize it's simply impossible to hail one here. My best bet is finding the nearest Métro station. And there it is, on a busy and dirty junction a few hundred metres along the street,

Barbès–Rochechouart. I cling to the wall map of the Métro and plan the route: line number 2 to Charles de Gaulle–Étoile and change for number 1 to Franklin D. Roosevelt. This, I hope, will take me more or less back to the hotel. I'm sure there's a faster way of getting there, but my nerves are frayed and I opt for the route that looks the simplest on the map. I have enough change from the Montmartre crêpe in my pocket to buy a single ticket. Both trains are hot and smelly, but they get me to the hotel at last. I speak to the concierge about the incident. As nice and apologetic as he is about my *'expérience terrible'*, all he suggests is going with my passport to the *commissariat de police* of the arrondissement in which the theft took place and filling out a *constat de vol*. This means going back to Barbès–Rochechouart, which is the last thing I want to do. I thank the concierge and go to my room. I'm upset and tired. I'll deal with the whole issue when I'm back in London, I decide. I open my laptop and see a solid block of unread emails. I can't be bothered with them right now. I just email Claire, letting her know my phone got stolen in case she tries to get in touch with me tomorrow morning before I get to the office, and close my laptop. I lie down on the bed, thinking of my unfortunate escapade. I chased a guy because I thought he was someone I knew. I'm not even sure who I thought he was. Andrew? James? Someone from work? Tom? Now I see how stupid the whole thing was, imagining that a young guy in his hip-hop gear was some kind of a stalker. I realize I've been seeing glimpses of 'the guys I know' all over the place. Now I know they've all been figments of my imagination. I can sort of understand my brain trying to trick me into believing James was close by. Perhaps subconsciously I still haven't separated from him. Or maybe I want him back? I must admit that in moments like this it would be comforting to have him around, full of his masculine protectiveness, making sure 'his lady' was all right. But seeing Andrew who, as far as I know, is four thousand miles away in New York? Or Tom, most probably tucked up in bed with Samantha as we speak? Well, lady, you wanted your freedom, and now you have it: you're on your own. With a flick of a switch I turn off all the lights in my deluxe room and fall asleep.

Four Days Later

Just as I thought, the morning train to London is full of French businessmen going on a work day trip across the Channel. I nibble on my breakfast, working on the meeting report for Julian. I'm supposed to meet him at 11 a.m., which means I have to have the whole thing ready before I get off the train. Going back seems faster and before I know it the train is entering St Pancras. I let all the businessmen disembark in a hurry and then I grab my bag and get off. I join a stream of passengers on an escalator going down and follow the crowd as they file though customs and border control. No one is being stopped, but there are a couple of official-looking plain-clothes guys watching people. I'm just about to pass them when I hear my name.

'Ms Wright?'

I stop and look at them.

'Yes?'

The taller of the guys, with mousy hair and tired eyes, shows me his ID.

'I'm DI Brown and this is DS Kapoor. I was wondering if you could accompany us to our office in the station.'

'Is it about the theft of my phone?' I look at my watch, wondering how they'd know about it so quickly. 'I have to be at work by eleven.'

'I'm afraid this is rather urgent,' says DI Brown.

They don't say anything else as I follow them through the station to the British Transport Police office. We enter a small room with a table and four chairs around it. DI Brown pulls one of them out for me and we all sit, facing each other.

'My apologies for stopping you like this, but we're aware that your phone was stolen while you were in Paris, so we didn't have any means of contacting you earlier.'

Ah, so it is about my phone, I think with relief. DI Brown clears his throat and continues.

'I'm afraid there's been a murder.' He pauses as if to give me time to process what he's just said. Still, I wonder what it has to do with me. 'We understand you are a friend of Ms Belinda Young.'

'Bell? Something happened to Bell?'

'Her body was found on Hampstead Heath yesterday morning.'

What he's just said doesn't sink in straight away. I look at him, half-expecting him to smile, to apologize for his terrible joke, to reassure me she's fine. But his tired eyes are unsmiling, his expression sombre.

'We'd like you to accompany us to the station.'

'Am I under arrest?' I ask stupidly.

'Of course not.' There's a hint of some feeling, perhaps compassion, in his eyes now. 'But your help would be invaluable to our investigation.'

A wave of weakness hits me and for a moment I'm afraid I'm going to faint. DS Kapoor, a slim, dark-skinned man with big, sad eyes, hands me a plastic cup of water. I take a sip. It's lukewarm and tastes of dust, but it does help me regain my composure.

'What about my work?' I ask, too shocked to realize the absurdity of my question.

'We've informed them of the situation.'

I nod, although I'm still not able to grasp the full extent of 'the situation'. DS Kapoor takes my suitcase and they lead me through the station to an unmarked car with a driver, parked right by the exit on double yellow lines.

No one says anything as we travel through London. I look out of the window, not registering where we're going, my mind churning around the few horrible facts I've been told, unable to make any sense out of it. We arrive at an ugly, concrete and glass building that turns out to be Kentish Town police station.

I'm led to a room that looks very much like the one at St Pancras and offered tea or coffee. I ask for tea, which DS Kapoor brings in a paper cup. It's milky and sweet. I take the first sip, then the door opens and a tall woman with short curly hair walks in. She's dressed formally, in dark trousers and a white blouse, but she's not wearing a uniform. I recognize her from the broadcast about the Heath rape.

'DCI Vic Jones,' she introduces herself and her handshake is dry and strong. 'I do appreciate you agreeing to come here.'

'I didn't have much choice.' It's more of a statement of fact, not a complaint on my part. 'But there must have been some terrible mistake.'

DCI Jones shakes her head sadly. 'I'm afraid not.'

'But it can't be true.' I want her to say something, to finish this awful game they are playing, but she says nothing. 'How . . . how did you find me?'

'We found a mobile phone in the pocket of Ms Young's raincoat and by checking her contact list and most frequently called numbers found you. We have also retrieved a voice message you left for her on Monday evening.'

Oh God, my message.

'Was she . . . was she already . . .' I can't finish the question.

DCI Jones nods. 'She was already dead when you rang her,' she says quietly.

I let out a sob I can't control. DCI Jones waits for me to compose myself.

'I'm so sorry,' she says quietly.

Eventually I take a sip of the sweet tea and look at her.

'Can you tell me what happened?'

She nods and pauses, as if deciding what to tell me.

'The body of Ms Young was found yesterday morning, about seven a.m., by a dog walker, in the area directly behind the Ladies' Pond on Hampstead Heath.' I feel a wave of nausea and force another sip of tea down my throat.

'We've established the time of her death between seven p.m. and ten p.m. the night before. Her body was partially hidden in the bushes, hence it remained undiscovered for so long, even though the area is not particularly isolated. But it was pouring with rain that evening and dusk, so not many people ventured out to the park. From your message we understood she was staying at your house while you were away, looking after your dog.'

'My dog . . .' I mumble.

'A chocolate Labrador named Wispa?' She looks at me with a tiny hint of a smile in her eyes.

'Yes.'

'She's fine. It was actually DS Kapoor who found her on the Heath yesterday.'

I sigh with relief, feeling selfish for being happy my dog is fine while my friend is dead. And then an awful realization hits me.

'It's my fault she's dead. I made her come to my house and look after my dog while I was away. If I hadn't asked her, she'd be alive.'

'No, Anna.' She reaches out and covers my hand with hers. 'You are not responsible for your friend's death. You shouldn't feel guilty.'

'But I do.' I can't control my sobbing again.

'It's not your fault,' she says quietly.

There's a knock on the door and DS Kapoor looks in. DCI Jones nods and he disappears, closing the door. We sit in silence as I dry my eyes with a tissue DCI Jones has given me. Then the door opens again and Wispa bounces in, followed by DS Kapoor. She runs straight to me, puts her front paws on my knees and licks my face. I can't help but laugh through tears.

'Oh, puppy, you're OK.'

She dances around the room, her tail wagging, runs to DS Kapoor, then comes back to me.

'Thank you.' I smile at him.

He nods, smiles back and leaves the room.

'Anna,' DCI Jones looks at me, 'I hope you don't mind me calling you by your first name . . .'

I shrug and shake my head.

'I'm afraid I have some more bad news. Your house has been burgled.'

I look at her, uncomprehending.

'It probably happened on Monday night and we have reasons to believe it's connected with Ms Young's murder. Our forensic team is there now, finishing their investigation. It means you won't be able to go back to it tonight.'

I just stare at her, completely numb.

'Is there anyone you could stay with tonight? We can, of course, provide temporary accommodation for you, if that's what you'd prefer.'

'Michael,' I whisper.

'OK.' She takes out a pen and opens her little notebook. 'Could you give me his surname?'

'Oliver. I'll call him . . .' I say and remember I don't have my phone. 'I have his number on my laptop.'

'It's OK, we'll get in touch with him for you. If you'd excuse me for a moment.'

She leaves the room and I'm on my own with Wispa, who looks at me, whining quietly. I hug her and kiss her big head. Then I realize she must have seen it happen. She knows who Bell's killer is. She paws me, as she always does when she's trying to tell me something.

DCI Jones comes back to the room and sits down again. She looks at me, her face kind and compassionate.

'I'm afraid there's one more thing. We've been trying to locate Ms Young's immediate family, without much success . . .'

'She was adopted by an older couple when she was a kid. Both her adoptive parents died a few years ago.'

'No brothers or sisters?'

'No.'

'A partner?'

I hesitate briefly, then say no again. DCI Jones nods and marks something in her notebook.

'You two were close?'

'Yes. She was . . . my family.' I feel the tears choking me again.

DCI Jones remains silent for a while, then clears her throat.

'In the absence of next of kin, I'll have to ask you to formally identify Ms Young's body. I know how hard it's going to be for you, but would you mind doing it for us?'

I don't say anything, just nod, trying not to think about what lies ahead of me.

'Thank you.' She sounds like she really means it.

'Did she . . . Was she—' My throat tightens with grief and I'm unable to speak. But DCI Jones seems to understand what I want to know.

'She was fully clothed and there were no signs of sexual assault. She'd been strangled.'

'Oh God . . .' I can't keep the tears in any longer. They come out in a flood, while I sob like a child. DCI Jones puts her hand on my arm and lets me cry. After a while, when my sobs begin to subside, there is a quiet knock on the door. DS Kapoor again.

'Mr Oliver is on his away.'

'Thank you, Navin.' She nods at him, then turns to me. 'Anna, we'll pick you up from Mr Oliver's tomorrow morning, if that's OK.'

I agree, my life suddenly being taken over by the police investigation.

Five Days Later

I wake up in Michael's guest room, heavy from the Ambien he gave me last night. For a few blissful moments I don't know why I'm here, then the awful memories of yesterday start flooding in. I lie in bed, staring at the ceiling, unable to move. Bell is gone. A part of me still hangs on to the hope that it's all been a terrible mistake that will somehow get explained soon. Perhaps if I stay in bed and don't let the reality in, I'll keep her alive in my mind. I hear a distant doorbell, some movement downstairs in the house, front door opening and closing. Then there are light footsteps on the stairs and a delicate knock on the door. Wispa, who is lying on the floor by the bed, gives a short bark.

'Anna?' It's Michael.

'Yes?'

He cracks the door open and peeks in. Wispa gets up to greet him, her tail wagging.

'It's for you.' He puts a small box on the bedside table.

'What is it?'

'Your new phone. All sorted out by Claire.'

'Oh, Claire . . .' Reality calls me and I know I'll have to get up and face the world.

'I'll be waiting for you downstairs with the coffee.' He closes the door.

I force myself to get up and stumble to the bathroom. I avoid looking at myself in the mirror because I know I look awful. Back in the guest room I find some clean clothes in my Paris suitcase, then follow the sound of a radio to Michael's kitchen, Wispa on my heels. Michael's on his laptop at the kitchen table, but closes it when I come in.

'Darling, your coffee.' He puts the mug in front of me as I sit down at the table. 'Would you like a fresh croissant with it?'

'No, thank you, coffee's fine.'

'DS Kapoor will be coming over soon to pick you up.' He speaks to me gently, as if to a sick child.

'Oh, DS Kapoor . . .' I remember what lies ahead of me today.

'Would you like me to come with you?'

'No, sweetie, thank you, I'll be fine.' I know I have to pull myself together.

'Would you like me to help you with anything, make some phone calls?'

'No, it's fine, really.' I try to sound as if I know what I'm doing.

'What about Bell's new girlfriend?'

I remember Candice.

'We have to get in touch with her.'

'All I know is that she lives in Moscow, Idaho, and works at the university there.'

'We'll find her.'

I recall my last conversation with Bell.

'She's supposed to come over in a couple of weeks. That's why Bell was decorating . . . She was so happy . . .' I feel tears welling up in my eyes. 'Oh, Michael, it's all my fault . . .'

'Shhh.' He puts his arm round me. 'It's not your fault, stop thinking that.'

We sit in silence for a long time. I feel the warmth of Michael's embrace and it makes the pain less acute. Eventually he looks at the kitchen clock and gets up.

'We need to get you ready for DS Kapoor. You can leave Wispa with me today, I'll be working from home.'

He takes a small brown bottle out of a kitchen cabinet and slides a pill across the table in my direction.

'Xanax,' he says. 'I use it for long-haul flights. Take one.'

I do what he says, swallowing it with a sip of cold coffee.

By the time DS Kapoor arrives the world seems distant and muted, the feelings of guilt and loss almost bearable. I know they'll come back, but numbness is what I need right now.

The next few hours are like a bad dream, but a dream, nevertheless, Xanax taking the edge off reality. DS Kapoor takes me to a nondescript building where DCI Jones is already waiting for me. They lead me to a small room and then I'm on my own with Bell, although I know that DCI Jones is standing beside me. Then I'm with DCI Jones in another room, drinking hot tea out of a paper cup. She talks to me in a quiet voice, something about Bell's clothes. She shows me a green raincoat and I'm surprised to see it, because it's mine.

'This is what Bell was wearing when she was found on the Heath,' she tells me.

The significance of it slowly sinks in and I start crying. Bell and I always used to borrow each other's clothes because we had such similar figures.

'It's my fault she's dead, it's my fault,' I keep repeating, refusing to stop.

And then I'm back at Michael's, crying into Wispa's soft neck while DCI Jones talks to Michael quietly in the hallway.

Six Days Later

Today is the day I'm supposed to go back to my house. The forensics guys have finished whatever they were doing there and the local glazier has fixed a broken window the burglars got in through. Michael called Sherie Lou, who offered to drop her regular jobs of the day and come to help sort out the mess. By the time Michael and I arrive, the house looks as if nothing out of the ordinary has happened there.

As Michael chats with Sherie Lou in the kitchen, I walk around the house, looking for any signs of someone being here. I can't see anything out of place and nothing seems to be missing. All the usual things burglars are interested in – camera, computer, flat-screen TV, iPod, jewellery – are still here. Even my CD and DVD collections remain untouched. Maybe my CDs aren't cool enough any more to be nicked. I check my safe, tucked away in one of the bedroom wardrobes, but it's locked and intact.

I join Michael and Sherie Lou and she tells me about the state she found my place in when she arrived this morning. According to her, apart from the forensics dust it was just very messy.

'It was as if Wispa went on a real rampage all over the place,' she says and Wispa trots to her, having heard her name.

'Everything was off the shelves, out of the drawers, books, clothes, papers, even your bedding was on the floor. Very, very messy. Wispa wouldn't do such a thing.' She pats her on the head.

'What the hell was that about then?' wonders Michael. 'Were they looking for something?'

'I really don't think there is anything here that could be something . . .'

Despite my casual tone, I feel deeply unsettled by it. I think of what DCI Jones said: 'We have reasons to believe it's connected with Ms Young's murder.' But how? Did the murderer come here?

'Oh, by the way, DCI Jones is coming over soon, she wanted to have a chat with you,' says Michael and I know he must've been wondering the same thing.

I thank and pay Sherie Lou, who promises to come back in a few days.

Michael is pottering about, making fresh coffee.

'Michael, you know you don't have to babysit me. I'll be fine on my own.'

'I know, babycakes. You're doing very well.'

We finish our coffees and Michael leaves, but only after he makes me agree he'll come back later and cook dinner for both of us.

I'm on my own for the first time since I've learnt about Bell's murder. My house feels empty and unfriendly, despite Wispa's soothing presence. I walk around, looking at objects as if they belonged to someone else. I can't see any of Bell's things and I assume the police must have taken them. I know I should get in touch with Claire, find out what's happening at work, report back to Julian about the Paris meeting, but the feeling of despondence that overwhelms me is so strong, all I can do is curl up on the sofa in a dull stupor, neither asleep nor awake. Bell. Bell, I'm so sorry. Wispa jumps on the sofa and stretches beside me, as if she knows I'm not going to tell her off this time.

I'm woken up by the doorbell and next I'm in the kitchen making a cup of tea for DCI Jones. She asks me to call her Vic.

'I need your help, Anna. I think you have some information that can help us catch whoever did this.'

'I'm not sure if I know anything that can be of any use to the investigation.'

'Is it OK if I ask you some questions?'

I nod.

'Can you think of anyone who'd want to harm Ms Young?'

'No, absolutely not. She was one of the most gentle, likeable, funny, generous people I've known.'

'No enemies? No disgruntled exes?'

I shake my head.

'No. She was a massage therapist, had her own practice, was actually helping people. And she'd been single for a while. Actually, no, she'd met someone recently, but this person lives in the States.'

For some reason I feel reluctant to disclose the fact that Bell was a lesbian. DCI Jones smiles.

'And you have no reason to believe that this . . . person wanted to harm her?' She leaves a small pause before the word 'person' and something about her look and her manner tells me DCI Jones might be a lesbian herself.

'No, they've only just met and they were very much in love. In fact, Candice was supposed to come to visit her in a couple of weeks. I need to find out her email address and let her know about Bell . . .'

I feel it's all too much for me and I'm welling up again. DCI Jones gives me a tissue and patiently waits for me to compose myself.

'We can give you her details if you want to get in touch with her,' she says eventually and I realize she's known all along about Candice. Of course, I think, the police have Bell's phone and her laptop.

'What about you? Is there anyone who might have wanted to hurt you?'

'Me? I don't understand.'

'We have to look at the crime from all angles,' she says gently. 'Bell had been staying at your place and was wearing your coat and walking your dog when she was attacked. It was pouring with rain that evening, it was likely she had the hood up.'

'Oh God, so it *was* my fault . . .'

'No, but we have to examine and exclude all the possibilities.'

DCI Jones watches me with her kind but penetrating eyes as I frantically try to think what to tell her. Or rather, what to omit.

'I'm not involved with anyone at present. I've recently split up with my boyfriend and I'm not ready for another relationship.'

DCI Jones nods.

'I'll need his details, it's just a formality. Anyone at work with a grudge?'

'Well, we're going through a major restructuring, some people are going to lose their jobs and I'll probably be the one who'll tell them about it.'

She nods again.

'Anyone else? Stalkers, weird callers, cyber trolls?'

Well, I've had my share of weirdos, including my ex-husband, poisoning my life over the years, but it's not something I want to share with the police right now.

'I really can't think of anyone,' I lie and for some reason I'm sure DCI Jones can read my thoughts. She watches me for a while in silence, as if waiting for me to change my mind, then gets up and puts her empty mug in the sink.

'Thank you very much for the tea, Anna. If you think of anything else, do give me a ring, anytime.' She puts her business card on my kitchen table. 'Even the smallest detail you find irrelevant might help us with the investigation.' It sounds a little like a rebuke, but maybe it's a slight feeling of guilt that makes me read something else into her words.

'Do you think I might be in danger?' I say, partly to ease my conscience and keep the conversation going for a bit longer.

'We've increased our presence in the area. There are uniformed police patrolling your street. Our chief super lives nearby, not that it's any reassurance. But if you see or hear anything suspicious, let us know immediately.' She sounds very formal now and I know she's annoyed with me for holding out on her.

I close the door behind her and go back to the kitchen. I realize she's neither confirmed nor denied whether she thinks I might be in danger.

Nine Days Later

The weekend disappears in a fog of Ambien and red wine. At some point I hear a doorbell, which I ignore. When I stumble to the door eventually I find a folded piece of paper someone's put through the letter box. It's a scribbled note.

> *Dear Anna, I haven't seen you for a while and was wondering if everything is OK. Do give me a shout if you fancy a morning run together. Tom xxx*

Thanks, but no thanks, I think and crumple it. I throw it into the bin outside as I leave the house to walk Wispa. It's only a stagger round the block and she's not happy about it.

On Monday I wake up early in the morning and I know it's time to face the world and reclaim my life. I can't keep on hiding in the safety of my own space forever. I get up and leave a message for Claire to let her know I'll be coming into the office today. I ask her to check with Laura if Julian's free to see me. I still haven't updated him about the Paris meeting. It seems it happened aeons ago and has lost its urgency and relevance, but, nevertheless, this is what work is about. Thankfully, Chiara is back from Italy and she's willing to walk Wispa.

It's been more than a week since my last encounter with

the Dior Man. I know I'll never want to risk meeting him on
the Heath again. That part of my life is over, I think and almost
immediately doubt my own conviction. Would I be able to resist
the experience if I saw him again? But what if he's Bell's killer?
It's too awful to contemplate, but there is a chance that he may
have seen Bell wearing my coat, walking my dog, and thought
it was me. He could've pounced on her as part of our sexual
game and realized too late it wasn't me. She gets spooked, tries
to fight him off and he accidentally kills her? No, it can't be
true, it's not possible. I reject the scenario partly because I don't
want to feel guilty about it.

The office welcomes me with an artificially hushed atmosphere. Everyone stares at me with curiosity dressed as compassion.
Claire updates me efficiently on the latest developments, telling
me only the things I need to know. Then she informs me Julian
is waiting upstairs. He greets me warmly and my hand stays in
both of his for what seems like an eternity, while he tells me
how sorry he is to hear what hell I've been through. When he
releases my hand eventually, he swiftly moves on to business.
My report from Paris seems to please him, but I detect a certain
change in his attitude towards me. It's as if I've been tainted
by the recent events, carry an incurable illness he wants nothing
to do with. He praises my Paris performance and wraps up our
meeting uncharacteristically quickly, telling me I should feel
free to take as much time off as I feel is necessary. I assure him
I'm fine and fit for work, which he dismisses with a wave of his
hand. As I step into the lift going down my alarm bells are
ringing. Whatever has brought on this sudden change does not
bode well for my future in the company. I try to concentrate
on the backlog of emails in my mailbox, but the feeling of
impending doom that seems to hover above my head is too

distracting. By six o'clock I feel I've wasted the whole day. I leave, feeling useless and anxious.

My phone rings just as I'm parking the car in front of my house. It's my old friend Sue, horrified by the news of Bell's death she's just heard from Michael. She also needs my advice on some work issue, she admits sheepishly, wondering if I'm up to getting together tonight. I agree readily, grateful for the prospect of her company. We arrange to meet at my local pizza place, which should be quiet enough to have an undisturbed chat.

She's waiting for me when I arrive at the restaurant and gives me a big hug that instantly makes me tearful. We fuss over choosing wine and ordering our food, which gives me time to compose myself. Our waiter arrives with a bottle of Montepulciano d'Abruzzo, opens it, pours the wine and disappears.

'Do you want to talk about it?' There's genuine compassion in her look.

'No,' I say, maybe a bit too abruptly. 'Can we please talk about something else?'

'Of course,' she says gently and takes a sip of her wine. 'I need to run something by you.'

A wave of relief washes over me. It feels good to be treated like a normal human being again.

'I've been approached . . .'

'By whom?'

She looks up, pointing at the ceiling. 'Tamara.'

'Big T?!'

This is exciting. Tamara Ashley-Sharpe is a corporate legend, making splashes on both sides of the pond. She knows everyone and everything there is to know about the media world. Sharp, as in her name, posh and without any manners, she is as ruthless as a hammerhead shark. And she is the best media headhunter in London.

'She approached you personally?'

Sue nods, not looking very thrilled.

'I don't know what to do, Anna. She is tempting me, quite unashamedly. I mean, I've flirted with the idea, but . . .'

'You don't want to sell your soul to the devil?'

'It's not that. You sell your soul working for any big corporation these days anyway. What worries me is that it's such a high-up job. I mean, it's Head of Production of a monster, not just a cosy little gig like I have at the moment. I won't be able to go to any shoots, do anything creative, it'll be meetings, meetings, meetings all the time. And what about Olive?' Olive is Sue's six-year-old daughter who she's bringing up on her own, having got rid of the hapless father of the child, who was nothing but trouble. 'I wouldn't have any time for her.' She falls silent and takes another sip of her wine.

'You've turned it down, then?'

She nods. 'But she's not taking no for an answer.'

Our pizzas arrive and we busy ourselves with food for a while.

'Did you talk money?'

'My department matched their original offer, so they came up with another sum, a ridiculously large amount. I know if I don't take it now I'll never be able to earn that much in my whole life.'

'But you won't take it.' I know Sue well enough to risk a guess.

'No.' She looks at me and I see stubborn determination in her eyes.

'Good.' I raise my glass. 'Here's to your gut instinct.'

'You really think I'm doing the right thing?'

'Yes,' I say and I mean it. 'Your gut instinct has never failed you before.'

She clutches on to my approval with relief.

'To freedom,' she says and raises her glass.

'Well, to relative freedom,' I correct her and we drink to that.

'All well at your work?'

'I'm not sure.' I tell her about the Paris conference and Julian's strange behaviour earlier today. She knows Julian from the past, when they both worked for a small production company in Soho.

'Don't worry about it. Julian is a cyborg, totally incapable of dealing with emotionally charged situations. I mean, look at him, he's never even been in a proper relationship with another human being. He avoids feelings like the plague. And here you are, marching into his office, all raw and emotional. He simply didn't know how to deal with it. But it'll pass, believe me.'

'I hope you're right. I really don't fancy looking for another job right now.'

'Remember my gut instinct?' Sue grins at me. 'It's never wrong.'

I get back home, my spirit lifted by Sue's youthful energy. But as soon as I close the door behind me and see the dark corridor, all the demons are back. Without turning on the light I go to the kitchen and open the fridge. Its light throws an eerily cold glow on the tiled floor. I reach for the Britta jug of filtered water and then I notice a half-empty bottle of Pinot Gris standing on the door shelf. I know straight away it was Bell who'd brought it in for herself, it was one of her favourites. I take it out and pour myself a glass.

'Bell, Bell, you have no idea how much I miss you,' I murmur and Wispa looks at me, startled by the sound.

I raise the glass, imagine clinking it with her, as we always used to do, then take a sip. Its crisp, citrusy acidity hits my palate and I know that from this moment on it will always remind me of Bell.

Ten Days Later

I'm going for a morning run with Wispa. Whoever it is trying to destroy the serenity and normal daily rhythm of Hampstead is not going to succeed for much longer. Part of me feels guilty and sad, as if I'm betraying Bell's memory. Am I selfish? Perhaps I am, but I need to pull myself out of the vortex of gloom and I can't think of another way of doing it. I need my runner's high, an injection of friendly endorphins, the natural morphine my body will produce to smother the pain and misery. Wispa, who's been watching me carefully, senses my determination and jumps up from her bed, ready for action. It takes me a while to find my running gear, but eventually I'm out of the door, an excited Wispa at my heels. As I reach the end of my street, my determination weakens and instead of turning right towards the Heath I turn left and head in the direction of Waterlow Park. I can't go to the Heath. I still can't deal with being in a place that in my mind is somehow responsible for Bell's death. It feels tainted, menacing, and I'm too weak to face its darkness.

There are people already in the park: a few runners, someone pushing a pram purposefully, a handful of dog walkers and a solitary man reading a paper on one of the benches facing the main meadow. As I run past him the smell of freshly brewed coffee hits me and I notice a paper coffee cup perched on the bench beside him. This instantly awakens my own coffee craving and I'm already looking forward to the first sip of espresso at home. It feels good to be out and running. Morning sunshine bathes the trees and the grass in a soft light that makes everything look clean and bucolic. Nothing bad can ever happen in a place like this, I think to myself as I run up the hill, my lungs filling with fresh air, my heart pumping at a steady rate. I should go out tonight, get some positive energy from other people – it's always been the best cure for sadness. I need someone who has a good vibe, someone who isn't connected with all the shit that's going on around me. Ray. A ray of sunshine, I smile to myself. I pull my mobile out of my bumbag and dial his number. Predictably, it goes straight to his voicemail. I leave him a short and breezy message, mentioning the possibility of meeting up for a drink tonight. This simple act of being proactive makes me feel even better. I continue my run. A small fluffy dog barks at Wispa and I exchange friendly smiles with its owner, a stumpy woman in a pink jogging suit. I do another small loop round the lake and head home through the Swain's Lane gate. Wispa, clearly disappointed by the shortness of our run, falls behind sniffing at something, ignoring my calls. I have to go back, grab her by the collar and drag her away from her smelly find. As I approach my house, something outside it doesn't seem right. The proportions are all wrong and when I get closer I notice that my car, parked in a lucky spot right in front of the house, is lower than usual. I stop and stare at it in disbelief. All four tyres are completely flat. As I take a closer look I realize this is not just some unlucky coincidence: someone has slashed all four of them. I circle the car slowly and when I reach the back a cold shiver runs through me. Someone has sprayed a word across the whole width of the rear window. Big, clumsy white letters spell out BITCH. I shout at Wispa who's dawdling again, wait for her to enter the house and slam the door behind us. I lean on the hall wall and slide down to the floor, unable to breathe. When I eventually manage to catch a breath it comes out as a sob. I sit on the floor until the coldness of the tiles makes me shiver, then get up and stumble to the kitchen. I rummage through bits of paper, old bills and mini-cab cards on the kitchen table until I find DCI Jones's business card. I dial her number. She answers almost instantly. I'm not sure I make sense telling her about the car, but she sounds serious when she replies. She wants me to come down to the station and she's sending DS Kapoor to pick me up in a car right now. I barely have time to have a quick shower and throw some clothes on before he rings my doorbell. I grab my phone and my bag, tell Wispa to be a good girl, lock the door and get into the police car. DS Kapoor smiles at me, but looks concerned. As he drives I leave a message for Claire telling her I'll be late for work. For once I don't even feel guilty about it. Perhaps I should've taken Julian's offer of stress leave, maybe I'm not ready to go back to work yet, I think, as we drive through the streets waking up to the rush hour. But I would've been perfectly fine this morning if some arsehole hadn't vandalized my BMW, I reason with my own doubt.

DS Kapoor parks the car right in front of the station and takes me straight to DCI Jones's office. She greets me with a smile and offers me coffee, which I gratefully accept. She asks me to repeat the story of the car, then nods slowly.

'It may be just a case of random vandalism, but it could also be the work of someone who has a grudge against you, Anna. And you have to tell me who that person may be.'

I look at her, uncomprehending.

'Anna, I have a feeling you haven't been entirely honest with me so far. No, maybe not dishonest, but you haven't made an effort to tell me everything. Please help me, walk me through your life. Give me a chance to understand what's really going on.'

I feel a hot flush rising to my cheeks. The last time I felt like this was in the headmistress's office at school. DCI Jones has a way of making me feel naive and guilty at the same time. I take a deep breath.

'There was a stalker who was obsessed with me and used to go through my rubbish bins and send me weird notes, but that was ages ago. The guy got sectioned in the end, I think.'

She nods. 'He died at Rampton Hospital five years ago.'

'Oh.' I can't believe she has managed to dig that up. 'Well, you obviously know about my ex-husband, Andrew . . .'

'Andrew Price,' she leafs through the printouts on her desk, 'lives in New York, for the past three months has been lecturing at the University of Buenos Aires. Politics and Management of Science and Technology,' she reads out from her notes.

'Oh well, you know more about my exes than I do.' I can't keep the sarcasm out of my voice. 'How is James, then?'

She picks up another printout.

'According to his place of work he's taken six months' unpaid leave to go travelling. South-East Asia I'm told. We're confirming with Border Control whether he's left the country.'

I try to hide my surprise. James had talked about taking some time off to travel, but I always thought he was too obsessed with his work to actually do it. Oh well, it turns out even overachievers can change. I wonder if he's taken the blonde with him.

'Anyone else?' DCI Jones watches me closely.

She knows I haven't told her the whole truth and I have to give her something she doesn't know about to get her off my back. So I tell her about Tom's wife, the seemingly innocuous encounter that started my acquaintance with her husband, their party, and how she came knocking on my door. I say nothing about my visit to the clinic.

'Is this behaviour still going on?'

'No, I haven't seen her for a while, actually.'

'Do you know why it's stopped?'

I shrug my shoulders. DCI Jones looks at me for a while, then nods.

'How would you describe your relationship with Michael Oliver?'

'With Michael?' I let out a small laugh. 'I've known him for ages. He's my best friend. Patient, reliable, understanding. Better than any girlfriend I've ever had . . .' I stumble over my words. 'Except Bell.'

DCI Jones gives me time to compose myself, then presses on.

'Anyone else you can think of?'

'There's Alden . . .'

I tell her about his strange visit to my place and how Tom came to the rescue.

'Tom again?'

'Yes – I didn't know what to do with Alden. He was completely drunk. Some girlfriend problems.' I remember what Tom had told me about him. 'That's a bit strange, actually. Alden talks about his girlfriend as if they are still together. But Tom told me that she'd left him ages ago.'

'It seems you've spent quite a lot of time chatting to Tom.'

She still doesn't believe a word I'm saying.

'It was mostly Tom doing the chatting. But I haven't seen him, or his wife, for a while.'

She looks at me as if waiting for me to continue. I shrug and regret the gesture almost instantly.

'Thank you, you've been very helpful,' she says at last and I'm not sure if she's being sarcastic or not. 'DS Kapoor will take you back home. Or would you rather he took you straight to work?'

'Home will be fine. I need to pick up a few things before I go to work.'

Not to mention sorting out my car.

As if on cue, DS Kapoor knocks and opens the door, and DCI Jones gives him a small nod. She gets up and shakes my hand. The interview is clearly over and she has no more time for me. DS Kapoor leads me through the station's corridors back to the main entrance.

We are heading towards the exit when a small group of men enters the building. I can't see their faces clearly against the light, but there are two uniformed policemen flanking a couple of civilians. As they approach us I gasp when I recognize one of the men in plain clothes and DS Kapoor looks at me in surprise. It's the Dior Man. The group passes us in silence, just as DS Kapoor touches my arm and asks me if I'm all right. I must look really bad because he directs me to a plastic chair in the reception and rushes over to a water dispenser. As I sip the lukewarm water from a plastic cup, disjointed thoughts frantically cross my head. What is the Dior

Man doing at the station? Is this why DCI Jones has brought me here? I half-expect DS Kapoor to take me back to DCI Jones's office. Or worse, straight to some dingy interrogation room. But he just stands there patiently by my side, the concerned look back on his face. I finish the water and decide to see what happens if I try to leave the station. DS Kapoor follows me closely as I approach the door. The fresh air hits me and I realize I've been holding my breath for far too long. As I breathe deeply the colour seems to come back to the world around me.

'Are you feeling better?'

'Yes, thank you.' For some reason the concerned face of DS Kapoor makes me want to giggle. But I know the whole situation is no laughing matter.

'Let's take you home then,' he says awkwardly and opens the car door for me. He doesn't say anything else and I'm grateful for his silence. As we are moving slowly through the streets clogged with traffic I try to understand what has just happened. Has DCI Jones arranged the whole situation to see my reaction? Could the Dior Man be the killer after all? Is he under arrest? How did they catch him? Has he noticed me? What is going to happen now?

DS Kapoor offers to walk me to my front door, but I thank him and send him on his way. He drives off and I'm left standing on my doorstep, still unable to understand what is going on. If the scene at the station had been arranged by DCI Jones, they wouldn't let me out of their sight, I decide. Which means they haven't made the connection between me and the Dior Man. But what was he doing at the station? Is he a suspect? I have no answers to the questions buzzing around in my head.

I open the front door and am greeted by an overexcited Wispa. I go straight to the sitting room and throw myself on the sofa. I feel almost catatonic, unable to face the outside world. I open my laptop and write a short email to Claire, inventing a story about the police needing my assistance for the rest of the day, then curl up and close my eyes, Wispa stretched on the floor beside the sofa. Sleep comes instantaneously, heavy and dreamless, as if someone has switched off the world.

I'm woken up by Wispa's growling, a low and menacing rumble I always forget she's capable of. She's still lying by the sofa, her head up, her ears pricked, staring in the direction of the hallway. I reach out and touch her neck. She growls again. I raise my head and listen for any sound that may have disturbed her. There's nothing for a while and then she growls again and I hear a slight creaking of the staircase, nothing more than a sigh of the old wood. Fear creeps up my chest and throat, the thumping of my heart roaring in my ears. There it is again. Wispa growls and I close my fist on the thick fur on her neck. Without moving my head I cast a look around, searching for something I could use as a weapon. There is a heavy candlestick on the mantelpiece, but it's on the other side of the room. Wispa gets to her feet and takes a couple of steps towards the sitting-room door, her movements slow and precise, her tail down between her legs. I hear another sound, the soft patter of feet and a delicate click, as if the front-door latch was quietly closing. I jump up, leap for the mantelpiece and, armed with the candlestick, rush out to the hallway. Wispa follows me closely. There is no one in the hallway and the front door is closed. I dash to the door and open it wide, the candlestick still in my hand. The street outside is empty, no passers-by, no moving cars. The neighbour's cat, who's been licking its paw on their windowsill, freezes with the paw up, staring at me contemptuously. I shut the door and turn the key in the mortice lock. With Wispa at my heels and candlestick in hand, I go upstairs and check every room, looking into wardrobes and the airing cupboard under the stairs. There is no one there and nothing looks out of place. I walk down to the kitchen and put the kettle on. As the sound of the boiling water fills the room, I sit heavily at the kitchen table, looking at the candlestick I've brought with me. Am I overreacting? Wispa was probably growling at the neighbour's cat and my house, as any old Victorian building, is full of strange noises. I need to pull myself together, sort out the car, think of work, face the world. I resist the temptation to call Michael. He's been helping me far too much, I have to start dealing with my life on my own.

Calling my car insurance is a start. I have a long discussion with 'John' from the insurance company about their definition of vandalism and what I need to do to arrange for the repair. 'John' assures me their damage assessor will come this afternoon and the car will be fixed by the end of today. I check my work emails, but there isn't much that needs immediate attention. It almost looks as if they've rerouted all the important emails for someone else to deal with. I feel a tiny sting of paranoia, briefly consider whether I'm on my way out, then decide I have more important things to worry about than losing my job.

My heart skips a beat when I hear someone at the front door. Wispa dashes to the door, wagging her tail. It's Chiara, unable to get in because of the key in the mortice lock. I open the door and an overjoyed Wispa greets her with so much enthusiasm I almost feel jealous. I tell her I'm working from home and I'll take Wispa for her daily walk. As I close the door behind Chiara a sudden thought hits me. Bell had a set of my front-door keys. They weren't in the pile of her possessions the police have shown me. Where are they? I pick up my phone to call DCI Jones, then put it down. If making me bump into the Dior Man at the station was some clever ruse, she'd be expecting me to call her at some point, to try to find out what's going on. Which is exactly what I'm tempted to do. Which is what I should avoid doing at all cost.

The Dior Man. My thoughts go back to him. I simply can't imagine he could be the Heath killer. Or maybe I just don't want him to be the one. I'm confused, unable to trust my own judgement. What is worse, there is no one I can confide in. Oh, Bell, I miss you! Michael knows about my Heath encounters, but there is a huge difference between having anonymous sex al fresco and having sex with someone who could be a rapist and a killer. He hasn't brought the subject up since I told him about it and it's best to leave it that way. I still don't know who the Dior Man is and I don't want to know. Or do I? I feel I'm going round in circles. I need to clear my head. I grab Wispa's leash and for the second time today we are heading towards Waterlow Park. The Heath still feels out of bounds.

It's a glorious afternoon and the park is filled with people who are not at work. Whenever I have a day off I'm amazed how many people are out and about when the rest of us are behind our desks. I walk round the lake, then choose a bench in a quiet, shady spot. There is a brass plaque attached to it that reads, 'To Adrian, who hated this park and all the people in it.' How refreshing, compared with all the people 'who loved this place'. I wonder what must have happened to Adrian in this park for him to hate it so much. In my present frame of mind I understand the sentiment totally. I hate the Heath and, maybe not all the people in it, but that one person who has poisoned it. My thoughts go back to the Dior Man and the unexpected encounter with him at the police station. Why am I so vehemently refusing to believe he could be the Heath killer? Because I trust my instinct? Perhaps I've developed some weird kind of bonding with him, a strange variant of Stockholm syndrome, and mistakenly interpret the fact that he hasn't killed me yet as an act of kindness? I should be telling DCI Jones about him and no one else, instead of wasting police time and spinning tales about other guys who I know have nothing to do with the attacks. But how can I be certain they are inno-cent? James is out of the country and out of the picture, but Samantha's behaviour has been suspicious. I could tell DCI Jones was interested in her and Tom. But my gut instinct tells me Tom isn't capable of prowling the Heath and attacking women. Could he be my stalker? I don't think so. I know the type.

A sudden scream somewhere behind me makes me jump. I hear a woman's voice shouting the word 'murderer' and my heart skips a beat. Unsure what to do, I get up from the bench and edge my way towards the cluster of bushes the voice is coming from. Suddenly the park seems deserted. Where are all the people when you need them? My phone in hand, I cautiously peek through the branches. There is a young couple in the clearing, a man and a woman who is talking loudly in a dramatic voice. I watch them closely, debating whether to intervene. It takes me a while to realize the woman's distress is theatrical. They must be actors, or students, rehearsing a scene from a play. The woman seems to be struggling with her delivery and the guy interrupts her and gives her directions. She starts her lines again.

'It cannot be but thou hast murdered him.
So should a murderer look, so dead, so grim.'

The rhythm of the verse and the woman's emphatic delivery tell me it must be Shakespeare. Trust my luck to pick a bench next to the people rehearsing a play about a murder. A police car's siren somewhere in Highgate mixes with the woman's voice and completes the scene. I'm ready to move on.

I remember there's hardly anything left in my fridge and decide to stop at Tesco in the village on the way back. I walk up Highgate Hill, resist the temptation to buy flowers at the expensive greengrocer's and check out the window display at the local bookshop. I'm about to cross the street when I see a familiar figure in front of Tesco. It's Tom. I stop, unsure what to do. He seems to be aimlessly hovering outside the entrance, looking around. And then, of course, he notices me looking at him and moves forward in my direction. A car honks at him when he steps off the kerb, he stops and moves back, just as the shop's doors slide open and Samantha comes out, shopping bags in both hands. Thankfully, she doesn't see me as she calls out to him. He rushes towards her and grabs the bags. I turn and walk away in the opposite direction, abandoning the idea of shopping at Tesco.

When I get back home curiosity gets the better of me and I Google the lines the woman was shouting in the park. They turn out to be from A *Midsummer Night's Dream*, a comedy with no real murder in it. I look at the lines, uttered by Hermia accusing Demetrius of having murdered the man she loves and looking like a murderer. What does a murderer look like? I

Google 'serial killers' and look at the mosaic of faces, some distorted and ugly, some bland and ordinary. Would I be able to tell if any of these people had killed another human being just by looking them in the eye? The answer is no. And still my conviction that none of the men I've met recently is a killer is unwavering.

A new thought enters my head and I cling to it with relief. Perhaps the Dior Man is a witness, just like me? This would explain the casual way he entered the station. He wasn't handcuffed or restrained, in fact he looked quite in control. But if he is a witness, is he going to disclose the nature of our encounters on the Heath? A cold shiver runs through me at the thought. If the police link me to him, then my game is over. I'll be branded a liar and accused of obstructing a police investigation or even perverting the course of justice. My legal knowledge gained from watching hours of *CSI* and *Law & Order* tells me I might be in big trouble.

I'm interrupted by the arrival of the damage assessor, followed in quick succession by a mobile tyre replacement van. Their efficiency is impressive, the tyres are changed and the rear window scrubbed clean. By five o'clock they are done and I'm left with no more distractions. My thoughts go back to Bell, the Heath, the Dior Man. I need to talk to someone who'd be able to understand the mess I'm in and offer sympathy. I'm reluctant to bother Michael again because I'm already so indebted to him for all the help he's given me and I'm not sure I'll ever be able to repay it. I consider calling Kate, but decide against it. She's too upright, too honourable, I'd be simply ashamed to show her my true colours. Ray? I hardly know the man, but this could be a plus. A perfect case of railway carriage honesty, when you reveal the most intimate details about yourself to a stranger on a train. Well, he's not a complete stranger, but we could disappear from each other's lives as quickly as we appeared in them. I dial his number but he doesn't answer. I decide against leaving him a message, as it would take away the element of spontaneity. I quickly put some make-up on, throw on a pair of skinny G-Star Raw jeans, a soft cashmere jumper and my Ted Baker cream leather jacket, grab my bag and car keys, tell Wispa to be a good girl and head out. I'm going to catch Ray as he leaves his salon tonight.

The rush-hour traffic seems to be going the other way and I manage to get to Islington in twenty minutes. I leave the car on a meter in a side street and stroll onto Upper Street. I casually walk by Ray's salon and quickly peer in. He's busy with a client, cutting her hair, talking to her reflection in the mirror. He hasn't noticed me and I don't break my stride. I find an outside table in a patisserie a few shops further down, order a latte and position my chair so I can see Ray's salon in the distance. I take out my phone and pretend I'm busy checking my emails. It's nearly half past six, so he should be closing soon. Ten minutes later his client leaves the salon, looking pleased with herself. I must admit, her hair looks good. Another five minutes pass and Ray appears in the street and begins to pull the shutters down over his salon front. I scroll down to his name in my address book and dial his number. Let's see how he reacts to seeing my name on his phone screen. It's ringing and I can see him pulling his phone out of his pocket. He checks the caller ID and a little smile crosses his lips. Bingo. He's just about to answer it when a woman appears behind him. She's young, glamorous and clearly very angry. I can't hear what she's shouting, but her words make Ray step back and raise his hands, as if trying to pacify her. She grabs the phone he's holding, waves it about angrily, then throws it on the pavement and kicks it. He says something back and she steps forward and slaps him in the face. An elderly woman with a little Shih Tzu dog stops and appears to intervene. Ray turns towards her and shoos her away. The old woman shakes her head and shuffles away indignantly, pulling her dog behind her. Ray grabs the young woman by both wrists, his face close to hers, his body language menacing. The woman tries to pull away, they struggle, he suddenly pushes her away and she slams against the closed shutters with her back. She is crying. Ray grabs her by the arm, picks up his phone from the pavement and leads her down the street, thankfully away from my table and the patisserie. What happens next makes me sit up in my uncomfortable patisserie chair. Ray and the woman get into a parked car. And no, it's not his BMW, but a blue Mini five-door hatch. And guess who's driving? Ray. As the car passes me I can clearly see a baby seat in the back. I exhale slowly as I watch the car head towards Highbury Corner. What have I just seen? A lovers' spat? Or a confrontation with an angry wife? His or someone else's?

Suddenly my impromptu escapade to see Ray seems like a bad idea. I leave a five-pound note by my coffee cup and walk away from the table. I don't feel like seeing Ray ever again. The anger and aggression of the scene I've just witnessed have left me disturbed and confused. Not to mention the baby seat. I didn't see it coming at all. So much for your killer instinct, lady man-eater. I realize I know next to nothing about most of the people I consider my friends and acquaintances. Any of them could have a flip side, a Jekyll-and-Hyde personality I haven't got a clue about. If I can't even tell a player from a decent guy, how can I be sure there is no killer among the people I know?

I quickly go back to my car and drive home, feeling alone

and tearful. I go straight to the kitchen and take out Bell's bottle of Pinot Gris from the fridge. It's nearly empty, but I pour the few remaining sips into a glass and sit at the table. I imagine Bell sitting in front of me, watching me nursing the glass with sparkles of amusement in her eyes. 'Hey, girl,' she says, 'don't feel sorry for yourself, only assholes do that.' It's a quote from her favourite Murakami novel, I don't remember which one. Oh, Bell, you have no idea what an asshole I am.

Eleven Days Later

I'm back at work and it feels as if I've been away for months. I notice belatedly that the restructuring machine has moved forward, mowing down its first victims. All the freelancers are gone. I'm sure they'll be back, as soon as Cadenca Global is done with us. No large media company can survive without freelancers, but for now their desks are empty, dirty keyboards and broken pens the only remainders of their fleeting presence. Freelance desks are quite different from those of permanent staff. They are impersonal: no cute mascots, no photos of spouses and kids, no secret stashes of nibbles or personalized mugs. It's partly due to convenience and partly to self-preservation. As soon as you bring a personal object to put on your desk, you're hooked. You develop an emotional relationship with your workplace and it hurts like hell when they let you go. And they always let you go at some point. I remember when I first started as a freelance producer and kept making the mistake of customizing the screen saver on my work PC with my favourite holiday snapshot. And how much it hurt to have to delete it once my services were no longer required. Now I'm the one who is supposed to let others go, but somehow the first cull seems to have happened without my knowledge, while I was off work yesterday. It's a bit worrying, but it doesn't take me long to find out how it happened. As I open the door to my office I see Gary parked in my chair, his legs splayed proprietorially under my desk, his fat fingers round the receiver of my phone. He jumps up and puts the phone down when he sees me, a false smile on his face. In fact, there is nothing out of the ordinary about him using my office, it's standard practice to utilize the management's glass boxes when they are not in use by their rightful occupants. But it's his body language that gives his true intentions away. Something has happened behind my back.

With Gary out of my office I quickly scroll down through my mailbox and find a chain of emails that explains his cocksure behaviour. Most of the emails come from HR, but the chain was originated by Julian a week ago, on the day I got back from Paris. The day I learnt Bell was dead. The email chain has been picked up by Gary who, it seems, was instrumental in the cull of freelancers. I sit motionless staring at the screen, processing the information.

There are two possible interpretations. The most likely is the apocalyptic one: Julian has decided to get rid of me and he's grooming Gary as my replacement. But Gary is the element that doesn't fit. He's a bumbling plodder with no management skills and Julian knows it. This points to scenario number two: Julian wants to keep me and is using Gary as an easy scapegoat, who will be sacrificed as soon as he ceases to be useful in the restructuring game. Of course, there might be scenario number three that only Julian is privy to. Time will tell. One thing is certain: I'm not going down without a fight.

I tell Claire to call in an urgent meeting of my department for 1.30 p.m. It's a bitch of a time for a meeting as it eats into people's lunch break, but that's exactly why I chose it: to show that my 'busy' is more important than other people's 'busy'. It's time to remind everyone who's the boss. And to embrace my inner bitch.

As the meeting starts I feel I'm back on top of my game. It gives me great pleasure to cut Gary down to size and re-establish the hierarchy of the place. I might as well enjoy my power while it lasts. I know I'm not a bad manager. I read somewhere that there are essentially three types of managers: those who need to be liked more than they need to get things done, those who need to achieve and don't care what others think about them, and those who are interested in power. It's the power-hungry ones who are in fact the most effective managers, in control of their goals and teams. I'd like to think I fall within the third category, of managers who gain power through influencing people around them. By the time the meeting is over I hope I've exerted my influence enough to last a few weeks longer without the need for more drastic measures.

I spend the rest of the afternoon catching up on emails, making sure I copy Julian into all the ones that work in my favour. I'm just about to wrap up for the day when my mobile rings. It's a US number I don't recognize. A woman with a Midwestern accent asks for Anna, and for a moment I think it's someone from the better, American side of our corporation.

'It's Candice,' she says and pauses, as if to give me time to place her. 'I got your number from Michael.'

'Candice, of course, Bell's told me about you . . .' I stumble awkwardly. 'I'm so sorry . . .'

We're both silent, not sure what to say next.

'Bell is . . . was very important to me,' she says eventually and I can hear she's on the verge of tears.

'I know . . . You were important to her. She's told me a lot about you.'

'I'd like to come over and say goodbye to her.'

'Of course,' I say and my mind is racing. Did DCI Jones say anything about releasing the body? When is the funeral? I need to speak to Michael . . .

'The funeral is on Friday morning,' she says as if hearing my thoughts. 'I've booked my flight for tonight and will arrive at Heathrow tomorrow lunchtime. It's all a bit last minute, but otherwise I'd miss her funeral.'

'I'll pick you up, just email me the details.' A wave of guilt is making me volunteer.

'Oh, it's fine, I can take the underground from the airport. I've found a room on Airbnb somewhere in East London. Errmm . . . Leyton? Would that be close to where she lived?'

'Bell lived in Stoke Newington. Leyton is not exactly round the corner. It would be much easier if you stayed at mine. Actually, I insist, I'll pick you up and you must stay at mine.'

'I don't want to inconvenience you.'

'No, it's no problem at all. It's the least I can do for Bell's . . .' Should I say girlfriend? Partner? Lover?

'It's very kind of you, thank you. I'll email you the details of my flight.'

I give her my email address, she asks again whether her visit won't inconvenience me and I assure her it won't. I put the phone down feeling totally ashamed of myself. What kind of best friend am I? How could I have not known when Bell's funeral is? I should be the one arranging it, getting in touch with Candice, calling Bell's friends. What is wrong with me? I feel I can't face Michael, who has clearly stepped in and taken over all the arrangements. Shame, shame on me.

As I drive home I mull over my egotistical nature. I've been so preoccupied with my own survival, my own grief, that I have totally ignored what my friends must have been going through. It makes me sick with shame to realize how wrapped up in my own little world I've become. It's unforgivable and I know Bell would have given me a right ticking-off. I promise myself to be less self-centred and to give more time and thought to my friends. I'll check on Michael, take care of Candice when she comes over, get in touch with Bell's friends, speak to Kate, find out if Sue's resisted the temptation of the Big T. I should probably get in touch with Nicole and see how she's doing and if she's going to come back to London and dog-walking.

There is a parking space free just in front of my house and I decide it's a sign I'm not all bad. I must have put some good karma into the universe and it's decided to come back at this very moment. I'm reversing into the tight space when I hear a sudden bang on the roof of the car. I instinctively step on the brakes, not sure what is going on. Have I hit someone? I buzz down my window and look out. There is a familiar man on the pavement, a can of lager in his hand, a bright red scarf round his neck, swinging his leg to kick the rear tyre of my BMW.

'Alden! What are you doing?'

'Yo, bitch!' he shouts at me in a bad imitation of Jesse from *Breaking Bad*.

I switch off the engine and get out of the car, just as he kicks it again.

'Alden, stop it!'

He turns to look at me and I can see he's completely drunk.

'Oh, yeah? And what will you do if I won't? Call DCI Dyke? So she can question me again?'

'Alden, you're drunk!'

'And I bloody deserve it! I've been helping with their

enquiries all day.' The lager spills from the can as he makes quotation marks in the air. 'I'm such a helpful guy—'

'Alden, go home.'

'You are evil.' He looks at me with the sudden clarity of a drunk. 'I thought you were cool, Anna, but you're a bad person, you are. Evil to the core. I know everything about you.'

'You know nothing about me, Alden.' I try to sound friendly, but firm. 'We hardly know each other. Why don't you go home, get some sleep, and we'll meet up for a coffee once you've sobered up?' I reach out and pat him on the arm.

'Don't touch me,' he yells, moving away, 'you evil bitch!'

'I'm not evil, but you are definitely drunk.' I let the bitch part slide, but he doesn't hear me, engrossed in his monologue.

'You nasty little scheming slut! He's warned me about you . . .'

My neighbours' outside light comes on and Patrick, the nosy accountant, pops his head out through the front door.

'Everything all right?'

'Yes, thank you, Patrick, my friend is just leaving.'

The neighbours' door slams shut. With all the comings and goings at my house lately, my neighbours probably hate me by now.

'Just go, Alden.' I infuse my tone with motherly calmness. 'Go home and sleep it off. Everything will look different tomorrow, you'll see.'

I move away from him and go up my front steps. I can hear Wispa barking madly behind the closed door. Alden leans against my car and looks as if he's going to fall over. I don't care if he does, I just want to get away from him and close the door behind me. I open my front door and block the exit, so Wispa doesn't rush out into the street. Two seconds later I'm in, double-locking the door from the inside. Wispa keeps barking and jumping up, nudging me with her nose. I go straight to the kitchen, pour myself a double whisky and drink it in a couple of gulps, neat. As its heat goes down my throat and settles in my stomach I rush to the front room and peer through the closed blinds. It looks like Alden has gone, but the window on the driver's side is wet, smudges of frothy liquid running down the door and onto the pavement. I only hope it's Alden's lager and not something else.

I let the blind drop down into place and go back to the kitchen. DCI Jones has clearly taken our conversation seriously and is interviewing all the men I told her about. I instantly feel a wave of guilt. Let's face it, my statement was more of a smokescreen to cover up my encounters with the Dior Man. I don't seriously think any of the men could be a rapist and a killer. But then again, what do I know about rapists and killers? Why has Alden reacted so violently to being questioned by the police? And how did he manage to connect it with me? Has DCI Jones mentioned my name while talking to him? That would be rather unprofessional of her, I think, drawing again on my knowledge of police procedure gained from watching too much *CSI*. Most importantly of all, why does Alden think I'm a bitch? Was it him who sprayed the word on my car and slashed my tyres? And who has warned him about me? Tom? I'm really tempted to call DCI Jones, to tell her about Alden's behaviour and the missing keys. But my will to keep the Dior Man secret is stopping me from contacting her. I open the fridge door, but Bell's bottle of Pinot Gris is gone. I finished it the other night. I pick up the phone and dial Michael's number instead.

'Darling, how are you?' He sounds pleased to hear me.

I tell him about my day at work and Candice's phone call.

'Yes,' he says, 'I gave her your number. I wanted to offer her board and lodgings at mine, but she said she was getting a room through some website.'

'Yes, in Leyton of all places. I persuaded her to stay with me. I'm picking her up at the airport tomorrow lunchtime.'

'She sounds like a really nice woman. It's so tragic that Bell's never going to . . .' His voice breaks.

'. . . be happy with her,' I finish his sentence and feel the tears welling up in my eyes. We both fall silent, then Michael clears his throat.

'I wanted to speak to you about her funeral arrangements. She wanted to be cremated and her ashes scattered from the cliff at Beachy Head.'

'Beachy Head?' I'm surprised, but then remember what Bell had told me. 'I suppose it makes sense. She lived in Brighton as a student and used to go to the South Downs a lot. She told me it was the happiest time of her life. How do you know it was her wish?'

'I'm her will executor.'

'Bell's left a will?' I'm taken aback. Why hadn't she told me about it?

'We spoke about it when Phil died and I suggested then she should make one. On account of her having no immediate family and being gay. I recommended my solicitor to her.'

'Why didn't she tell me about it?'

'She said she didn't want to worry you. Some people are funny about wills and talking about death.'

'I suppose she was right. The whole idea of preparing for your own death freaks me out.'

'I don't think one is ever really prepared for it.' Michael clears his throat again. 'I thought we might all drive to the cliffs with her ashes on Saturday. You, Candice, myself. Candice needs to fly back home on Sunday.'

'Of course, it's absolutely fine. I'll drive.'

'She also wanted Helen to be there.'

'Big H? Her mad ex? The one who cheated on her and always had three girlfriends on the go?'

'The same one.'

'Well, it's her will . . .' I must say Bell doesn't cease to surprise me, even after her death.

'I know you've never been very fond of her, so I'll contact her.'

'Not fond of her is the understatement of the year. Remember, I was always the one picking up the pieces when Bell's girlfriends turned out to be psychos. And Big H is in a category of her own in that department.'

'I know, but you'll have to put up with her just once more.'

'Do you think it's safe to put her and Candice together?'

'Apparently she's a reformed character these days.'

'It's a recipe for disaster, if you ask me.'

The sound of my doorbell makes me jump. Wispa rushes to the hallway, barking.

'Someone's at the door, Michael, I have to go.'

'Do you want me to stay on the line?'

'No, sweetie, thank you, I'll be fine. Talk to you later.'

I dash to the door, then stop, seeing a big dark silhouette behind the stained glass.

'Who is it?'

'Anna, it's DS Kapoor.'

I unlock the door, holding Wispa by her collar. DS Kapoor is in his uniform and looks official.

'We had a report of a disturbance at this address . . .'

Patrick, my nosy neighbour, of course.

'I just wanted to check if you're OK.'

'I'm fine, thank you.' I quickly calculate the risk of telling him about Alden and decide it's minimal. 'But why don't you come in and I'll explain.'

He takes off his cap as he walks in. He pats Wispa's head as she jumps around him, wagging her tail.

'Shall I put the kettle on?' I ask as I direct him to the kitchen.

'That would be lovely, thank you.'

We sit down at the kitchen table, waiting for the kettle to boil.

'It was Alden, one of the guys I mentioned to DCI Jones. I believe you talked to him earlier today. For some reason he's taken umbrage at me . . .'

'Has he threatened you?' DS Kapoor takes out his police notebook and a pen.

'No.' I busy myself making tea, my back to him. 'He did call me an evil bitch, though.'

I put a mug of tea in front of DS Kapoor and point to milk and sugar. He looks up at me from his notebook and I notice for the first time he's quite good-looking, especially with the five o'clock shadow on his chin.

'Do you know why?'

'No.' I take a sip of my tea. 'I thought you'd tell me.'

DS Kapoor raises his eyebrows, then nods slowly. 'He was a bit agitated when we spoke to him today.'

'Agitated enough to kick my car and call me a bitch?'

'Your name wasn't mentioned. Do you want to lodge a complaint?'

'Nah.' I shrug my shoulders. 'I'm in enough trouble as it is . . .'

'Trouble? Why do you say that?' He looks at me inquisitively and I can hear echoes of DCI Jones in his voice. Like a dog with a bone, I think to myself, and shrug again.

'It's a figure of speech, Navin. May I call you Navin?' He nods and I continue. 'I have never had so much contact with the police in my entire life. And as much as I like you and respect your boss, it's not something I want to develop into a long-term relationship.'

DS Kapoor suddenly looks flustered. I can see tiny droplets of sweat forming on his forehead. What have I said? He gets up, folds his notebook and carries his mug to the sink.

'Thank you for the tea, Anna. I'm glad you're OK. If you change your mind about filing a complaint, just give me a call at the station. I have to get going.'

'Of course.' I follow him to the hallway, taken aback by this sudden change in behaviour. I thank him for stopping by and close the door behind him. That was weird. Maybe I shouldn't have said I liked him. Perhaps he fancies me? He has been rather nice to me and he did look after Wispa, which in my book makes him a good person. Whatever it was, I have no time and energy to try to get to the bottom of it, I decide. A quick walk with Wispa, a long soak in the bath and bed, that's what I need.

Wispa already knows we're going out and waits for me in the hallway, wagging her tail. I rummage in the cupboard under the stairs for poo bags, grab her leash, the house keys, and open the front door. As I walk down into the street a police car stops in front of my house. The passenger door opens and I expect to see DS Kapoor again. What now? But the policeman looks quite different, tall and blond-haired, in a white short-sleeved shirt and a black vest. His colleague gets out from the other side, a wiry Indian guy, but not DS Kapoor.

'Miss Wright?'

'Yes?' I stop and put the leash on Wispa.

The blond-haired policeman squeezes himself between the parked cars and approaches me.

'We've had a report of a domestic disturbance at your house.'

His voice reminds me of Gary Sinise, minus the American accent.

'Another one?'

'Excuse me? You are Miss Wright, right?'

I'm not sure if he's trying to crack a joke I heard a million times when I was at school, but I dislike him instantly.

'Yes, I am Ms Wright and it was my neighbour who called you.' I feel a wave of anger bubbling inside me. Patrick will pay for this. 'I was arguing with a friend outside my front door. He must've misconstrued it as a disturbance.'

'So you don't require assistance?'

'No, thank you, as you can see, I'm perfectly fine.'

'We'd appreciate it if you could let your neighbour know to call the non-emergency number 101 in the future.'

'Why don't you tell him yourself, as you're here.'

I march up my neighbour's front steps and ring his bell.

'His name is Evans. Mr Patrick Evans. Goodnight.'

I pull on Wispa's leash and walk away indignantly. As I cross the street I can hear Patrick unlocking his door and the nasal drone of the blond policeman enquiring about a report of a disturbance.

What a waste of police time, I think, as I walk down Swain's Lane. And to have them call at your house twice in half an hour, just when you don't need them at all. But then a different thought makes me stop and Wispa looks at me impatiently. Why did they come twice? The visit from the Gary Sinise lookalike and his sidekick seemed genuine, but what was DS Kapoor doing at my house? No, I'm getting too suspicious, I decide as I start walking again. Kapoor was obviously on duty, knew about the call made by Mr Evans, probably recognized my address and decided to check if I was OK. Sinise and Co. on the other hand were sent to my house by a dispatcher. There, mystery solved. There is a distinct chill in the air and the musty smell of wet earth and rotting leaves heralds the beginning of autumn. I haven't even noticed the summer colours starting to lose their vibrancy and the mornings becoming wrapped in fog.

Twelve Days Later

It turns out Candice arrives on the 11.15 a.m. United flight from Chicago, having caught a local flight from Spokane to Denver, and then connecting onto the London flight in Chicago. She is going to be exhausted. It'll take her at least an hour to go through passport control and customs, so I should get to the airport by noon. Which doesn't leave me a lot of time at work in the morning. Luckily, the office isn't far from the M4, but still, I'll have to leave by 11.30 at the latest. I kick myself for offering to pick her up. I should've booked a cab for her and asked them to take her straight to Michael's. But it's too late to change the plan and I feel I owe Bell this at least – taking care of her girlfriend while she's in London.

The office is unusually quiet, with most of the producers out on shoots or in edit suites. My work mailbox isn't quiet at all on the other hand. Since last night over a hundred new emails have arrived, most of them carrying red flags of urgency. I check my diary and it doesn't look good. I'll miss a big departmental meeting in the afternoon. Claire tells me Julian wants to have a one-to-one with me tomorrow morning, another date I won't be able to keep. But surely my friend's funeral warrants one more day of compassionate leave. She also reminds me that today is the last day to submit our company's entries to this year's Promax UK. It's that time of the year again! I can almost measure the length of my professional life by the number of Promax conferences I've attended over the years. From a bright-eyed and hungry-for-awards young promo-maker to begin with, to the jaded and cynical know-it-all I am now. A TV promotion, or a promo, is a weird beast. Its aim is to drive ratings but often it's far superior creatively to the programme it's supposed to promote. What do Promax judges take into account then? Accuracy, effectiveness or creativity? A promo that does exactly what it says on the tin usually has the creative value of a pint of wood stain. A promo that's truly unique and brilliant often wouldn't be able to sell water to a thirsty man in a desert. Luckily, my task this morning is not hindered by such dilemmas. Our creative department hasn't produced any masterpieces this year, so I go for a selection of humorous spots that fit safely into categories like Best Use of Humour or Something for Nothing. Better than nothing, I think, as I pass on my selection to Claire who is going to take care of the paperwork. Then I write a short and apologetic email to Julian, excusing myself from our tête-à-tête tomorrow, and head out of the door.

There is hardly any traffic on the M4 and I reach the short-term car park at Terminal 3 at five past twelve. The information board in the arrivals hall says that the flight from Chicago has landed and the bags are on their way to the baggage hall. I position myself at the barrier to crowd-watch. The sliding doors disgorge passengers in various states of disarray, from fresh and energetic European hoppers to blurry-eyed and crumpled intercontinental travellers. A clutch of disorientated Japanese tourists is followed by a gaggle of overexcited American pensioners, then the doors remain closed for a while. They open again to reveal a colourful couple: a large woman in a bright, flowing dress and a small man dressed in black, pushing a luggage trolley filled with a stack of suitcases. They make such a captivating picture that I almost miss the woman who appears right behind them, carrying just a small cabin bag. She is quite petite, slim but muscular, with straight highlighted hair pulled back in a ponytail and blue eyes that look striking in her tanned face. I instantly know it's Candice. She recognizes me at the same moment and walks towards me, smiling.

'Anna?'

'Candice!'

We hug as if we've known each other for years.

'Thank you so much for meeting me.'

'It's a pleasure, Candice, really.'

I stop to pay the parking fee at the machine, then lead Candice to the car.

'Good flight, or should I say flights?'

'I feel my carbon footprint has grown dramatically within the last twenty-four hours,' she laughs. 'But it hasn't been that bad. I managed to sleep on the flight from Chicago.'

Unlike most Americans I know, she's softly spoken and has a gentle manner about her. I like her instantly. As we drive towards London I ask her if this is her first trip to the UK.

'Actually, I lived in Canterbury for a couple of years.'

'Canterbury?' I repeat, wondering if I heard her right.

'I did an MA course in Social Anthropology at Kent.'

'Wow, so you're no stranger to this part of the world.'

'No, this visit would feel quite nostalgic, if only the circumstances were different . . .'

We both fall silent for a while. Then Candice clears her throat.

'What was she like?'

Even though I'm driving, I can't help looking at her. She stares back at me, her blue eyes serious and pleading, as if she's asking me to divulge a secret.

'What was she like,' I repeat, my gaze returning to the road in front of us. 'She was a good person, honest, trustworthy . . . singular. You know, with most people you get the feeling that there is another person hiding behind the facade you see. With Bell you never got that: she was exactly who you saw, no hidden agendas, no Mr Hyde to her Dr Jekyll. She was kind, open, warm. And very funny. We'd had so many good laughs over the years.'

'She talked a lot about you. You were her best friend.'

'I hope I was . . . I tried to be . . .' A tearful feeling wells up inside me. 'But I failed, I let her down badly—' I stop, searching for words, wondering why I'm sharing my most intimate thoughts with a woman I met ten minutes ago. She waits for me to go on and I feel I have to. I realize I've been carrying a terrible burden of guilt around with me and I have to share it with someone. 'She died because of me, Candice.'

Tears suddenly flood my eyes; I can barely see where we're going. I step on the brake and turn off abruptly onto a side road leading to Heston Services. The car park is almost empty and I stop right in front of Costa Coffee. I switch off the engine and take a deep breath.

'I'm so sorry, Candice. I don't know what has come over me. This must be so weird for you . . . ending up in a foreign country at a motorway service station with a stranger having a nervous breakdown . . .' I try to make light of what's just happened.

Candice puts her hand on my shoulder.

'Let's have some coffee,' she says.

I lock the car and we walk over to the coffee shop. Candice makes me sit down in an armchair in a quiet corner of the shop and goes to order the drinks. A few minutes later she puts a big steaming mug in front of me and sits in the armchair opposite. As I pick up the mug, the smell of hot chocolate hits me. Candice smiles.

'I thought we needed this more than coffee.'

I take a sip and decide she's right. The taste of chocolate is both indulgent and soothing.

'Thank you. I'm so sorry.'

'There's no need to apologize.'

'I feel so silly. Here you are, exhausted after your flights, having to witness my sudden outpouring of confused emotions. This is not how it was supposed to happen.'

'Sometimes we just can't help it. When your cup becomes too full, you have to empty it . . .'

We drink our hot chocolates in silence.

'I was in love with Bell. I still am. It all seemed crazy at the beginning, the whole Internet dating thing. I'm really not into it, don't even know why I joined the site in the first place. And then suddenly there was Bell, filling my life with hours of Skype conversations, just being together, in this weird long-distance way. I didn't know what to expect when she came over, wasn't sure I'd like her in real life. The Internet is such a deceptive tool of communication. I remember waiting for her at the airport and thinking to myself, what if she turns out to be a complete psycho? What if she isn't who she says she is? But when she appeared at the top of the escalator in the arrivals hall, all my doubts melted away in an instant. My stomach did a little flip and I was filled with this inexplicable joy. She felt so . . . familiar and exotic at the same time.'

Candice falls silent, stirring her chocolate absentmindedly.

'You know, I really thought we'd spend the rest of our lives together.'

Her eyes glaze over with tears, she shakes her head and takes a sip of her chocolate. I reach out and touch her hand. I know there's nothing I can say that would make her feel better. There is nothing I can think of that would make me feel better.

Thirteen Days Later

We meet just inside the main gate of the New Southgate Cemetery. The morning sun is already quite hot and I decide against leaving Wispa in the car. I'm sure it's OK to take her with me, as long as she stays outside the chapel. There's just a handful of us, no more than twenty people, most of whom I know. Marianne, Bell's old friend from uni, a smattering of friends from her teaching days, a few of her Stokey cronies and a couple of her exes, with Helen hovering on the edge of the gathering, muttering to herself. This does not bode well for the confrontation with Candice. My phone starts ringing and I rummage through my bag to find it. I recognize the work reception number, which always comes up instead of any particular extension, and I switch it off. Michael, who's taken upon himself the role of host, invites everyone to proceed to the chapel, which houses the crematorium. To my relief I see that Helen hasn't been talking to herself. She removes a phone earpiece and puts it in her pocket. As we walk along the main alley I'm overwhelmed by the stark beauty of the Victorian gravestones, the peaceful and contemplative nature of the place. It carries the wisdom of inevitability, forcing one to realize that no matter how hard we fight death, it still defeats us at the end. We move slowly forward, a motley crew of mourners, united in grief. Old oak and chestnut trees scattered along the alley begin to shed their leaves, which rustle under our feet. I tie Wispa to a stone bench outside and we enter the chapel through heavy wooden doors. The chapel's Gothic exterior contrasts with the straight and unadorned lines of the interior, which feels quiet and peaceful.

As we settle in the pews it becomes clear that Michael is continuing his role of host and he's going to make a speech. I feel a pang of guilt. This is yet another thing I haven't thought of doing, being much too self-absorbed lately. Again I feel I'm letting Bell down. Michael's eulogy is simple, warm and beautiful. He speaks of Bell as a great friend, a good and generous human being. It's all true, I think, welling up at the sound of Michael's soothing voice.

'As some of you know,' he continues, 'something truly wonderful happened in Bell's life not long ago. After years of searching and heartache, she'd met someone who transformed her life. Candice.' Michael pauses and smiles warmly at Candice, who smiles back at him through tears. Out of the corner of my eye I can see Helen shifting uncomfortably.

'Candice brought love and hope into her life. Hope for the future, a new life in a new place. I know it'll come as a surprise to most of you, even to her closest friends, but Bell was actually planning to move to the States to join Candice.'

A flutter of astonishment goes through the gathering. I'm surprised and taken aback. Why didn't she tell me?

'Being an overcautious old bore, I questioned the rashness of her decision and she simply said she had no time to waste. She wanted to grab happiness while it was there. I must say, I envied her such certainty of feeling. She talked of throwing a huge party for all her friends here, not a farewell, but a celebration of the past, the present and the future. While going through her papers, a sad obligation I was bound to fulfil by her will, I came across a notebook. And I discovered that Bell, who favoured pen and paper over the erasable nature of computers, had started jotting down short messages for her friends, clearly with the idea of reading them out at her party. They are fragments of poems, snippets of dialogues or lyrics of songs, dedicated individually to the people who were close to her heart. I'm sure Bell would agree with me that this is a very opportune moment to read them out.'

Michael pauses to take his reading glasses out of his breast pocket, then opens a blue Moleskine notebook.

'To Anna, my best friend.' He looks at me over the top of his glasses. 'Remember the Madonna song, the one that was practically on a loop in the cassette deck of your old banger as we drove around the Lake District one rainy summer? The one about pushing someone to see the other point of view, pushing them so they are not complacent, making them get up and keep going even when they've had enough? Thank you for pushing me, Anna, when I felt like giving up. This song will always make me think of you.'

Suddenly I'm blinded by the tears, my chest constricts in acute pain and I'm unable to breathe. I jump up from the pew and dash towards the exit, barely seeing where I'm going. As I push the heavy doors I'm no longer able to contain my sobbing. The brightness of the daylight hits me and I see a man in a dark hoodie crouching next to Wispa. When he sees me he gets up abruptly and walks away. Blindly, I stumble towards the bench and put my arms round Wispa's neck. The memories of that Lake District holiday with Bell flood in and I'm consumed with grief. My obsession with the song made Bell tease me endlessly until it became the leitmotif of the whole trip. But hearing the lyrics read out in the chapel makes me understand the true nature of our friendship, a unique bond I will never be able to recreate with anyone else. More acutely than before, I feel I'd let Bell down badly, let our friendship slip away while I took it for granted. She died walking my dog, wearing my coat, helping me out, as always, while I was away thinking only of myself. I will never be able to forgive myself for my own utter selfishness. Would trying to make up for it change anything? It won't bring back Bell and I won't be able to earn her forgiveness. But would an attempt to become a better human being bring any consolation? I should do everything I can to help the police find her killer. I have to tell DCI Jones about the Dior Man, I decide, overwhelmed by the feeling of guilt. There is music coming from the chapel now and I drag myself from the bench and walk in, wiping my tears. Annie Lennox's velvet voice flows from the chapel's discreet sound system. I recognize it instantly, it's 'Lifted' by Eurythmics, Bell's favourite song. I feel it's a message from Bell and when I look at the faces of her friends gathered in the chapel I know everyone is going through the same emotion. As the music fades, we all get up, hug each other and reluctantly leave the chapel, leaving our friend behind.

Fourteen Days Later

Saturday morning disappears in a flurry of rushing around. I leave Candice at home and drive to New Southgate to pick up Bell's ashes. By the time I get back, Michael and Helen are already at my house, ready to set off on our trip to Beachy Head. I decide to go through town and take the A23 and M23 towards Brighton. This proves a bit of a mistake as we get stuck in traffic as soon as we hit Brixton. The atmosphere in the car is tense, Helen's hostile silence clearly directed at Candice. I'm glad I have driving as an excuse for being quiet and I'm grateful to Michael for trying to keep a friendly conversation going. He chooses the safe subject of work and it turns out that Candice is an expert on funeral traditions around the world. She tells us about Tana Toraja, a region in eastern Indonesia, where funerals are lavish and loud occasions lasting sometimes for weeks.

'As the family save up for the occasion, the deceased continues to "live" with them and is referred to as the one who is asleep or ill.'

'We have the same tradition here when the family don't want their dole to be cut off.'

I'm not sure if Candice gets Helen's sarcasm, but she doesn't seem to be offended.

'I remember when my gran died,' Michael fills in a lull in the conversation. 'I must've been six or seven at the time and just about coming to grips with the idea of death and close people passing away. She was a fierce lady, inspiring terror and awe in all the wee bairns in the family.' Michael comes from a large Scottish family, with five sisters and one older brother. 'She was laid out in the lounge for a whole day and night, which I found incredibly exciting. I somehow figured out that I no longer had to be scared of her and this was a true revelation. I waited until everyone was asleep, then crept downstairs in my pyjamas, snuck into the room she was in, put a little stool beside her so I could reach her, grabbed her nose and shook it vigorously. You have no idea how totally liberating it was! Till this day I can feel the elation of the experience, and no guilt at all . . .'

We all chuckle at Michael's story, then fall silent as our thoughts go back to Bell.

As we approach Brighton I turn left onto the A27 to avoid traffic jams and head towards Lewes, then take the picturesque route down to the coast through Alfriston. It's a crisp and sunny day and the Cuckmere Valley looks stunning. We reach East Dean in surprisingly good time, then turn onto Birling Gap Road. As I park in the National Trust car park I'm glad the tourist season is over and the usual summer crowds are gone. My passengers pile out of the car, stretching their legs, and I let Wispa out of the boot. She does loops around us, barking madly, excited by the proximity of the sea. Although the day is clear, the wind is sharp and the bite of the cold sea air makes us head unanimously for the cafe before we face the climb up Beachy Head. We emerge fortified by mugs of strong tea and gather by the gate to the path. I go back to the car to collect

Bell's ashes. When I rejoin our group, Helen looks at the tube in my hand incredulously.

'What the fuck is that?'

'It's a scattering tube. The guy at the crematorium recommended it when I told him we were going to scatter her ashes.'

'You mean you put Bell's ashes in a fucking cardboard tube? I can't believe it!' Helen's bad temper I've been so wary of is back in full swing. 'Why spend money at all? You could've put her in a recycled toilet-paper tube, it wouldn't cost you a penny! This is a fucking farce!'

'It's not disrespectful at all,' Candice pipes up before I can stop her. 'It's very common in the States. It's biodegradable and—'

'And you,' Helen sticks her finger in Candice's face, 'you better shut up. You have no fucking right to be here. You think you can waltz into Bell's life, eat her pussy a couple of times and, what, it gives you some special right to her? So you can swoon around like some entitled widow? You can take your fucking biodegradable grief and fuck off back to the States!'

The commotion has attracted the attention of a group of Japanese tourists who have just arrived in a luxury coach. A mother with a small daughter is pulling the child away from us.

'Helen!' Michael grabs her by the arm and she pushes him off.

'You never really knew her. I spent YEARS with her! I was ready to give her my WHOLE LIFE!'

One of the Japanese tourists comes a bit closer and snaps a picture of our group with his compact camera. Before any of us can react, Helen throws herself at him with a roar, yanks the camera out of his hand, throws it on the ground and stomps on it with her hiking boot. A few ladies in the Japanese group start screaming as Michael grabs Helen and pulls her away from the stunned tourist. I rush forward and pick up the camera. It's covered in mud, but looks intact. I wipe it with the sleeve of my jacket and give it back to the guy. Helen turns round and storms off towards the public toilets outbuilding. Michael raises his hands in a pacifying gesture.

'It's all right, ladies and gentlemen! Apologies for the little disturbance. It's over now and we can all go about our own business. As for the damage to the camera . . .' Michael turns to the Japanese tourist, puts his arm round the man's shoulders and leads him away from the group.

I look at Candice, who's been watching the scene in shocked silence, her face the whitest shade of pale, her eyes black with enlarged pupils.

'You OK?'

'I think so . . .' She takes a deep breath.

'So sorry, Candice. Helen is . . . volatile. She's been through some shit in her life and has a funny way of dealing with it. She's very upset about Bell's death. Her anger wasn't directed at you, but at the situation.' I know my attempt at justifying her behaviour must sound lame.

'It's OK, Anna. I'll be all right.' Candice gives me a weak smile. The crowd around us disperses slowly.

'Let me get you another cup of tea . . .'

'No, thank you, I'm fine, really.'

Michael's finished his little chat with the Japanese tourist and comes back to us, putting his wallet in the breast pocket of his jacket.

'All sorted.' He sounds almost cheerful.

'Did you have to give him some money?'

He shrugs his shoulders. 'Forget about it.' He looks around. 'Where is Hell?'

Michael uses Helen's old nickname, which reminds me of what she used to be called behind her back when she was Bell's girlfriend: 'Hell-on-Legs'. Indeed.

'I think she's gone to the loo. Shall I go and get her?'

'No, let her be. She'll come around. Let's start walking up.' Michael leads the way. I whistle at Wispa, who's been rummaging about near the cafe's rubbish bins, and we follow Michael through the stiles.

As we climb up the path I can feel the stress ebbing away. It's a glorious autumn day, unusually clear for this time of the year. The view of the white cliffs is spectacular and the sea shimmers in the sunshine.

'Look!' Michael points at a couple of yellow butterflies chasing each other above the meadow of small lilac flowers. 'It's Clouded Yellows! Believe it or not, they come here all the way from North Africa.'

'The butterflies?' asks Candice incredulously.

'Yes, they set off from Tunisia in early spring, go to Italy, then east around the Alps, through France and arrive here in Kent, Essex, Suffolk and Dorset.'

'It takes them all summer to get here?'

'Oh no, they start arriving in May. These two are the second-generation immigrants, born here.'

'How do you know all this?' I'm always amazed by the amount of knowledge Michael retains on all conceivable subjects.

Michael laughs at my awe.

'I did the graphic design for a short documentary on butterfly migration a few years ago. You know, title sequence, all the charts and maps. It was quite interesting.'

I catch a glimpse of Helen following us at a distance. In front of us looms the circular tower of the Belle Tout lighthouse. As we near the top of the headland, we slow down and gingerly approach the edge of the cliff.

'The trick now is to try not to slip,' Michael warns us as we shuffle forward. 'It's over five hundred feet down in a straight line.'

'Be careful, folks! Hope you're not planning to jump!' We all turn towards the voice behind us. It belongs to an older man, dressed head to toe in the most stereotypical hiking gear, including the obligatory green fleece, Berghaus Gore-Tex jacket, zip-on trousers and thick woollen socks sticking out of his heavy Merrell boots. 'It's quite a drop down there.'

'Thank you for your concern, we have no intention of jumping.' I turn away from him, hoping he gets the message and keeps walking.

'Good. Do you know it's been the most popular suicide spot on the coast since the 1600s?'

We don't reply, but the man carries on, undeterred.

'Around twenty people each year try to jump off here. Twenty people! In the seventies they even installed a telephone box near the clifftop with a number for the local Samaritans. I've been coming here for years—'

''Scuse me, mate,' Helen joins us suddenly, 'it's a private party. We'd like to have some peace here.'

'Oh, right, dear.' The man looks at her, taken aback. 'I'll leave you alone then.' He marches off in a huff.

Instinctively we form a little circle at the edge of the cliff. Everyone's looking at me and it reminds me I'm the one carrying the scattering tube. I hold it out, unsure what to do. Michael gently takes it out of my hand and opens it.

'I think we should all do it individually . . . Let's give each other some privacy.'

Everyone agrees with relief. Michael hesitates, then passes the tube back to me.

'Anna, you go first.'

Smart move, avoiding escalating the conflict between Helen and Candice, I think, moving away from the group towards the edge. I tip the tube slightly and a handful of ash comes out, surprisingly heavy, like sand, not floating in the air as I've expected. It is picked up by the wind, nevertheless, and carried over the cliff towards the sea.

'Forgive me, Bell, please forgive me,' is the only thought relentlessly echoing in my head. And then another one: 'I miss you.'

I stand facing the sea for a while, taking in the view, intense sadness and loss in my heart. The gesture hasn't given me the relief I've been hoping for. There is no answer to my silent plea and the void I feel remains achingly real and inconsolable.

Eventually I turn away from the sea, give the tube back to Michael and walk down the slope. A flock of swallows takes off from the bushes, their white bellies shining against the glossy blue wings. They circle gracefully, then swoop low over the greenery, as if practising air acrobatics before their long flight back to Africa. I watch them flutter and disappear behind the horizon as quickly as they appeared and I know that from this moment on the sight of a swallow will make me think of Bell.

Here today, gone tomorrow.

Fifteen Days Later

It's an early start on Sunday. Candice is catching the 11.05 United flight to Chicago and I'm taking her to the airport. The alarm clock on my iPhone wakes me up at 6.45 a.m. and I stagger to the kitchen, bleary-eyed and exhausted, still reeling from the emotional roller coaster of yesterday. Candice is sitting at the kitchen table in her pyjamas, warming her hands against a mug of steaming coffee. She points to the other mug on the table.

'Freshly brewed. I love your Nespresso machine.'

I pick up the coffee gratefully and take a sip. I slide into a chair next to her and we both sit in silence, holding on to our mugs as if they carried answers to all the problems in the world.

Yesterday was traumatic. After the ash-scattering ceremony we went for a late lunch at the Golden Galleon near Seaford, which was a bad idea. It turned out it used to be Bell's hang-out when she was a student at Sussex and Helen was her girlfriend. Just as our food arrived Helen threw another fit, accusing us of being emotional imposters desecrating Bell's memory, and stormed out of the pub. Three hours later, tired of waiting for her and aware that Candice had to catch an early flight the next morning, we decided to go back to London without Helen.

Then, feeling responsible for her in her distressed state, I drove up and down the A259 and Beachy Head Road, eventually finding her wandering aimlessly along the village green in East Dean. It took some persuading to get her into the car, but finally she relented and sat in stony silence throughout the whole trip back to London. I was relieved when I dropped her off by her flat in Walthamstow, wondering what made Bell put up with her for so many years.

'Thank you for taking such good care of me while I've been here.' Candice breaks our pensive silence.

'Don't mention it. I'm sorry if things didn't go exactly as planned . . .'

'No, it was good. I'm glad I came.'

'I'm glad, too. And I'm glad I've met you.'

We leave the house at quarter to eight and get to the airport well before 9 a.m. Surprisingly, there is just a short queue at the check-in that moves forward smoothly. Then I walk Candice to the entrance to the departure gates and we hug goodbye.

'Do you think we'll stay in touch?' she asks.

'I'd like to. It's up to us, isn't it?' I say, aware that often even the best intentions of keeping in touch fail to keep the acquaintance going.

'Yes,' she says and I know she's thinking the same. 'Let's try.'

She turns once before disappearing behind the sliding door and waves at me. I wave back and wonder whether I'll ever see her again.

I'm back home at ten and decide it's still early enough to go for a run. I feel I've neglected my body long enough and it's screaming for its fix of adrenaline and endorphins. It's not a great day for running, it's damp and overcast, but as long as it isn't pouring down I should be fine. Saying goodbye to Bell has marked a shift in my perception of the Heath. I think I'm ready to go back there. Wispa drops her rawhide bone when she sees me putting my running gear on. She positions herself by the front door, wagging her tail excitedly. You and me, girl; the prospect of a proper run in a beautiful open space makes my heart sing.

My legs seem to know the way when we jog down Fitzroy Park. Despite the autumnal hue, the Heath looks strangely monochromatic, seen through the colour filter of the moisture hanging in the air. Even the diehard Heath lovers are few and far between today. I can feel I'm out of shape, but I press on up the hill, Wispa's effortless trot putting me to shame. Halfway up the hill I'm beginning to feel the rhythm and my breathing stabilizes, the first rush of endorphins making me high. I turn right towards Kenwood, instinctively following my favourite route. It feels great to be back here. I follow the path through the woods, lined with a soft layer of wet leaves, then go through the gate to the estate. I slow down to negotiate a muddy stretch, then reach the open space of the West Meadow. The expanse of many shades of green, yellow and red takes my breath away. It's one of the most beautiful views on the Heath. I turn off the path onto the meadow and run across it, careful to avoid rabbit holes. Wispa overtakes me, galloping through the wet grass.

A sudden feeling of dread catches me out when I hear footsteps behind me. No, this can't be happening again, I think as my pace falters and my breathing becomes strained. I keep on running, scared to look back.

'Anna!' I hear an urgent voice.

Without slowing down, I half turn and see the Dior Man. He's about fifty paces behind me, his face intense.

'No,' I gesture and keep running. I don't want to see him. I don't want to go back to the madness of it all.

'Anna, wait!'

Fear mixed with anger is propelling me forward, my feet barely touching the ground as I thunder across the meadow. Fear that he'll catch up with me and I won't be able to resist him, anger because in my head he's suddenly become the reason for all the disasters in my life. There is a gate ahead of me – if only I can reach it, there will be people on the other side. Through the pounding of blood in my ears I can hear his voice again.

'Anna, we need to talk!'

I slip in mud, recover, reach the gate, open it long enough for Wispa to get through, then follow her towards Kenwood House. My silent prayer has been answered: there are some people in the distance, they'll probably hear me if I scream. And if he comes near me I *will* scream. There is a mechanical screech behind me, I see a large green shape out of the corner of my eye and nearly collide with a park ranger's electric buggy.

'Whoa, lady, got a death wish!'

The ranger, an older guy in a green uniform, is clearly furious. I bend over, desperately trying to catch my breath.

'You have to be more careful, madam! You can't just run willy-nilly like this! You could hurt yourself or other people.'

'I'm so sorry . . . I think I saw a flasher back there . . .' I improvise, waving vaguely in the direction the Dior Man might come from.

'A flasher?' He looks at me, instantly alert.

'I think he was chasing me.' I keep going with the lie. For a split second I debate giving him a description of the Dior

Man, but change my mind. I think the presence of a ranger looking for a flasher is enough to put him off approaching me.

'This sounds serious, madam.' The ranger looks around, clearly unsure what to do. 'I'll . . . er . . . better go and investigate.' He jumps off the buggy and whips a walkie-talkie out of his pocket. 'And I'll need to report it . . .'

He starts for the gate to the meadow, then turns back to me.

'Please can you stay by my vehicle, madam. I'll need a description of the perpetrator.'

I nod at him eagerly. As soon as he disappears into the bushes, his walkie-talkie squeaking, I turn round, whistle to Wispa and run towards Kenwood House. It looks different from usual, intricate scaffolding surrounding the facade of the main building. As I trot up the hill I can feel the adrenaline of the chase slowly ebbing away. My legs suddenly feel like jelly. I reach the main path. It looks like the long-overdue refurbishment of Kenwood House has just begun in earnest. I head towards the Brew House Cafe, which I find, to my relief, still open. I desperately need an injection of sugar. Thankfully, there is a ten-pound emergency note folded neatly in a small pocket of Wispa's poo-bags pouch. No dogs are allowed inside the cafe, so I leave Wispa by the entrance and go in. I pick a lemon drizzle cake from the impressive display of sweets and savouries, accompanied by a cup of English Breakfast tea. I park my tray at a secluded table in the corner of the cafe and sit down heavily on the wooden chair.

He called me Anna. He knows my name. He probably knows who I am and where I live. I notice my hand is shaking when I raise the cup. As the sweetness of the cake dulls my nerves, I begin to think more rationally. Where did he get my name from? An obvious answer would be the police station. I definitely saw him there, accompanied by the policemen who are probably working on the Heath attacks. Was he a witness or a suspect, I ask myself again? If he was a suspect, he wouldn't be roaming the Heath freely now. Unless he's been released due to the lack of evidence . . . The *CSI* expert in me takes over. A more likely explanation is that he is a witness, just like me. He came to the station voluntarily and overheard my name being mentioned by someone connected to the case. No, it doesn't make sense. Which leaves the other option, much more sinister. He is a stalker. I put my teacup down with a loud clunk. An elderly lady at the table next to mine looks at me reproachfully. Her make-up is impeccable; so is her hearing, it seems. If he's a stalker, he knows everything about me. Why would he wait till I go to the Heath to confront me then? He's probably had many opportunities to accost me, hurt me, even kill me . . . He could've killed me. Why am I still alive then? This scenario doesn't add up either, I decide. He said we needed to talk. Talk? What about? To compare notes about our encounters in the bushes? This is the first time in days I allow myself to go back to them in my thoughts. I feel nothing but embarrassment and shame. The sense of edgy eroticism I found so irresistible has evaporated completely. I don't want to have anything to do with this man ever again. What we did feels sordid and tarnished by all the violence that has happened on the Heath. Why doesn't he leave me alone? Oh God, have I inadvertently started some insane chain of fatal attraction? I push away my half-eaten cake and the old lady looks at me again.

'Enjoy the rest of my cake,' I say to her and leave her sitting at her table, rigid and judgemental.

Wispa greets me outside as if I've been gone for days. Her

joy reassures me, and for a moment I think everything is fine, as it's always been. Then I remember the ranger and my lie. Shit, he's probably looking for me. And, God forbid, he may have called the police. I have to disappear from the scene as quickly as possible. As I bend over to untie Wispa's leash I see something white attached to her collar. I throw myself at her and she yelps in surprise. It's a small piece of paper. A note.

'Please call me,' it says, followed by a mobile number.

In a flash of anger I crumple it and throw it in the nearest bin. Why doesn't he leave me alone? He must've followed me all the way here. I'm not surprised Wispa let him attach the note to her collar. She's such a slut when it comes to cuddles that sometimes I think she'd walk away with a stranger as long as she got plenty of tickles behind the ears. But the thought of him touching my dog makes me feel violated. I'm amazed at my double standards. I let this guy fuck me in the bushes, but when it comes to petting my dog it's a different story. The moment of flippancy is over and I feel dread creeping in. What does he want from me? Pretending I'm calling Wispa, I take a discreet look around. Of course I can't see him, but I know he's watching me. What kind of a nightmare have I unleashed? My heart is pounding and I'm shaking again. I can't face going back through the Heath, so I whistle to Wispa and we trot towards the gate leading onto Hampstead Lane. It's going to be a longer walk home, but I hope the steady flow of traffic will make me feel safer. Just when we reach Hampstead Lane I see a 210 bus coming in the direction of Highgate and make a dash for it. The driver takes pity on me as I make a show of fumbling around for my Oyster card, and lets us on for free.

REBOUND

We get home in record time. I slam the front door shut behind me and sigh with relief. The world outside seems like an alien and menacing place yet again. But as I stand in the hallway watching Wispa trotting off to the kitchen I realize that even my own house doesn't feel safe any more.

Sixteen Days Later

The morning drive to work seems like a welcome relief from the claustrophobic inertia of yesterday. I spent most of the day curled up on the sofa with a bottle of Malbec, trying to understand what was going on. The wine eased the tension and produced some surprising interpretations of the morning's events. After one glass I was debating calling DCI Jones and telling her everything about my encounters with the Dior Man. After two I was ready to go back to the Heath to retrieve the note with his number and confront him. Three glasses in I felt sorry for myself and sobbed inconsolably until the fourth glass started to kick in. By then I was staggering around the house, checking all the windows and barricading the front door, determined never to set foot outside again. The memories of the fifth and the sixth glass are blurry, but the empty bottle of wine I found by the sofa this morning seems to suggest that I'd managed to complete the full circle of drunken paranoia.

I don't recall going to bed, but remember waking up in the middle of the night covered in sweat, my heart pounding from too much alcohol and a nightmare. In my dream I am jogging along the cliff path at Seven Sisters. Someone is chasing me and, as I try to run, the path turns into a swamp, the mud sucking my feet deeper and deeper. I can feel my pursuer's breath on my neck and suddenly I am on the edge of the cliff, wrestling with the Dior Man, who is trying to push me off into the sea. I scratch his face and his skin sticks to my fingers. I pull my hand away and with it comes his face, revealing someone else's features underneath. I'm suddenly winning the struggle, he doesn't fight when I push him off the cliff and when he starts falling I realize it's not the Dior Man any more, it's Bell. She looks at me as she's falling, calm and resigned, and she says something, but I can't hear her, the roar of the waves below drowning her words. It was the roar that woke me up, not of the waves, but of blood pulsating in my head.

It took me ages to calm down and get back to sleep and when I woke up at 6 a.m. my head felt as if it was about to explode and splash my brains all over the Farrow & Ball Lulworth Blue walls of my bedroom. A hot shower, two Paracodol tablets and three Arpeggio coffees from the Nespresso machine brought some comfort to my sore body and soul and by 8 a.m. I was brave enough to sit behind the wheel of my BMW without the fear of ruining the upholstery.

It's 8.37 a.m. and I'm driving into the work car park, buzzing with the mixture of caffeine and codeine. The office greets me with a strange sight. A handful of men in suits are walking about, looking at walls and desks, and marking things on sheets attached to their clipboards. Claire is on hand to provide an explanation. They are assessors from Utispatial, a company hired by Cadenca Global to introduce a new, highly organized work-space run by space-management software. In other words, hot-desking. I hide my extreme annoyance and ask Claire to call whoever is in charge from Utispatial to my office. After some delay, one of the clipboard minions knocks on my door. From his demeanour I can tell he's quite low rank, but dying to impress and get promoted. I know talking to him is going to be a waste of time, but I indulge my curiosity. I ask him to explain the logistics of the workspace transformation and for the next twenty minutes he draws a vision of the brave new world of space allocation and management. He goes on about the simplification of the work flow, swift management of employee moves, reduction of costs and a new level of efficiency. When he tries to dazzle me with the idea of a centralized repository of office-space information, I interrupt his monologue.

'So, how many desks are there on this floor at present?'

'One hundred and seventy,' he replies without hesitation.

'And how many are you going to cut it down to?'

'A hundred.'

'That leaves seventy people without workspace, right?'

'Yes, but they are mostly non-desk-owners.'

'Non-desk-owners?'

'They are either home-workers or mobile-workers.'

'Do you actually know what we do here in this office?'

He twitches nervously, shuffling papers on his clipboard. 'You make television programmes?' Without his specialized workspace-related vocabulary he seems rather lost.

'Do you know what it actually entails?' I don't feel like explaining it to him.

'Erm, filming, editing . . .' He clearly has no idea.

'Do you see that empty desk there?' I point through the glass wall of my office and he follows my finger like a puppy waiting for a ball. 'It belongs to Gary, who, I believe, is on a shoot today. Shoots don't happen very often and Gary spends a lot of time at his desk.' Too much time in fact, I think, and continue. 'Next to him sits Caroline. As you can see, she's not at her desk because she's in edit, two floors below. But she will be back later, to prepare scripts for an audio session tomorrow. And look who's there!' I go on in the most patronizing tone I can muster. 'It's Linda! She will stay at her desk for a while, filling in music details and finishing paperwork that accompanies every promo, but she may be gone this afternoon, to a meeting with a graphics company. We don't know when she'll be back . . .' I look at the guy. 'Can you see where I'm going with this? This office is not a call centre in Staines. It is not an accountancy firm. It's an evolving, creative environment. It's difficult to predict "employee moves" as you put it. It's impossible to implement any computerized space-management system. So why don't you kindly gather all your colleagues, tell them to pack their clipboards and leave this office right now. And when you get back to your own no doubt highly organized workspace, you can tell whoever is in charge to put their centralized repository where a suppository normally goes. Have I made myself clear?'

The guy nods and backs out of my office. I can see him talking to the other suits, then they all pack their clipboards and leave. A result. I sigh with relief, pick up my phone and ask Claire to bring me a double skinny latte from the canteen downstairs. My head is pounding and my bladder is bursting from all the coffee I drank at home. I dash to the toilet, where I catch sight of myself in the merciless bathroom-light-special mirror. My eyes are bloodshot, my face puffed up, and my hands are shaking. The blouse I put on this morning is the wrong shade of hangover green. It's going to be a tough day.

I spend the rest of the morning catching up on emails that seem to be multiplying like germs in a toilet bowl. At midday Claire comes into my office and tells me Julian wants to see me. Immediately. A bad taste in my mouth after too many coffees gets instantly complemented by a bad feeling in my stomach. In the lift I feel the weight of my phone in the pocket of my trousers. I take it out, put it on silent and slide it back into my pocket. There is nothing Julian hates more than being interrupted by someone else's phone.

He greets me with a warm handshake and leads me to his leather sofa. He seems very much at home at his London office; I wonder how much time he has been spending here lately. He kindly enquires how I feel, asks about the funeral. I tell him a little about the ceremony and the trip to the coast, skipping the incident with Helen, and feel a surprising relief while talking about it. Julian is a good listener and acts as if he really cares. They don't pay him a six-figure salary for nothing, after all. Then the pleasantries are over and he gets down to business.

'I hear you had a little contretemps with our guys from Utispatial this morning.'

Ah, so they are 'our guys' now.

'I told them to stop what they were doing and leave.'

'That's rather unfortunate.' He plays with his Breitling watch as he speaks. Strange, I'd expect him to be more of a Rolex man.

'Is that so? I've made it clear to Cadenca Global, time and time again, that hot-desking is not appropriate for our work environment. Whoever made the decision now—'

He raises his hand to stop me.

'I made the decision, Anna.'

This silences me.

'Implementing a new system of space allocation and management goes hand in hand with our restructuring vision and it's fully supported by Cadenca Global. It's not only about saving money, Anna, lots of money, but also about optimizing employee efficiency, eliminating time and resource wastage. Utispatial is going to help us with creating a new production village down-stairs, a brand-new infrastructure of facilities, editing pods, audio studios, a graphics suite. We are fully entering the twenty-first century at this juncture, Anna. It'll make us proud. And Utispatial are instrumental in making it happen.'

I don't know what to say. It appears I've put my foot right into Julian's pet project. Should I admit I've made a terrible mistake?

'Of course, Julian. I'll see that the Utispatial guys are re-invited to assess our floor.'

Julian waves his hand dismissively. 'It's already been taken care of. They are coming back after their coffee break. Why don't you take some time to drill down, so you're in the loop on all aspects of restructuring?'

In a patronizing gesture, he reaches for my hand and pats it gently.

'As a very wise man said, hold on to the old just as long as it's good, and grab the new as soon as it becomes better.'

I'm being dismissed. Drill down, I think as the lift door closes behind me. Have I been away from the office for too long?

I spend the rest of the afternoon drilling down to the very last word of every memo I've received in the past few weeks. By the end of play, as Julian would put it, I feel I've regained at least some understanding of what's going on in the company 'at this juncture'. It's almost 9 p.m. It's time to go home to Wispa. As I pack my bag I realize I can't find my phone. Then I remember feeling it vibrate in my pocket as I was sitting on Julian's sofa. It must've slipped out. I grab my things, close the door to my office and take the lift up to the executive floor. It's dark there, but the ceiling lights come on as I walk down the corridor towards Julian's office. I push the glass door, hoping it isn't locked. Triggered by the movement, the light comes on and I turn towards Julian's leather sofa. I gasp in surprise when I see someone sitting on it. In fact, it's two people, one of them kneeling awkwardly in front of the other. They must be as surprised as I am, jump apart and face me. It's Julian. And Gary. Not knowing what to do, I turn back towards the door.

'Anna.' I hear Julian's voice and I stop.

He comes towards me, blocking my view of Gary, who is still sitting on the sofa.

'My phone . . .' I mumble.

'Yes, you left it here,' he says, sounding totally in control. 'I meant to ask Laura to take it back to you. But it slipped my mind.' He has the audacity to smile, then reaches towards his desk and gives me my phone back.

'Thank you,' I say quietly.

'You're welcome,' he says, his voice relaxed and friendly. 'And goodnight.' As I back towards the door he adds, 'Have a safe drive home.'

Thankfully, the lift is still there and the door opens immediately. I stab the U button for the car park and lean against the wall as the lift starts descending. I get into my car, close the door and let out a sigh of relief. As I turn the key in the ignition, my brain is still trying to process the scene I saw upstairs. Julian and Gary. I'll be damned! I turn the radio on and turn the music up loud to drown a giggle I feel building up in my chest. I laugh so hard I have to pull over right by the exit from the car park. And then the song fades and the news comes on. There's been another murder on the Heath. The police are not releasing any details at present. I switch the engine off and sit behind the wheel, numb, unable to move. When I start driving again I barely register the traffic around me. My mobile keeps ringing, relentlessly amplified by the car's audio system. I get home on autopilot, stagger to the front door and let myself in. Wispa greets me by the door, but without her usual song-and-dance welcome routine. Just a few wags of the tail and she goes back to her bed. Strange. Maybe she's pissed off with me for staying so long at work.

There are messages on my answerphone, but I ignore them. I go straight to the sitting room, curl up on the sofa and fall asleep. I wake up in the middle of the night, stumble upstairs, throw myself on the bed and fall asleep again, my brain escaping reality into a dark and dreamless slumber of nothingness.

Seventeen Days Later

I open my eyes and I know something is wrong. The house is eerily quiet. I don't hear the soft snoring from Wispa that I usually wake up to. She is not by my bedside, where she normally sleeps.

'Wispa!' I call her and my voice echoes in a house that seems empty.

I get up and cautiously walk down to the kitchen. In the dull, morning light I see a dark, unmoving shape on the kitchen floor. I let out a cry and rush in. It's Wispa. She's lying on her side, her eyes closed, blood seeping from her nose. There's more of it on the tiles, little puddles that look like urine mixed with blood. I kneel down by her and touch her neck. She doesn't move but I think she's alive. Quick, I need to get help for her. I grab my mobile and scroll down to Wispa's vet, Beaumont Sainsbury Animal Hospital in Camden. To my relief they answer almost immediately. When I start chaotically describing Wispa's condition, the receptionist interrupts me and tells me to bring the patient in straight away. I throw my tracksuit on, grab a blanket and roll Wispa as gently as I can onto it. Then I pull the blanket with Wispa on it to the door. She lets out a little moan but doesn't open her eyes.

'It will be all right, puppy, just hang on in there,' I whisper as I look for my keys.

She is a big dog, much bigger than she should be, but fear for her life gives me Herculean strength. I carry her down the steps, lift her up and lie her down in the boot of the car. Within seconds I'm on the road. The traffic is bad, I've hit the eight o'clock rush hour, but I honk and push aggressively, overtaking slow drivers and breaking the speed limit all the way to Camden. I park on the double yellow line just outside the hospital and run into the surgery.

'I have a sick dog, could someone give me a hand?' I shout and a young, freckled receptionist rushes out with me. We carry Wispa in and the receptionist buzzes us straight into one of the examination rooms. The doctor is already there, waiting for us. He immediately starts to examine Wispa, then turns to the young receptionist and asks him to take me to the waiting room outside. When I protest, he gently moves me towards the door and tells me it will be better if I wait outside.

For the next twenty minutes I pace around the three waiting rooms, for dogs, for cats and for little furry animals, unable to sit down. Eventually the freckled receptionist calls me inside. We go to the same examination room, but Wispa isn't there any more. I hold my breath, expecting the worst.

'The vet will be with you in a minute,' the receptionist tells me and asks me to sit down on one of the blue plastic chairs. Oh no, please don't tell me she's dead, I repeat like a mantra in my head. After what seems like an eternity, but is probably just a couple of minutes, the doctor enters the room.

'It looks like Wispa may have eaten some rat poison,' he says quietly.

'Is she going to be all right?'

'We don't know yet, but we are doing everything we can to save her.'

241

I let out a sob and he puts his hand on my arm.

'We're conducting a complete blood profile to determine the severity of poisoning. We know from her history she's a strong and healthy dog, which obviously works in her favour. Can you think of when and where she might have got hold of the poison? It usually comes in pellets, blocks or granules of any colour, teal, blue, green or pink. It's grain- or sugar-based which makes it irresistible to rodents and dogs, unfortunately.'

I shake my head.

'My dog walker takes her for a walk in the daytime and they usually go to the park.' I hesitate. 'Actually, she didn't seem well last night . . .'

'She may have ingested the poison several days ago without you noticing it. Two to five days usually.'

I shake my head again, unable to think that far back.

'There are several types of rat poison: some of them kill instantly and some are cumulative and require multiple feeding to kill a rodent. We are hoping this is the kind she's ingested: an anticoagulant that thins the blood and causes spontaneous and uncontrolled bleeding. Her bleeding nose and gums would suggest that. This is actually good news. If she had ingested another type of poison she'd be dead by now.'

I gasp and he gives me a tiny, reassuring smile.

'We are giving her a blood transfusion and Vitamin K to restore normal blood clotting. It's a very common type of poisoning in dogs and most of them, given the right care, manage to pull through. In Wispa's case I hope we've caught it in time. But she'll have to stay in intensive care for a while.'

Overwhelmed by a tearful wave of gratitude, I thank him profusely. He walks me out to the reception and tells me they'll ring me later today to update me on Wispa's progress.

As I drive back home, I'm trying to think where Wispa might have picked up the poison. It most likely happened on Chiara's watch and I'll never know. But wait, two days ago – the mad chase on the Heath and the note behind Wispa's collar. The Dior Man. Why on earth would he want to harm her? I slow down and the car behind me honks and flashes headlights in annoyance. Was this supposed to be a message for me? Meaning what? No, this is crazy. As I pass Highgate Cemetery another image flashes in my memory. Bell's funeral. A guy in a hoodie crouching next to Wispa. Oh God. It was him. He looked vaguely familiar, but who was he? Is it possible that someone actually gave Wispa the poison? That it wasn't her penchant for eating any old rubbish that nearly killed her? Is it possible that someone was evil enough to want to kill my dog?

Deep in thought, I park the car and walk to my front door. I jump when I see a figure sitting on my doorstep. It's DCI Jones, strangely informal in a pair of black jeans and a purple fleece. It strikes me she looks very much like Bell's lesbian friends in their fifties: fleece, no frills, make-up free, avuncular.

'Good morning, Anna.' She gets up and notices my puffed-up face. 'Are you all right?'

'My dog has been poisoned.'

'Oh, I'm so sorry. . .' For once I can see she doesn't know what to say. 'Wispa, isn't it? Is she all right?'

'Don't know yet. I found her in the kitchen this morning. She'd had a haemorrhage . . . I've just come back from the vet . . .'

'Are they looking after her?'

'Yes.' I don't want to talk to her, but it doesn't look like I'll be able to get rid of her easily.

'Anna, we have to talk.'

243

'What time is it?'

She looks at her watch. 'Nearly ten.'

Shit, I'll be late for work again.

'I'm afraid you will be late for work,' she voices my thought. 'But it's rather urgent.'

'Do come in.' I unlock the door and let her in. 'Would you mind helping yourself to some coffee in the kitchen? I need to take a quick shower. It'll only take five minutes.'

Without a word she looks at her watch again and nods. I dash upstairs and jump into the shower. As the hot water runs down my head and body, my stress eases off enough for me to remember the bloody mess in the kitchen. But when I come down the floor looks like it's been wiped clean and there is a wet mop standing in the corner.

'Thank you.' I smile gratefully at DCI Jones and she instantly goes up in my estimation.

She gestures towards the kitchen table. It looks like she's made coffee for both of us. Even more points for her. As we sit down she gives me a quick appreciative glance, taking in my fresh-from-the-shower look, and I know there's still life in the avuncular DCI Jones. Then, it's all business.

She opens a black folder and removes a postcard-sized photograph. She slides it across the table, until it's by my coffee mug.

'Do you know this man?'

As I look at the picture, my heart stops for a second, then starts thumping as if it wants to jump out of my chest. It's a photograph of the Dior Man. I pick up the photo, biding my time. I notice that my hand is shaking and I put the photo back down. Have they caught him? Is he the Heath killer after all?

'Why do you ask?'

'I'm afraid it's my turn to ask questions.' She sounds stern.

I look at the photo again. It's a casual snapshot. He's smiling at the camera, hands in his trouser pockets, some blurred office furniture in the background. I've never seen him smile. DCI Jones is watching me closely. I have to give her something.

'I may have seen him while jogging on the Heath . . .'

'When?'

'I'm not quite sure . . . Definitely before . . . it all started.'

'Could you try to concentrate and give me a more specific timeline?'

'What is it all about? Have you caught him? Is he the Heath killer?'

She looks at me without saying anything, as if mulling a decision over. Then she reaches for the photograph.

'You have probably heard that there was another killing on the Heath last Sunday. This man,' she points to the photo, 'was the victim.'

Suddenly the surface of the table, DCI Jones and my kitchen seem very far away. I take a deep breath, aware that I might faint. Slowly everything comes back into focus and I see DCI Jones's expectant face.

'I . . . I don't understand,' I mumble. 'He's dead?'

'We believe he was killed by the same person who attacked Belinda and all the other women in the park.'

'But he is . . . was . . . a man.'

'Yes.' She nods and a strange expression flickers across her face.

'It . . . doesn't make sense . . .'

'No, it doesn't.' She puts the photograph down. 'Anna, I believe you haven't been honest with me.'

'What do you mean?'

'I think you know exactly what I mean. I think you've been withholding vital information. You know something about the Heath killings. You are somehow linked to the deaths. And,' she taps the photograph, 'you know this man.'

'Are you going to arrest me?' The more she pushes me, the more belligerent I feel.

'If need be.' She shrugs her shoulders. 'Anna, listen to me. I'm not saying you are responsible in any way for the killings. Absolutely not. You are not a suspect. But you know there is a link between the killings and yourself. And this is the thing you're not telling me.'

She picks up her mug and gets up, trying to hide her frustration.

'Do you mind if I make myself another coffee?'

'Help yourself.' I wave in the direction of the Nespresso machine. 'Actually, I'll have one too.' I get up and join her. As the coffee maker goes through its slurping cycle, she looks at me.

'I'd like you to accompany me on a walk through the Heath. And a visit to the latest crime scene.' She puts her hand on my shoulder when she sees me recoil in horror. 'Don't worry, the forensics are done with it. It's just a piece of grass cordoned off by white and blue tape.'

'When?'

'Now would be a good time.'

'I need to go to work . . .' I protest feebly.

'I'm afraid this takes priority over work. Please let them know you'll be late. Unless you want me to contact them on your behalf?'

'No, thank you.' I get up in search of my phone. There are eleven unanswered calls and six new voicemail messages on it. I speed-dial Claire's number and leave her a message.

'Well, we might as well go now, if you insist.' I'm not attempting to hide my annoyance.

'Thank you.'

As we leave the house I'm expecting DS Kapoor to be waiting for us in a marked car. Instead I'm being led to a red Mini Roadster. There's definitely more to DCI Jones than meets the eye. She's a fast and confident driver and she clearly enjoys the drive. She parks the car in Merton Lane, exactly where I'd park if I ever drove to the Heath.

We walk down towards the pond. I'm determined not to say anything and eventually she breaks the silence.

'I do appreciate you coming here with me, Anna. As you may have guessed, this is not an official enquiry, more of an informal chat.'

She leads the way, following exactly my usual running route.

'In order to catch the bastard who's killed all these people I need your cooperation, Anna. I need your help.'

There is something so sincere in her voice that my belligerence begins to evaporate.

'I don't know what you want me to tell you, Ms Jones.'

'Vic, please.'

'What do you want me to say, Vic?'

It feels strange calling her by her first name, but somehow appropriate now.

'You knew Belinda. And I know there is a connection between you and the last victim.'

'Who was he?'

'You don't know?' She looks at me incredulously.

'I have no idea,' I say honestly.

She stares at the horizon, hesitates.

'What I'm going to tell you is still confidential, but it's bound to come out in the media soon.'

She hesitates again and I can barely contain my curiosity. Who was he?

'The last victim's name was Mark Thomas. Detective Chief Superintendent Thomas.'

It slowly sinks in.

'You mean he was a policeman?'

'My Chief Super.'

This is too much to take. I stagger towards a bench and sit down heavily. DCI Jones sits down beside me. I'm desperately trying to think, to make some sense of what she's just told me, but my mind's gone blank.

'He was your boss?' I ask her at last.

She nods.

'Was he involved in the investigation?'

'Not directly. But he was kept informed of all the developments.'

I struggle to comprehend what I've just heard.

'I can see it's come to you as a shock. Why?'

I shake my head and say nothing.

'Anna, we have evidence that links you to DCS Thomas,' she says quietly. I look at her, uncomprehending.

'Evidence?'

Vic doesn't answer, observing me. I feel my arms and legs go numb as I try to breathe normally. That's it then. There's no point lying any more. I don't even want to speculate what kind of evidence they've got.

An unexpected sense of relief washes over me as I start telling her about the Dior Man. At last I can unburden myself, share my secret with someone who's not going to run away screaming or moralize. Vic may charge me with obstructing the police investigation or withholding information, but I know she's not going to pass judgement. I skip a few steamy details, but stick to the story pretty much as it happened. I'm not hiding the fact that I instigated the encounters and try to be succinct and matter-of-fact.

Once I finish, she doesn't reply for a long time. I know my story has put her in a very awkward position. She's learnt something about her deceased boss that she probably didn't want to know. Is she going to disclose it to the rest of the department or keep it to herself? Can she keep it to herself? Surprisingly, now that the story's out, I don't care whether the whole CID knows about it. Well, that may not be entirely true.

Eventually she looks at me and I can tell she has a plan.

'Thank you for being honest with me, Anna. Finally.' There is a sparkle of emotion in her eyes, perhaps reproach, then she looks away. 'I'd like you to do something for me.'

'Yes?'

'I want you to go home and make a list of all the encounters with Chief– DCS Thomas. I want dates and times – try to be as precise as you can. It would also be helpful if you could pinpoint the locations. Do you think you can do it?'

'Of course.'

She gets up with new energy, a woman on a mission.

'Let's get going.' She starts walking back to where we came from.

'We're not going to the crime scene, then?'

'It's no longer necessary.'

We walk down in silence, then stop by her Mini. There is a parking ticket behind the wiper on the windshield, which she removes, folds and puts in the back pocket of her jeans, without any sign of annoyance.

'Would you like a lift back?'

'No, thank you, I think I'll walk back.'

She nods and opens the driver's door.

'I'll be in touch this afternoon. Please try to have the list ready by then.'

'Vic?'

'Yes?'

'Was he married?'

She gives me a heavy look before replying.

'Yes.'

I lean on her red Mini as she gets in and slams the door shut. She starts the engine and I move away. She drives off without giving me another glance. So that's what she really thinks of me.

He had a wife. He'd go home after our dirty sex in the bushes, have a shower and snuggle up to his wife. God, what a mess.

DCI Jones hates me. Of course she does. I'm this privileged slut who seems, in some inexplicable way, linked to the deaths on the Heath. What is she going to do? She strikes me as a righteous person, a solid and grounded policewoman, who is not going to try to hide anything in order not to tarnish the name of a fellow police officer. Would my story really tarnish his memory? The romanticized notion of the Dior Man has all gone, replaced by Detective Chief Superintendent Mark Thomas. Trust my luck to stumble upon a policeman in the bushes. A married policeman. A policeman who is now dead. A cold shiver runs through me. She thinks I'm linked to the attacks on the Heath. Am I in danger? I instinctively pick up pace and cast a glance behind me. The lane is empty. If I were at risk, wouldn't she be sending a guardian angel, preferably in the form of DS Kapoor, to watch over me? I have a feeling I'm straying into the realm of *Murder She Wrote*. This is real life, and Jessica is not going to come to the rescue. But there is something I can do to help the woman who hates me right now.

When I get home I go straight to the kitchen and get a clean sheet of paper. Then I fetch my Filofax from the bedroom. My well-worn, leather-bound personal organizer is a nostalgic throwback to the eighties, totally obsolete and practically unknown to most people under the age of forty. But it's served me well over the years and I have no heart to throw it away. So each year I faithfully go on Amazon and buy a Filofax Diary Refill, then spend hours painstakingly marking the birthdays of all my friends on its pages in green pen. This is also where I mark all the events that would never, ever make it into my iCalendar. And this is where I've written four tiny letters in the right top corner of each day I encountered the Dior Man on the Heath. DIOR. I count five DIORs, but I'm pretty sure I saw him twice before I started marking the dates in the Filofax, when I first saw him and the second time, when we bumped into each other while running. Something tells me it's the DIOR days that will be of utmost interest to DCI Jones. What will she do with them? Check them against the dates of the attacks on the Heath? I grab my laptop and Google 'attacks on the Heath'. It turns out there are plenty of places called the Heath in the world that have been witness to all sorts of acts of violence. I keep narrowing my search until I have the right Heath and the right attacks. I check the two sets of dates, the attacks and the Dior Man encounters, against each other. The sequence that emerges makes my blood run cold. The first rape happened four days after I had sex with the Dior Man for the first time. The second, on the day after I met him for the second time. The rapist struck again two days later. I returned to the Heath after a break of nearly two weeks and ended up with the Dior Man at the Ladies' Pond. Two days later Bell got murdered. I put the pen down and look out through the kitchen window. There is a bird frolicking on the Japanese maple bush that seems on fire with its orange and brilliant-red leaves. It makes me think of Bell. Fighting the tears, I get up and put the kettle on. Is the pattern I've just discovered coincidental or is there really a connection between my encounters with the Dior Man and the horrible crimes on the Heath? With a mug of tea I go back to the table. There is one more DIOR mark in my Filofax. It's on the day I saw the Dior Man for the last time. The day he left a message under Wispa's collar asking me to call him. Twenty-four hours later he was dead.

Now I know how he knew my name. He was a police officer, indirectly involved in the investigation into the death of my best friend. What was he trying to tell me that day he chased me in Kenwood? Had he worked out the connection himself and was trying to warn me? There is, of course, another possibility. I put the mug down as the thought strikes me. The violence on the Heath had nothing to do with me, but with him. He was a policeman after all, dealing with all sorts of shady characters who probably held grudges against him. And who were capable of committing terrifying acts of violence.

I need to speak to DCI Jones, tell her what I've discovered, talk to her about my suspicions. There is no point in hiding the remaining details: Samantha's strange visit, Alden's recent freak-out, Ray's behaviour which I witnessed in Upper Street, anything that can help solve this gruesome case. I must admit I'm also curious what DCI Jones will make of my theories.

My phone rings. It's Claire, asking whether I'm coming into work today. I glance at the clock. Good grief, it's nearly one. I know I should be there, keeping my finger on the pulse while all the fighting and scheming goes on, but I'm so preoccupied with my own investigation that I tell her I'll be working from home for the rest of the day. Then I call DCI Jones's mobile number and leave a voicemail message asking her to get in touch as soon as possible. Chiara, who's come to pick up Wispa, is horrified by the news of her poisoning and swears to me that she always keeps an eye on the dogs when she takes them out. I have no reason not to trust her. Once she's gone I eat some nondescript pasta dish defrosted in the microwave and find myself pacing around the house, waiting for my phone to ring. When eventually it does, I grab it and answer without checking the caller ID. But instead of DCI Jones's baritone I hear a different female voice. It's Laura, Julian's assistant. She's asking if I will be able to pop into Julian's office tomorrow morning at 9 a.m. Of course, I say, too distracted to ask her what it's about this time. As I put the phone down I suddenly remember the embarrassing scene in his office last night. Julian and Gary, what a sight. This explains, of course, Gary's recent transform-ation from an office plodder to a corporate star. I try to imagine Sue's face when I tell her about it. Then I check myself: this is something I should probably keep to myself.

My phone rings again and it's the Beaumont Sainsbury Animal Hospital with an update about Wispa. She's responding well to treatment and the vet is hopeful, but we're not out of the woods yet. I put the phone down with a cautious sigh of relief. Then it rings again and this time it is DCI Jones. I tell her I have the list and some new theories and she promises to come by within the hour. That's fast; she must think that whatever I know, consciously or not, about the case, is important. Which makes me feel both flattered and anxious.

She arrives exactly forty minutes later and I begin to wonder whether the Heath attacks are the only case she is dealing with at the moment. We go straight to the kitchen and she accepts my offer of coffee, revealing she's as addicted to it as I am. I present her with the list of dates I've made and she studies it for a long time in silence. When she puts it away I tell her about Samantha's visit, Alden's abusive behaviour and my acquaintance with Ray. She listens carefully to everything I say, but I can tell she doesn't consider my revelations as important as the dates linking me to the Dior Man. Then I put forward my theory of the attacks being somehow linked to his life rather than mine and she nods.

'We're looking into it right now. But we have to bear in mind that you were linked to two of the victims, and DCS Thomas, as far as we can tell, only to you.'

She rubs her forehead and I notice that she looks tired. Having your boss murdered on your watch must be a nightmare. She finishes her coffee, puts my list away in her black notebook and gets up.

'Thank you, Anna, I really appreciate your help,' she says and I know that this time she means it. 'Do give me a call if you think of anything else. I'll be in touch anyway.'

I close the door behind her, feeling that I've done something useful and right.

Eighteen Days Later

I wake up in the middle of the night, screaming. Another nightmare. I find myself looking for Wispa, but of course she's not in her usual place by my bed. The house feels so empty without her. I turn the bedside lamp on and pad barefoot to the kitchen to get a glass of water. The dream is still vivid in my memory: a man was trying to break in through the bedroom window, pounding on the double-glazed pane, leaving dirty handprints on the glass. I screamed at him and just as he managed to break the window and started climbing in, I pushed him out and he fell from the first floor to the ground. When I looked out of the broken window he was lying on the patio below, spread-eagled on his back, a dark pool of blood seeping out from under him. The Dior Man.

I haven't had so many nightmares since I was a child. But then I kept dreaming about monsters hiding under my bed, ready to snatch me as soon as I stuck my leg even an inch outside the duvet. The nightmares were getting so bad that I started wetting my bed until one day my mum gave me a small brown bottle with a yellow label. 'Anti-monster spray' it said on the label and it gave detailed instructions about how much spray one should use depending on the size and the type of the monster. I'd spray my bedroom generously every night and it worked like magic. The monsters disappeared and my sheet and mattress remained dry. It took me years to realize the spray was the lavender water my mum used to make herself. Till this very day I connect the smell of lavender with my childhood, monster-free bedroom. I wish I had the spray now.

It takes me hours to get back to sleep and when my alarm rings at 6.30 a.m. I feel exhausted. But I force myself to go for a short run, which feels sad and lonely without Wispa, take a long hot shower, limit myself to two Arpeggios from my coffee machine and get to work half an hour before my meeting with Julian at 9 a.m. I have barely enough time to skim through the subjects of my emails, opening a few that seem urgent.

He greets me cordially, enveloping me in the cloud of his aftershave. I'm pretty sure it is, ironically, Eau Sauvage by Dior. He leads me to his pristine leather sofa and the image of him and Gary flashes through my mind. Is that why he invited me here? To somehow strike a deal about what I saw on Monday night?

'Anna.' His voice is full of compassion. 'I'm afraid I have a bit of bad news.'

He pauses and I brace myself for whatever might come.

'Your position has been made redundant.'

'Excuse me?'

For a moment I think this is some kind of an elaborate joke and in a second we'll both be laughing at it. But he is not laughing; there isn't a hint of smile in his face, just ruthless satisfaction.

'Your position is no longer viable in our new structure.'

'I don't understand.'

He sighs and opens his hands in a gesture of hopelessness, so incompatible with his face.

'I know. It's been such a hard decision. Believe me. We greatly value your experience, your skills, your honesty and sincerity, and it will be a great loss to our company. And to me personally. I have really enjoyed working with you and I'll be very sad to see you go. But such are the times. They call for change, for tough austerity measures, for a new slim-lined structure, and even for letting go of our best people.'

I tune him out and try to understand the implications of what he's just said. Julian keeps talking and I watch his stony face, his hard, uncaring eyes and his thin mouth moving eloquently, delivering my sentence.

'. . . is a thankless task,' he continues. 'It is an emotional process and we've set up measures to help you go through it. I've arranged a follow-up meeting with HR for you on Friday. Anthea will go through all the details with you, the redundancy package and your rights, of course. You'll see how much we've appreciated your hard work.' It's intended as a promise but sounds like a threat. 'In the meantime, go home, take the time to think of the future. Don't bother coming in tomorrow. Anthea will be in touch regarding Friday.'

He gets up and I have no choice but to get up as well. The meeting is clearly over. He takes my hand in both of his and looks into my eyes with the compassion of an alligator.

'I'm so sorry, Anna, but you'll find it's for the best.'

Shell-shocked, I leave his office and take the corridor to the emergency access staircase at the back of the building. I swipe my card and pull the heavy door open. The staircase is the office sanctuary, used only occasionally by the maintenance staff and a few fitness freaks who prefer the stairs to the array of lifts at the front of the building. One can spend hours here without being accosted by a single soul. I sit on the vinyl-covered step at the top of the stairs. As the initial shock subsides I see the reality of the situation. It's really quite simple. I'm out of a job. Just like that. And I'm dying for a cigarette. I haven't smoked for years, but the sudden craving takes me all the way down to the underground car park and the office of the security guys. I bum a Marlboro Light off one of them and stand outside by the car exit, inhaling the smoke greedily. As soon as the nicotine buzz hits me, I begin to feel better. I'm ready to face the world. Well, almost. I take the back stairs up to my floor and go straight to my office. Gary passes my door and raises his hand in greeting. I wonder if he knows. Not that it matters one way or the other. Soon everyone will know and the place will be rife with gossip and speculation. It's better to leave as soon as possible, Julian was right about that. I log off my laptop, pack my bag, grab the picture of Wispa that has been sitting on my desk since I started the job and leave, closing the door behind me. Luckily, Claire is not at her station, so I don't have to invent a lie about leaving work so early.

Once I start driving, the nicotine rush dissipates and suddenly I'm on the verge of tears. I drive on, looking for a place to stop. But the streets are busy, there are people everywhere, and the only place I can think of that would give me some solace is the Heath. On autopilot I drive towards it and find a parking space off Highgate Road. I remember I'm in my work clothes and shoes, which are not the best walking gear, but I don't care. A path I choose without thinking takes me to the top of Parliament Hill. It's a crisp, windy day, and the clouds are swiftly moving above the city skyline. I take in the view framed by the autumnal trees, stretching from the Gherkin on the left up to the BT Tower on the right. It normally makes my heart sing, overwhelms with the beauty of this mad, sprawling

city. But today all I can think of are the people in office buildings everywhere, as far as I can see. Together they create this
tight, humming network of workforce: striving, achieving,
winning, losing, always in a rush, forever on a treadmill. As I
take the view in I slowly begin to comprehend that the network
has spat me out; I'm a small cog that has broken off, useless,
discarded. Where is the fight in me, what's happened to my
usual resilience? I hope it'll come back, but at the moment I
feel defeated.

I rummage through my bag, find my phone and speed-dial
Bell's number. It is only when I get the 'disconnected' message
I realize what I've done. Fighting back the tears, I put the phone
back in my bag. I miss you Bell, more than ever before.

A tiny Chinese tourist, dressed in colourful woollen clothes,
asks me to take a picture of her with her camera. I oblige her
and can tell she's dying to have a chat.

'You dressing like business, you no work?' she asks me.

'No, I don't work,' I tell her, the first person to learn of my
new employment status.

'You come here a lot?'

'Yes, I do.'

She looks at me with her smiling, sparkling eyes. Then the
smile is gone.

'You alone in the soul,' she says.

'Yes, I suppose I am,' I reply, taken aback.

'London dark place.' She puts her two tiny fists together.
'People push, people fight. But this place good for soul. Let the
light in your soul and you see harmony.' The smile is back. She
puts the camera in her bag, pats my arm and turns round. I
watch her walking away, a small colourful dot against the greying
landscape. Perhaps she's right, but even the Heath is not giving

me any light for my soul today. I look around, searching for Wispa, then remember where she is. Please, please, let her be all right. I need her.

By the time I walk back to my car I'm frozen to the bone. I turn the heating on full blast and drive home, shivering. My street seems to be packed with cars and I keep driving around until I get tired of hunting for a parking spot and dump my car on Highgate Hill. I walk up the hill, huddled against the wind, and when I get to my house I see a man standing in front of my door. My heart instantly begins to pound. I'm ready to scream for help when he turns towards me and I see a huge bouquet of flowers in his hands.

'Ms Wright?' he asks and smiles with relief when I nod. 'Flower delivery from Liberty's.'

I take the bouquet from him and unlock the door. The flowers are stunning, a mixture of purple hydrangeas, lilac roses, blood-red dahlias and purple clematis. The letters on a silver ribbon tying them together say 'Wild at Heart'. I pull out a small envelope tucked in-between the flowers. 'Wishing you all the best, Julian,' it says. I put the note back in its envelope, take the flowers to my rubbish bin outside and dump them, heads down. I slam the front door, go to the kitchen and pour myself a glass of Aberlour whisky. I'm shaking, not from the cold, but anger. How dare he, that evil cyborg of a man, invade my private distress? With a few more gulps of Aberlour my anger subsides. It's being replaced by a new feeling, of determination. I'm not going down without a fight.

I pick up my phone and scroll through my contacts. I stop at Sue's number and dial. She picks up almost immediately.

'Sue, am I interrupting anything?'

'No, it's fine. Olive's got a bit of a cold and I'm working from home. What's up?'

'I need the best redundancy lawyer in town.'

There is a long silence in which I can hear distant TV in the background.

'You've been made redundant? When?'

'This morning.'

'Shit. Haven't they given you any notice?'

'Nope.'

'When is your last day?'

'Today, I think . . .'

'They've put you on gardening leave straight away? That's hard core.'

I say nothing as my anger subsides and is replaced by feeling sorry for myself. Sue picks up on my change of mood.

'Don't worry, old girl. Leave it with me. I'll do some research and get back to you. Actually, do you want to pop over for dinner tonight? I don't think Olive's lurgy is contagious.'

'That would be great, thank you.'

We arrange I'll come by at 7 p.m. and I put the phone down. What now? I look around my kitchen and am overwhelmed by the feeling of purposelessness. It's as if all the urgent tasks that I've been putting off because of work have suddenly disappeared and there is absolutely nothing left to do. I don't even have the energy to call any of my friends to let them know my news. What's left? Wispa. I pick up the phone and dial the vet's number. Good news. Wispa Wright is doing much better. The vet is optimistic. If she keeps improving I might be able to take her home in a day or two. I put the phone down. What now? Daytime TV. I go to the lounge and put the TV on. I skip a couple of game shows with miserable-looking people wearing name tags, watch a bit of tennis, am amused for a while by the silliness of *NCIS*, then stumble upon a rerun of seventies nostalgia galore, *Kojak*. Once the awesome baldy has managed to catch a psychotic killer in Manhattan, I go on channel hopping until I hit the news. It's live coverage of a press conference. According to the helpful crawler at the bottom of the screen, the speaker, Commander Bob Rowland, is saluting the memory of Detective Chief Superintendent Mark Thomas. I turn up the volume.

'The murder of a police officer is a particularly appalling crime. It strikes at the very core of our society. As police officers, it is our duty to protect, to catch criminals who go against everything we stand for. It's a tough and dangerous job and we are fully aware of the risks we encounter on a daily basis. We know that some of us will have to pay the ultimate price. Detective Chief Superintendent Mark Thomas was a great leader, a respected and valued police officer, a devoted husband, loving father—'

I grab the remote and switch the TV off just as a photograph of the Dior Man in his police uniform appears. I stare at the blank screen, stunned. Loving father. This is the bit DCI Jones withheld when I asked her about him, that's why she despised me so much. He had a child, maybe children, who are now left without a father. An intense feeling of guilt and shame washes over me. I go to the kitchen and pour myself another glass of Aberlour. Then I sit at the kitchen table sipping the whisky, hating myself, waiting for the alcohol to dull my senses. My phone's ringtone pulls me out of the stupor. It's Sue, who launches into a monologue straight away.

'Hon, I've found you the best redundancy lawyer in town. She helped Giles Welsh when he got booted out last year and on the strength of one letter from her they doubled his redundancy offer. Apparently she's absolutely brilliant. Even the biggest corporate sharks are scared of her. I've called her already and she can see you tomorrow at ten a.m. This is really lucky, because she's busy as hell. Hon, we're going to kick their arses so hard they won't be able to sit down for months. Here are her details, have you got a pen? Her name is Gillian Foster . . .'

I make some noises as I look for something to write on.

'Hon, you OK?'

I muster all the energy to focus.

'I'm fine, Sue, thank you so much for doing this.'

'You're still coming over tonight?'

'Actually, I was just thinking that I should probably stay home and have an early night . . .'

'You sure you want to be on your own?'

'Yes.' I try to sound as upbeat as I can. 'I really need to absorb everything, get a full picture . . .'

'Sure, I understand. But do call me if you change your mind.'

She gives me the details of the lawyer, which I scribble on a piece of paper, and promises to ring me tomorrow morning. I switch the phone off and pour myself a glass of water from the tap. Sue's call has sobered me up. The irony of what I'm doing doesn't escape me. I had no qualms about making other people redundant, but here I am, screaming blue murder because the same thing is happening to me. Am I being just a tad hypocritical? Well, what goes around, comes around. It doesn't mean I should take whatever comes lying down.

Nineteen Days Later

As promised, Sue wakes me up bright and early, with plenty of time to get ready for my 10 a.m. meeting in Tower Bridge.

Ms Gillian Foster is in her late forties, looking striking with her short auburn hair and deep-red lipstick. Her green eyes are sharp and her handshake is strong. She invites me to her office straight away and her secretary, a tall transsexual with a deep voice and too much make-up, brings us a tray with a carafe of water and two glasses. Once the water's been poured, she asks me to tell her in my own words what has happened. She listens to my somewhat chaotic story without interrupting, jotting a few things on an A4 pad. Then she puts her pen down.

'Dealing with redundancy is at the same time hard and easy. The hard part is the emotional side of it, going through all the stages from the initial shock, through denial to anger. This is the part I won't be able to help you with. It is very likely that your employer has included some "help package" in their redundancy offer, which would include counselling, help with readjusting, retraining. There are companies that specialize in this kind of help, offering even an office space with your own desk you can go to every day if you have problems with adjusting to the absence of work routine in your life.'

'I'm sure I won't miss sitting at my desk every day.'

'You'd be surprised how strongly we've been conditioned to be workhorses. If they offer you a help package my advice would be – use it. But it's entirely up to you. The other part of dealing with redundancy, the easy one, is the legal side of it. This is where I come in, and that's why I say it's going to be easy. Before we go any further, let me ask you a question: do you want to be made redundant?'

'Excuse me?'

'You have the right to appeal against your redundancy. You can try to contest it informally by offering for instance a change in your working conditions that might be attractive to your employer. Or you may feel you have grounds to dispute the redundancy decision and take your case to an employment tribunal. Again, it's entirely up to you.'

'Would I want to fight to stay on with the company that has sucked me dry and spat me out? My answer is: over my dead body. I want to take them to the cleaners and run with the money.'

Ms Foster smiles for the first time and it's the smile of a hungry shark.

'Wonderful. Let's make it happen, then.'

I'm overwhelmed by a feeling of gratitude. It feels good to have a hungry shark on your side.

'When making employees redundant, every company is legally obliged to follow strict procedures. I am going to make sure the process has been fair and unbiased, and that it is a genuine redundancy and not just a ploy to get rid of you.'

I debate whether to tell her about having caught Julian and Gary on the couch and decide against it. Even if it was the real reason for Julian to get rid of me, I'm not prepared to stoop as low as him.

Ms Foster moves on to a much nicer subject: compensation.

She outlines the scope of my 'exit pay', as she calls it, including redundancy and notice pay.

'Once we get your redundancy offer, I'm going to scour it for everything we can use to our advantage. We want enhanced pension, share payouts, extended medical insurance. Do you have a company car?'

I shake my head.

'But you do have a company mobile phone. And you're going to keep it.'

'Isn't it a bit petty?'

'You'll be surprised when you see how petty the other side can get. As your payout is likely to exceed the tax-free limit, instead of asking for a higher redundancy settlement, we'll go for higher non-cash benefits. I'll also ask you to consider signing a non-compete clause.'

'Non-compete?'

'In case you want to join the competition.'

'The way I feel at the moment, I don't want to work for television ever again. A landscape gardening course sounds tempting right now. Or perhaps I could open an art gallery.' I can already see myself with a glass of champagne in my hand, entertaining exquisite guests at a private view.

'Yes, but they don't have to know about it. Offering to sign the clause, even for as little as six months, can double your exit package,' she says with barely disguised glee. 'It's going to be so much fun, Anna.'

Although a bit unnerving in a lawyer, I find her enthusiasm contagious. For the first time since my meeting with Julian I actually begin to feel my redundancy might not be such a bad thing after all.

I leave Ms Gillian Foster's office having agreed I'll be in

touch tomorrow, right after my meeting with HR, which she isn't going to attend. I feel I'm in good hands. Gillian versus Julian, I think, it's going to be an interesting game to watch.

Instead of catching the tube home straight away, I head towards St Katharine Docks and stroll around the marina, looking at the luxury yachts moored there. I could probably get used to this kind of life of leisure. But then I remember my monthly mortgage repayments and feel a flutter of anxiety in my chest. I won't be able to retire yet, no matter how good Ms Gillian Foster is.

I'm considering an early lunch at the Dickens Inn when my phone rings. It's DCI Jones, asking me if I could call at Kentish Town station to see her, preferably as soon as possible. I'm not overjoyed, feeling that my meetings with DCI Jones are becoming a touch too frequent. But as I have nothing better to do, I reluctantly agree. The tube journey is surprisingly smooth and I'm entering the station forty minutes later.

DS Kapoor takes me straight to DCI Jones's office. She looks official today, the fleece and jeans replaced by a black tailored suit with a pair of designer reading glasses perched on her nose. She acts official, too, when she asks me take a chair opposite her at her desk. DS Kapoor leaves, closing the door quietly behind him.

'Thank you so much for coming, Anna. I do appreciate you making time for us at such short notice.'

'Oh, I have lots of time at the moment,' I say rather flippantly.

'Really?' She throws me a glance above her glasses.

'I've been made redundant. As of yesterday.' I take strange pleasure from telling her about the misfortune which has befallen me.

'I'm very sorry to hear that.' She takes her glasses off. 'Has it been on the cards for a while?'

'No, it was completely unexpected.'

'Gosh.' She shakes her head. 'I hope they'll pay you off handsomely.'

'I hope so, too.'

'The reason I've asked you to come in today is that we've had an interesting development. I'm not entirely sure of its relevance, but I thought it was significant enough to discuss it with you.'

She pauses and my heart begins to beat faster, even though I don't know what to expect.

'It transpires that Mr James Morgan, your ex-partner I believe –' she looks at me for confirmation and I nod – 'is not in South-East Asia as we'd previously assumed.'

I wait for her to continue, not sure where she's going with this.

'According to the UK Border Agency there is no record of James Morgan leaving the country. There is also no record of him ever reaching South-East Asia. And yet his employer, as well as all his friends we've spoken to, are under the impression that that's where he is. This appears to be a conjecture, as in fact no one has heard from him or seen him since he went on leave over a month ago. Have you had any contact with him since your break-up?'

'No. Well, I spoke to him on the phone a few days after we'd split up, but nothing since then. What does it all mean?'

'It means he's disappeared,' she sighs. 'And we need to consider all the possible scenarios.'

'Has something happened to him?'

She smiles thinly. 'There are plenty of possible explanations for his disappearance. Most of them entirely innocent. He could've changed his mind and decided to spend his career break in . . . Scotland, for instance. Or he could've hopped on the Eurostar using someone else's ticket and is travelling in Europe as we speak.'

'But you don't know for sure?'

'No. None of his debit or credit cards has been used since he disappeared. There was, however, a large withdrawal of cash from his account on the last day he was seen at work.'

'That's strange. He never uses cash. He relies totally on plastic, even for ridiculously small amounts.'

'How did you two split up?'

'What do you mean?'

'Was it amicable?'

I shrug my shoulders. 'It was very civilized. We had dinner at Roka. He didn't want us to break up. He said we were perfect for each other.'

'So it was you who dumped him?'

I raise my eyebrows, taken aback by her bluntness. But she goes on, unperturbed.

'Would you say he took it well? Or badly?'

'No.' I feel irritated by her questions. 'James doesn't take anything badly. He's quite unflappable. And he's very sure of himself, with women, I mean. I might have caused a slight dent in his ego, but I'm sure he recovered pretty quickly. In fact, I know he's dating someone else. Is this why you've asked me to come here? To discuss James's state of mind?'

'We have to consider the possibility he may have self-harmed . . .'

'James?' I laugh.

'Has he ever harmed you?'

'No, never.'

'He hasn't been violent in any way?'

'No. Why do you ask?' A cold shiver runs through me. 'God . . . what are you suggesting?'

DCI Jones raises both her hands as if to stop me. 'As I said, we have to consider all the possibilities.'

'Including the possibility that he is a rapist and a killer!'

She doesn't answer.

'I'd been with the man for three years! I know him. He can be a bit of an arrogant arsehole at times, self-absorbed and with a huge ego, but who isn't these days? He is also generous, funny and caring. He is a *normal* guy, not some deranged psycho attacking people on the Heath.'

She nods. 'I hear you.'

'Is that all you wanted to ask me about?' I get up abruptly, my chair making a scraping noise on the floor.

'Yes, thank you, I have no further questions.' DCI Jones gets up as well.

'Good.' I go towards the door.

'I do appreciate you stopping by, Anna. Oh, I hope your dog is better. And good luck with the redundancy.'

'Thank you.' I look at her coldly. 'And goodbye.'

I leave her office and almost immediately get lost trying to find my way out. When I eventually find the exit, my anger has gone. Why did I react so emotionally to DCI Jones's questions about James? Is it because she's implied something that I have been suppressing in my thoughts from the very beginning? Could James really be the Heath attacker? Is he on some insane revenge trip following our break-up?

I cross the street, but instead of taking the tube I decide to walk home. I turn left and follow Highgate Road. Then I stop abruptly as I remember the teddy-bear incident. A man who's been walking behind me nearly bumps into me. He mumbles something when I apologize, then turns and walks away in the opposite direction. A Kentish Town weirdo, I think as my mind goes back to the teddy bear. It was strange from the start, the way it got nicked from my car, to reappear in the window of a charity shop. Could it have been a sign from James, a message that I'd been unworthy of his presents and his love? No, I decide, it would have been completely out of character. James doesn't do big, dramatic gestures. His emotional imagination doesn't stretch beyond ordering a stuffed toy delivery on the Internet. Is he capable of a jealous rage? The more I think about it, the less likely it seems. My relationship with James was fun at the beginning, but it had always been lukewarm. James is not a man of great passion, he's reserved and guarded emotionally. Under the cuddly *cagnolino di peluche* facade sits a rather withdrawn, repressed even, cautious man. Not a deranged rapist.

I decide I deserve a treat for my efforts today and stop at the Bull & Last for lunch. Their menu overwhelms, as usual. After a long deliberation I choose handmade ravioli of cavolo nero, with ricotta and hazelnut, raisins, radicchio and brown butter. And I don't regret it. Good food takes my mind off killers and redundancies, and I don't think of either until I get home and check my phone for messages. There is a voicemail from Anthea, the HR goddess, inviting me for a meeting tomorrow at 11.30 in the morning. It is for real, then, I haven't dreamt the whole redundancy thing up. It's time to let my friends know I'm becoming jobless.

Twenty Days Later

It feels weird driving to work with no purpose of working at all. At the car park my space has been taken by a white Lexus RX 450h. Dead-man's shoes, I think, although I know perfectly well it's standard practice to take someone else's parking spot if the person isn't there by 11 a.m.

As I take the lift to my floor, I brace myself for a collective display of sympathy. In fact, the office seems strangely empty, with just a couple of heads barely visible from behind their computer screens. But Claire is there and she greets me with genuine distress in her eyes.

'Anna, I've just heard, I'm so sorry . . .'

'It's OK, darling, I'll live. In fact, I'm looking forward to a life of leisure.' I keep it light, to avoid the unnecessary tears. 'Where is everybody?'

'Downstairs in the conference room. Julian's called in an urgent departmental meeting.'

'He's probably announcing my redundancy. Clever timing, I must say. Everyone's out of the way when I come in, so no one will get contaminated by my bile.'

'I don't know what to say . . . It's been such a shock.'

'Don't worry, Claire. It happens, probably more often than we think.'

'But you've been here from the start, it's your baby.'

'Well, obviously the baby's grown up and it doesn't need me any more.'

'Everyone will want to say goodbye to you. Will you want a farewell party?'

There is nothing I want less than the humiliation of my own redundancy party.

'Probably not, but thanks for thinking about it. Just a card signed by everyone and an engraved clock for my mantelpiece will do.'

Claire is so distressed she doesn't seem to be able to appreciate my joke. I give her a hug and it actually feels good. The idea that someone needs comforting more than I do makes me feel stronger.

I take the lift upstairs and knock on Anthea's door. She opens it instantly, as if she's been waiting for me with her hand on the doorknob. So keen to get rid of me.

The meeting is short and polite. I stick to Gillian's advice: 'Keep it soft, don't agree to anything, don't sign anything, take their offer and bring it to me.' Instead of discussing details I try to draw Anthea into a conversation on a more personal level. But when it comes to the emotional implications of redundancy, the queen of HR shows the empathy of a concrete wall. I quickly realize there is no point prolonging the superficial exchange. I've read somewhere that HR employees are like estate agents. They always pretend to be on your side, but ultimately cover the back of whoever pays them. And since I'm out of the game, I'm no longer of interest to Anthea. I collect the offer documents and leave. I take the lift straight to the car park, having managed to avoid meeting anyone on the way down. I get into my car and go through the papers Anthea has given me. The offer seems good, amounting to nearly a year's salary. But let's wait and see what Gillian has got to say about it. I pick up the phone and dial her number. The deep-voiced secretary tells me Ms Foster will see me this afternoon at 4 p.m.

I'm leaving the car park for what I hope is the last time when my phone rings, relayed via Bluetooth to my car speakers. It's the vet surgery and the news is good. I can pick up Wispa today. Great, I'm on my way, I tell the receptionist, quietly acknowledging the fact that there are good sides to being un-employed. Like being able to pick up your dog from the vet in the middle of the day, for instance. When I arrive at the Beaumont Sainsbury Hospital Wispa greets me with a display of happiness so intense I burst into tears. She seems fine, perhaps slightly surprised by my strange behaviour. She'll have to take it easy for a week or two, I'm told, and I assure the nurse who's been looking after her that Wispa's middle name is 'taking it easy'. As I pay the bill I make a mental note to look into dog insurance. But even the hefty sum I've had to fork out just now doesn't cloud the joy I feel at having Wispa back. She curls in her usual place in the boot of my car and suddenly my life feels almost complete.

The detour to the vet still leaves me with plenty of time to do some shopping for an impromptu dinner I've arranged for tonight. Sue and Michael are invited, and Michael is bringing a 'new man' with him, a guy he met recently through mutual friends and whom he actually likes a lot. I stop at Waitrose on the way home and luxuriate in browsing the empty aisles that are normally packed with irate middle-class people at weekends. Despite having spent a small fortune, I realize I've forgotten a few vital ingredients for my dinner and decide to stop in the village High Street on the way. There is a parking space right at the top of Highgate Hill, so I leave snoozing Wispa in the car and walk up to the shops. I subconsciously pick up the leisurely rhythm of a midday stroll with nowhere to rush to and stop by the bookshop, checking their window display. I might actually have time to read books now, I think, and I go inside. I emerge with a handful of exciting new titles: Margaret Atwood, William Boyd, Donna Tartt and Sebastian Faulks. This should keep me happy for a while. I'm just about to cross the street when I hear someone calling my name. I turn and see Tom, waving at me.

'Long time no see!'

'Yes, it's been a while.' I remind myself I have no reason to run away screaming from him, the man hasn't actually done anything bad except try to be friendly. And as to his wife's ridiculous request, well, I have been avoiding him long enough.

'I was so sorry to hear the terrible news.' He looks genuinely concerned.

'Oh well, it was a bit of a shock, but I'm getting used to it.' I wonder how he knows about my redundancy.

He looks at me strangely. 'What a tragedy. She was your very close friend, wasn't she?'

'Oh . . . Bell . . . yes, I'm sorry, I thought you meant . . .' I instantly hate myself for forgetting about her for a moment. I'm clearly turning into a self-absorbed monster, shallow and uncaring. Whoever called me a heartless bitch was right.

'Are you all right?' He puts his hand on my arm.

'Yes . . . no . . . I'm fine, thank you, Tom.'

'Samantha and I meant to call you, to offer our condolences . . . and help . . .'

'That's very kind of you.'

'But at least your partner's back, so you don't have to deal with it on your own. There's nothing worse than—'

'My partner?' It comes out a bit too aggressively.

'Your . . . boyfriend?' He looks at me strangely again.

'Oh, you mean Michael?' Of course, he's seen him at my house a couple of times.

'No, not the gay guy . . .' He stops, embarrassed. 'I'm sorry, I didn't mean . . . It's just that I saw your ex leaving the house just now and I thought—'

'My ex?'

'Erm . . . I don't know his name, but I'd seen him around in the past—'

'You saw a man leaving my house just now?' I scream at him.

'Well –' Tom, clearly taken aback, looks at his watch awkwardly – 'five minutes ago . . .'

'Oh God . . .' I turn away from him and start running in the direction of my street.

'Anna!' I hear Tom's voice behind me. 'Are you OK? Do you want me to come with you?'

'No, I'm fine! See you later!' I shout back as the books slip out from under my arm and scatter on the pavement. I quickly pick them up and trot up the hill.

My street is empty, there are no passers-by and no moving cars. I reach my house, run up the front steps and try the door. It's locked. I unlock it and walk in cautiously. It's quiet inside. I take out my phone, dial 999 and hold my finger above the green dial button as I walk into the kitchen. Everything seems as I left it this morning. The same quiet stillness greets me in the sitting room. I slowly walk upstairs. There's no one there and nothing looks out of place. I go down to the kitchen and check the back door. It's locked and intact. The same goes for all the windows downstairs. I switch off my phone, go back to the front door and inspect the lock. There is nothing wrong with it, no signs of tampering or forced entry. Then I remember the set of keys Bell had with her when she was attacked. I look through recent calls on my phone and dial a number. She answers on the second ring.

'DCI Jones – Vic – this is Anna Wright.'

'Yes, Anna, how can I help you?' There is a lot of background noise, as if she's in a busy office.

'I think James has just been to my house.'

'Have you seen him?'

'No, I haven't, but he was seen leaving my house.'

'By whom?'

'By Tom. I've just bumped into him in the High Street and he casually mentioned he'd just seen my boyfriend leaving the house.'

'Tom Collins?'

'Yes.'

'Does Tom know James?'

'No . . . yes . . . I don't know. He said he'd seen him around. He was adamant it wasn't Michael.'

'OK.' I can hear doors closing and Vic's voice is clearer now. 'Why would Tom volunteer this information?'

'He was concerned I'd be upset after Bell's death. And said it was good my boyfriend was back.'

'It is a rather odd thing to say.' DCI Jones falls silent and I must admit I'm beginning to agree with her. 'Have you checked the house? Is anything missing or disturbed?'

'No, not as far as I can tell.' I'm beginning to have doubts about the whole thing. 'But, Vic, the keys . . .'

'Yes?'

'The set Bell had with her when she got attacked. The set you've never found. Whoever murdered her must have it. And if James . . .' I can't find the words to finish the sentence.

'Yes, I see. We'll speak to Tom to confirm what he saw exactly. Would you like me to send DS Kapoor to check on you later today?'

'No, thank you. I have friends coming over for dinner, I'll be fine.'

'Good.'

I put the phone down, feeling silly about calling her. It does seem strange that Tom should stop me to tell me about James. How does he know who James and Michael are, anyway? But what if he was right and James really was at my house? A cold shiver runs across my back. No, I can't let it wind me up again. It's all supposition, without a shred of tangible proof. But, to be on the safe side, I'm going to call the locksmith and change my locks once again.

I remember Wispa and the shopping I've left in my car and dash out to retrieve the car from Highgate Hill. When I get back home I have just enough time to start dinner preparations and then I have to go out again to see Ms Foster. It's amazing how quickly a day goes when you don't have to work.

Gillian greets me warmly, offers tea and biscuits, then goes quickly through the documents I've received from Anthea. She puts the papers down with a triumphant glint in her eyes.

'It's a good offer, way above the statutory minimum.'

'Are we accepting it, then?'

'Oh, no. We're going for the jugular.'

'The jugular?'

'When did you learn about your redundancy?'

'Two days ago.'

'And you had no inkling it was going to happen? No warning? No one had talked to you about it?'

'No, never.'

'Fabulous.' Gillian takes a sip of her tea. 'We are going to get them for the lack of consultation.'

'Consultation?'

'Employers should always consult with you before making you redundant. They have clearly failed to do that. I'm really surprised such a huge corporation would trip over something so basic. We are going to wave unfair dismissal at them and see what happens. We have them by the short and curlies, Anna.'

I leave Ms Foster's office with this image in my head.

My guests arrive just as I'm putting my Parmigiana di Melanzane into the oven. They have all brought little treats for Wispa to welcome her home and I have to heartlessly hide them from her, as I know she'd eat them all at once. Michael's new man is called Giorgio. He's tall and lean, with the youthful energy of someone who wants to do too much at once. He's brought an exquisite bottle of Barolo, which will go nicely with my aubergine dish. I like him instantly. Michael goes straight to my Bose sound system and chooses Max Richter as our background music. As we nibble on olives, bocconcini and Italian bread, I tell them about my visit to Gillian Foster and my redundancy.

'Here's to Ms Foster having them by the short and curlies.' Michael raises his glass.

'And that Julian character, he deserves the wrath of a thousand harpies,' adds Giorgio.

I haven't mentioned walking in on Julian and Gary, but the image I've painted of the man is enough for anyone to dislike him.

'I'm sure she's capable of that.' Sue clinks her glass with mine. 'You'll see, even though it feels devastating now, it'll turn out to be one of the best turns in your career. You've been in that golden cage for too long.'

'You're probably right. But it's the sudden loss of power that feels humiliating right now. One moment I'm fine and the next I feel this cold fist tightening in my stomach.'

'Fear.' Michael nods his head. 'I know the feeling. It's one of the paradoxes of our lives. Having a permanent job gives us a totally false sense of security. We believe the job is going to last forever, and of course it never does. But take away this fickle safety net and we suddenly crumble to the ground, paralysed with fear.'

'It takes a lot of guts to go freelance,' says Sue.

'Yes, but at least you know what to expect from freelance life.'

'Permanent insecurity?' Giorgio smiles at Michael.

'Well, it doesn't come as a shock when the work's suddenly not there.'

'I think it's always a shock. We're only adapting to the increasing voltage.'

'What do you do, Giorgio?'

'I'm a light rebel.'

'And you happen to be a very talented architect,' throws in Michael.

'Oh, that,' Giorgio dismisses it with a wave of his hand, 'that's just a day job. Light rebellion is my passion.'

'Light rebellion?'

'It's a form of street art. I use light to reclaim the streets, to introduce colour and life into the dullness of urban landscape.'

'It's quite fascinating.' It's Michael again, unable to hide his awe of Giorgio. 'He has this van, equipped with state of the art lighting gear, all computerized and motion controlled. Thousands of lumens on wheels.'

'How do you do it?'

'It's a bit like architectural lighting, but with an added dimension. I started with simple shapes that I'd colour with spotlights. I'd go out at night, looking for derelict buildings, shabby exteriors, black and white street art pieces, then I'd fill them with colour, photograph them and scram.'

'Tell them about your 3D video projection mapping,' Michael chips in again.

Giorgio smiles shyly. 'I have to warn you, once I start talking about it I won't be able to stop.'

'Oh, go on, give it to us in a nutshell.'

'All right, but I think I need a smoke first.'

'Go out to the garden through the kitchen back door. The ashtray's on the windowsill,' instructs Michael, well versed in the rules of my house. Once Giorgio is out of the room, Michael continues. 'He creates 3D animation on his computer and then maps the visual onto the chosen building. He's shown me a video of the projection he did in Shoreditch a couple of weeks ago, it's absolutely amazing.'

'It looks like you've fallen for him, hook, line and sinker.'

Sue sounds just like my aunt Janet, the scourge of my teenage years.

'I think I have, darling . . . Isn't he the cutest thing?'

'He is,' both Sue and I agree.

Suddenly there is a shout outside, followed by the sound of something falling and breaking. Wispa barks sharply and runs out of the room.

'In the garden!' shouts Michael, jumping to his feet.

I follow him to the kitchen. The back door is wide open, the whole garden flooded by the cold light of a security lamp. There are two men swaying in a clinching hold on the lawn. Wispa jumps around them, barking fiercely, her sickness long forgotten. I recognize Giorgio, who is just swinging a punch at the other man's chin. The other man staggers backwards and Giorgio moves swiftly forward and catches him in a shoulder lock. I call Wispa, who comes to me wagging her tail excitedly, and I grab her by the collar.

'A burglar! I caught him red-handed!' Giorgio shouts triumphantly, turning towards us. The other man is clearly in pain in his tight lock, blood streaming from his nose.

'Tom?' I look at him in disbelief.

'What the hell are you doing here?' Michael takes a step forward as Tom tries to pull out of Giorgio's grip.

'You know him?' Giorgio doesn't seem willing to release his shoulder lock. 'He was trying to climb either in or out of your first-floor window.' He points at my bedroom window with his head. 'I caught him by the ankles. I think part of the guttering came down with him.' Indeed, there are some broken bits of black plastic guttering lying on the ground.

'Tom! What the fuck is going on?!' I shout, anger building inside me.

'I'm calling the police.' Michael pulls out his mobile.

'Wait!' I grab his hand. 'Tom! Answer me!'

Tom tries to pull out of Giorgio's grip again, his face contorted with rage and smeared with blood.

'Maybe call an ambulance as well.' I hear Sue's voice behind me.

Michael doesn't answer, dialling a number.

I stare at the two men on my lawn, unable to comprehend the situation.

'Anna, you're all shaking, come inside.' I feel Sue's hand on my shoulder.

'But . . .' I point at Giorgio and Tom.

'It's all right, I've got it under control.' Giorgio flashes a smile at me.

'He's a black belt,' whispers Michael, interrupting for a moment his conversation with the 999 operator.

Sue and I go inside, followed by Wispa, who carries her rawhide bone around excitedly.

'Who is that guy?' asks Sue as I reach for Giorgio's bottle of Barolo.

'Want some?'

She nods.

'He's my neighbour.' I pour wine for both of us.

'Your neighbour? What was he doing out there?'

'I've no idea.' I sit heavily at the kitchen table.

'Maybe he's locked himself out and was climbing over the fence to get—'

'No, Sue, he doesn't live next door. He doesn't even live in my street.'

'Oh . . .' Sue takes a gulp of her wine.

'I have no idea what's going on.' I start sobbing uncontrollably.

Sue comes over and puts her arm round me. She hushes me like a mother would her baby. We sit at the kitchen table until the shrill sound of the doorbell breaks the silence. Sue rushes to the front door and lets two policemen in. One of them is the Gary Sinise sound-alike who came to my house a few days ago. He seems nicer now, almost friendly. The other policeman looks shockingly young, with a clean baby face and blond, almost white, short hair. They stop briefly in the kitchen, then Sue leads them to the garden. I can hear raised voices and sounds of struggle. Then everything goes quiet, the silence interrupted by the squawking of the police radios. After what seems like an eternity Michael and Giorgio appear at the back door, followed by the two policemen who lead Tom between them. He is wearing handcuffs.

'He's refusing to say anything,' says Gary Sinise.

'Even to confirm his name,' adds Michael.

'His name is Tom Collins. And I can give you his address —'

'No!' Tom interrupts me and tries to pull himself free.

'Easy, mate.' The baby-faced policeman holds him tightly. 'You know him?'

'He lives a few streets down from here. He found my dog once in the street and brought her home. I've met him casually a few times since then. And I've been to his house for a party and met his wife Samantha —'

'Shut up!' shouts Tom.

'Oi, move it.' Baby Face pushes him out of the kitchen and into the hallway.

'Do you know what he was doing in your garden?'

'I've no idea.' I'm beginning to sound like a broken record.

'You haven't invited him over?'

'No.' I shake my head. 'He definitely hasn't been invited.'

'OK.' Gary Sinise smiles at me reassuringly. 'We'll take him to the station and process him. You are pressing charges, aren't you?'

'Yes,' Michael says firmly. 'The guy was trying to get into her house.'

He looks at me and I nod.

'How long will you keep him in custody? I mean . . . he's not going to come back here tonight?'

'Oh, no,' he laughs. 'No need to worry about that, madam. He won't be coming back.'

The front door closes behind the policemen and Tom. The guests gathered in the kitchen stare at me with concern. I feel suffocated by their attention.

'Sorry, guys, I just need to go to the bathroom.' I get up shakily.

'You all right?'

'Thanks, Sue, I'm fine. Back in a flick.' I try to sound as light-hearted as I can.

In the bathroom I stare at my face in the mirror. What the hell is going on? Why would a man who seemed so friendly, so normal, want to break into my house all of a sudden? What was he trying to do? This is all too much. I can feel another wave of tears welling up inside me and I splash cold water on my face to stop myself from crying. When I look up again my make-up is all smeared, mascara running down my cheeks. I wipe all the smears off, not bothering to reapply make-up.

As I walk back into the kitchen the smell of burnt cheese hits me. My guests are gathered around the remains of the Parmigiana di Melanzane, which looks charred and inedible.

'OK, guys,' says Michael cheerfully. 'Why don't I take you all out to dinner at the Spaniards Inn tonight?'

'Actually, I was just about to suggest the same thing. Can I invite you all to celebrate meeting the lovely friends of this amazing, charming and sexy man?' Giorgio puts his arm round Michael, who is radiating happiness.

'Sounds like a great idea,' I say with relief, glad no one has mentioned Tom again.

Twenty-one Days Later

It's still dark outside when I wake up, my Siberian-duck-down duvet stiflingly heavy, my heart pounding. I'm convinced I've been woken up by a noise in the garden and I lie in bed, petrified and sweating, listening out for any sign of an intruder. But the house is quiet and Wispa is snoring peacefully on her bed by the bedroom door. I look at my iPhone. It's five o'clock. I read somewhere that this is the 'fearful hour', when our cortisol levels are at their highest and the blood sugar at its lowest. The fight or flight hormone makes our mind produce anxious and negative thoughts that exacerbate the feeling of restlessness and panic. As the memories of yesterday begin to flood in, the feeling of stress and anxiety intensifies. I must speak to DCI Jones, try to find out what's going on. But it's too early to speak to anyone. I feel painfully lonely and helpless. What has happened to my usual buoyancy, my fighting spirit that has served me so well all these years? It may have served me well, but look where it has got me, I think bitterly. I'm jobless, unimportant, single and stalked by a dentist. My ex-boyfriend might be missing, my best friend has been murdered and my illicit Heath lover is dead. And I can't get rid of the feeling that I am somehow at the very centre of all these tragedies. But why and how? My bed doesn't feel like a safe sanctuary any more. I get up and shuffle through the dark house to the kitchen, where I'm greeted by the burnt remains of the Parmigiana di Melanzane. The baking tray it's in is beyond salvaging. I wrap the whole thing in a plastic bag and put it in the bin. Then I sit at the kitchen table, waiting for the coffee to percolate. Why isn't DCI Jones calling me, I think, staring at my phone. But it's not even six o'clock and my phone will remain silent for a few more hours. So this is what it has come down to: I'm waiting for a phone call from a woman I hardly know, a woman who cares about me only in her professional capacity. Is this where I turn for comfort now? How pitiful and alone I've become.

The coffee is ready and I take the first sip of my daily caffeine ration. As it burns my stomach and jerks at my nerves I feel my body slowly waking up. I need to shake off this feeling of gloom, try to think rationally about my situation. In my present state of mind I consider myself unemployable. Or, at least, unable to find a job that would sustain my present lifestyle. I have to consider selling my house, moving out to affordable suburbia, somewhere in Finchley or Southgate perhaps, swapping my BMW for something cheaper, a Ford or a Vauxhall. I must, to use the hateful Americanism, downsize. Moving house may not be such a bad idea; perhaps it'll break the madness my personal life has become lately. Yes, the anonymity of suburbia is what I need, I decide, and open my laptop. A quick look at what's on offer on Zoopla and Rightmove cools my enthusiasm for the move out of Highgate. I remember all the reasons I moved here for three years ago, taking out a mortgage for a ridiculously high sum of money. Nothing has changed since then. If you're on a tight budget, you can buy a studio flat in Erith or 'purchase an exciting development opportunity' in Purfleet. I shiver at the thought, then realize I'm frozen to the bone. The heating, set to the later weekend hours, hasn't kicked in yet and the house is freezing. I shuffle back to bed and crawl under the duvet. As my body begins to warm up, I fall asleep, dreaming about estate agents and car salesmen from hell.

I'm woken up by the Piano Riff ringtone of my iPhone. It's Michael. He asks how I am and then we move on to last night's bizarre incident.

'There's been a development,' says Michael lightly. 'Tom is pressing charges.'

'What!' I'm not sure I heard him correctly.

'He's accusing Giorgio of causing ABH. Actual Bodily Harm.'

'I don't believe it!'

'Well, it's true. It's a step up from Common Assault and it carries a maximum penalty of five years' imprisonment or a fine, on indictment of course.'

'But that's absurd! OK, he ended up with a bloody nose, but it was justifiable.'

'I know, it's quite mad, but he claims Giorgio's actions have given him whiplash. And, wait for this, he's caused him psychological harm.'

'God, the man is crazy. What was he doing in my house anyway?'

'I don't know what his excuse is. I'm sure his wife has come up with something plausible. Apparently she's firmly standing by her man. And they do have a good lawyer.'

'I'm so sorry, Michael, I feel awful. None of this would've happened if—'

'Don't worry, sweetie, it's all right. I'm sure we'll have a good laugh about it once it's over.'

'I really don't feel like laughing now.'

'It'll be fine. Listen, do you fancy coming over tonight? Giorgio and I are having a small party.'

'Thanks so much, honey, but I think I need some time to myself. To count my sheep . . .'

'. . . instead of your blessings. Or was it the other way round in the song?' Michael chuckles. 'I totally understand. But do come if you change your mind.'

'I will, thank you.'

Before I put my phone down I check the time. Good grief, it's nearly 11 a.m. I've slept for five hours. I'm surprised Wispa didn't come to wake me up, demanding her morning walk. I jump out of bed, driven by a feeling of guilt. Before I take Wispa for a run I dial DCI Jones's number. My call goes straight to her voicemail, but I don't leave a message. I'm actually not sure what to say to her.

It's a glorious autumn day outside and Wispa and I are heading for the Heath. As we trot down Fitzroy Park, my mind begins to clear and I'm able to focus on the events of the last twenty-four hours. Why was Tom trying to break into my house? He'd always seemed like a nice and friendly guy. And then there is Samantha, the quiet powerhouse of the Collins household, standing by her man, for better or worse. The woman who knows my secret. Except it's not a secret any more, since I spilled my guts to DCI Jones. I have a feeling all these elements are somehow connected, that there is some devious logic to everything that's been happening to me recently but, whatever it is, it eludes me.

As we enter the Heath, its autumnal beauty takes my breath away. The pond shimmers in the warm sunshine, black coots dotting its surface. There are a lot of people milling around, dog walkers, joggers, families with kids, all grabbing the last rays of sun before the winter gloom descends on the scene. I run up the hill at full speed, then slow down before turning off into the woods. It's much darker here and almost empty, most of the walkers staying out in the sunshine. A shiver runs through me and I stop abruptly. The damp chill smells of rotting leaves, decaying matter, mouldy earth. The smell of death. Somewhere in these woods the Dior Man spent his last moments, fighting for his life, gasping for breath, slipping into unconsciousness, darkness closing in around him. I don't know how he died; the details have been kept confidential by the police and I haven't asked DCI Jones. I don't want to know. I want to remember him alive. I suddenly feel cold, despite my heart pounding furiously. I can't shake off the feeling there is someone lurking in the shadows of the bushes, watching me, following my every step. I know there is a rapist and a murderer still out there somewhere, and yet I'm drawn to the place, unable to resist its pull. I whistle quietly at Wispa, who's rummaging in the damp leaves ahead of me. She comes back instantly, her tail wagging. Whatever I feel must be a product of my imagination then, I tell myself, but the sense of danger persists. I cast a quick glance behind me and start walking backwards towards the brightness of the open space. I keep my eye on the dark bushes, listening for any noise, bracing myself for something terrible I'm convinced is just about to happen. A branch cracks under my foot, I slip in the mud and fall backwards, landing hard on the ground. I'm back on my feet instantly, breathless and shaking. The safety of the open meadow with other people in it is only a few steps away. I turn and run towards it, followed by a bouncing Wispa. The brightness and warmth of the sunshine hits me, but I keep running at full speed until I see other people – a teenager with a kite, a female runner in a pink outfit, an elderly couple with an elderly dog, a family with screaming kids. I run towards noise and movement, towards safety and life.

I don't stop until I'm back by the ponds, where a small crowd has gathered by an RSPB tent. I walk towards the display board, purely to feel the proximity of other people. I surround myself with the comforting fraternity of birdwatchers and stare at the display board, not seeing any detail, concentrating on my breathing and heartbeat. Once my pulse slows down I continue up Merton Lane, careful to have other people in my line of vision all the time.

When I get home I look up the number for the local locksmith and request an emergency visit to change the locks. They seem very busy, but when I say I don't mind paying double the call-out charge to have it done as soon as possible, they agree to send someone straight away. I must also call Dennis, my handyman, to have a look at the guttering damaged in last night's scuffle. I'll have him check the garden fence and maybe install some barbed wire in the most vulnerable spots. I know that if an intruder wants to break into my house he'll find a way anyway, but having done something about the security of my home makes me feel better.

The locksmith is the same guy who came to my house before. If he is surprised by the frequency with which I change my locks, he doesn't show it, just gets on with the job. Twenty minutes later he hands me a new set of keys, takes my cheque and tells me with a grin that he'll see me again soon. I lock the door behind him, check if the garden doors are locked as well, and get into the shower. I stand under the hot stream of water until all the mirrors are steamed up and the bathroom feels like a sauna. The rest of the house seems cold compared with it. I go to the kitchen and make scrambled eggs with chorizo and mushrooms. As the comfort food settles in my stomach I begin to relax at last. I'm determined to have a normal Saturday, catch up on calling friends, cook a simple dinner, watch a movie on iPlayer.

The doorbell sets my heartbeat racing again. Wispa rushes to the hallway, barking, but with her tail wagging. It's someone she knows. I put the chain on and crack the door open. It's DCI Jones, in her fleecy weekend attire. When I open the door for her I catch a glimpse of her red Mini parked behind my car. She apologizes for calling in unannounced, but I assure her it's fine. I offer her a coffee, which she accepts, and settles at my kitchen table.

'We've got Tom Collins in custody,' she says without preamble.

'Oh, I'm surprised his wife hasn't got him out yet. As you probably know, she's accusing Michael's boyfriend of causing Tom Actual Bodily Harm.'

'Yes.' She dismisses it with the slightest of shrugs. 'Anna, what I'm going to tell you isn't official yet. But I think you deserve to know.'

She pauses and I hold my breath. Her phone blips, but she ignores it.

'We've sent Tom's DNA sample for analysis to Forensic Science Service. They can process urgent samples in eight hours. We've just had the results back.'

She pauses again and I wait for her to continue, unsure where she's going with it.

'It's a match, Anna. A match with the Heath rapes.'

I stare at her, speechless. This can't be true.

'This is serious, Anna. We're checking his alibis for all the dates but it looks like he might be the Heath attacker.'

'But that's impossible. He's got a wife and kids . . . He's a dentist . . .' As soon as it comes out of my mouth I know how ridiculous it sounds.

'I know.' DCI Jones smiles sadly. 'Most rapists appear ordinary and innocuous. Until they attack.'

'Is he – Has he—' I can't bring myself to ask whether he's responsible for the murders as well, but Vic guesses my question.

'We don't know at this stage, but it's likely.'

'Oh my God.' A wave of extreme exhaustion washes over me. I don't feel shocked or angry, just desperately sad. 'If only I'd known . . . I could've stopped him.'

'No, Anna.' Vic puts her hand on my shoulder. 'You couldn't have. Don't blame yourself.'

'But why?'

'Why do people commit violent acts?' She sighs. 'There are a thousand answers. Because that's human nature?'

'What happens now?'

'The usual process: he'll be charged and kept in custody until the court hearing.'

'He won't come out on bail?'

'Unlikely, given the seriousness of the crimes.'

'Do you really think he did it?' I still can't get my head round what she's just told me.

'That's what the evidence is telling us.' Her phone blips again and she looks at it this time. 'I'm afraid I have to go. It's a busy day for us.'

I close the door behind her and go back to the kitchen. Tom is the Heath rapist. This is not what I'd expected, even after his strange break-in yesterday. I don't know whether I should allow myself to feel relieved. So much has happened within these last couple of months. Will anything good ever come out of this period of my life? I doubt it.

I unlock the door to the garden and step out onto the stone-paved patio. The garden looks peaceful, though slightly unkempt. If not for the pieces of broken guttering someone's put in a neat pile by the fence, there are hardly any signs of yesterday's struggle. It's as if nothing has happened here. This is life, I think, erasing any traces of turmoil, growing scar tissue over the wounds, self-healing. I remember Pia is due tomorrow for her gardening blitz. After her visit the garden will look even more tranquil and immaculate, a blank canvas, ready to be painted over with my moods. But it's not blank, I realize. Even though it looks almost perfect, it carries the memory of yester-day's fight, the anger and aggression of it. I go back to the kitchen and close the door behind me, but the feeling persists. The house seems claustrophobic and cold, full of menacing vibes, as if some stranger who hates me has moved in, unbe-known to me. I crank the heating up and turn on my Bose sound system. The smooth jazzy sound of Hidden Orchestra fills the rooms, but it's unable to shift the gloom. I need to get out, clear my head, get some positive energy from other people. I grab my car keys and head out through the door, unsure why I'm doing this or where I'm going. Wispa follows me closely and I have no heart to leave her behind. We both get into my car, one of the rare occasions Wispa's allowed on the front passenger seat, the place she loves. I drive off, nearly hitting another car that has to brake suddenly to let me out. We go down Highgate Hill, meander around the Archway Gyratory then continue along Holloway Road. Surprisingly for a Saturday afternoon there is very little traffic and we breeze through Highbury Corner, Islington and Shoreditch, and soon reach my improvised destination, Brick Lane. This is where I used to come when I was a fresh-faced and eager freelance producer with no money but plenty of time and ideas that were supposed to lead me onto the red carpet at the Cannes Festival. The red carpet never happened; the dreams of youth got stifled by the pragmatism of comfortable, corporate life.

I leave the car in a side street, just outside a derelict building decorated with beautiful street art, a combination of paste-up, spray-painting and tags. With Wispa on a short leash, we walk past newly refurbished arty shops and merge with the pedestrian traffic of Brick Lane. It's busy here, the colourful locals mixing with awestruck tourists, snapping photographs of London life at its most vibrant and genuine. I head straight for the bagel shop at the top of the street and get their salt-beef special with a large dollop of mustard, which I eat outside on a small bench, next to an old man in a bowler hat, who's been a permanent fixture outside the shop for as long as I remember. It's Wispa's lucky day – she gets a big chunk of the beef, which she swallows in one greedy gulp. Our hunger dealt with, we walk back down Brick Lane at a leisurely pace, window shopping. I stop at a quirky clothes shop run by two Italian guys who sell drop-crotch trousers of their own design. Encouraged by the moustachioed Marco, I impulsively buy three pairs of different fabric and design. It's time I ditched the corporate look and regained some of my past cool street flair. Then it's time for two stunning jackets in the shop opposite. My retail therapy complete, I head for the cafe at the Vintage Emporium in Bacon Street, a Victorian-style tea room and one of the few places in the area that welcomes dogs. Wispa immediately befriends the resident shaggy greyhound, while I order a cappuccino and a piece of scrumptious-looking coffee and walnut cake. As I soak in the bohemian atmosphere of the place, refusing to look at my iPhone, I feel the stress that has held my body in a vice for the last couple of days is beginning to ease off. This is what I've missed all these years stuck behind the corporate desk. And this is what I'm going to regain now. I'll start an art gallery, I decide. There are still plenty of vacant places for rent in the area. I'll look for artists who defy pigeonholing and curate exhibitions of urban art, graffiti, paste-up, stencil, spray-paintings, installations. I'll organize workshops, create a space where artists will be able to work and hang out. That's what I'm going to do. Perhaps I can rope Michael into my project. Maybe Sue will be tempted as well, although I doubt she'd want to abandon the security of a full-time job because of Olive. As the sugar rush provided by the cake hits me, I feel I'm ready to face the new life head-on.

By the time Wispa and I emerge from the Vintage Emporium the weather has turned and it's beginning to rain. We trot back to the car, getting completely soaked in the process. I turn the heating on full blast, enjoying the warmth emanating from the driver's seat. London traffic follows the changes in the weather, and the rain means instant traffic jams. We crawl back towards Old Street, the car smelling of wet dog.

An epic hour later we reach Highgate, with an average speed for the whole trip of six miles per hour, the car's computer tells me. I love weekends in London, but the amount of time one wastes in traffic almost kills the joy of being out and about. Because it's wet and miserable outside, there isn't a single parking space free in my street. I drive out to the High Street and do a small loop, returning to my street. Still nothing. I make a bigger loop and suddenly find myself in Tom and Samantha's street. I cast a glance at their house as I'm passing it. It looks dark and abandoned. Perhaps Samantha has taken the kids to some relative in the countryside, I wonder. That's what wives of disgraced men do in crime novels, don't they? There is a car coming in the opposite direction and it means one of us will have to reverse all the way to the end of the street to let the other one pass. I hate reversing, so I just stop, hoping the other driver is more accommodating. The other car stops too and turns on its headlights. This doesn't bode well. I'm checking my rear-view mirror to see if I can reverse after all, when the car in front jerks forward and stops, inches from my front bumper. I can see the driver's face, pale and twisted in anger. It's Samantha. She glares at me with hatred and I stare back, unsure what to do. Then she opens her door and gets out of her car. I instinctively check if all my car doors are locked. Wispa lets out a warning bark as Samantha approaches my car. She pulls at my door handle, then hits the window with an open palm.

'Are you happy now?' she shouts at me through the window. 'Have you come here to gloat?' I jump as she hits the window again. 'It's all your fault, you evil, manipulative bitch! You destroyed him!'

I sit, paralysed, as Wispa barks madly at Samantha, trying to get to the window, climbing over me.

'He's not your first, is he? It's your usual pattern, isn't it? You play with decent men, you goad them, until they can't take it any more! I bet it wasn't your first time at the clinic either!' Her spit lands on the window, inches from my face. 'How I wish you never walked into our lives! How I wish you were dead! You malignant, dirty whore!'

I put the car in reverse and start driving frantically backwards, trying to get away from Samantha. She follows me, hitting the car's bonnet with her fists. I press on the accelerator pedal, the car veers to the left and the left-hand side mirror catches one of the parked cars. Crystals of broken glass and bits of plastic crunch under the wheels as I keep going back, until I reach the end of the street. As I glance ahead I catch a glimpse of Samantha, standing motionlessly in the middle of the street. Someone's running towards her, pointing at my car. I reverse into the main street and drive off, wheels screeching on the asphalt. It takes me a while to gather my senses. I find myself driving down Hampstead Lane way above the speed limit, both hands on the wheel, knuckles white. When I try to loosen my grip I realize I'm shaking. Wispa stares at me from her seat, whimpering quietly. I slow down, pull over and switch the engine off. Why on earth did I drive down their street? I want to believe it was a genuine mistake and not some nasty trick of my subconscious. No, I really didn't think where I was going, I was just looking for a parking space. What a mess. I bet Samantha is going to report it to the police; God only knows what story she's going to invent about it. That's all I need now. It's not enough she blames me for Tom's behaviour, now she can add a tale of Anna Wright, the deranged stalker, to her list of accusations. I need to call DCI Jones to give her my side of the story before Samantha files her complaint. She's probably on the phone right now. I'd better act fast. As I turn the engine on, I remember the car I hit while reversing. I should go back and sort it out. I don't want to set foot again in Samantha's territory, but it has to be done. I park a few streets away, scribble a note of apology with my phone number on an old postcard I've found in the glove compartment, leave Wispa in the car and make a dash for it. At least it's stopped raining. I tentatively peer into Tom and Samantha's street. It looks empty. I trot along the parked cars until I see the pieces of broken side mirror on the road.

Thankfully, the damaged car is still there. I quickly stick my note behind one of its wipers and run back. I don't stop until I'm back at my car, where Wispa greets me ecstatically.

'Let's go home,' I tell her and she seems to agree.

This time I manage to find a parking spot right in front of my house. Without inspecting the damage to my car I head straight for the door.

The house feels cold and damp. I lock the front door and put the safety chain on. That's it, I'm done with the outside world for the day. I turn the heating on and, as the radiators begin to tick with a promise of warmth, I bury myself under the blankets on the sofa, a generous glass of Aberlour in my hand. I know I should call DCI Jones, but I can't be bothered. The comforting heat of the whisky spreads in my stomach, relaxing my body. As I take another sip, my eyelids start to droop, the shapes of the furniture in the room become blurred and I fall asleep.

Through the haze of sleep I can hear my phone ring, but my body feels almost paralysed, my limbs too heavy to move. I try to open my eyes, but that too seems like too much of an effort. I float away again, to be woken up by Wispa's warning bark. She hasn't moved from her place by the sofa, but her ears are pricked up, her wise eyes alert.

'What is it?' I want to ask her, but barely manage a mumble. My head is spinning and my body is still too heavy to move. Wispa lets out a low growl, looking at the open door to the hallway. I try to focus, but it's too dark to see clearly. My heart begins to pound, I push myself up, but my legs fold when I attempt to stand. I fall back on the sofa, panting. Something is wrong with me – food poisoning or maybe I'm having a stroke. Whatever it is, I need help. I frantically search for my phone and find it on the floor by Wispa's front paws. It takes me a while to focus on the screen, but eventually I manage to dial 999. As the operator enquires which emergency service I need all I manage is a long wail. In desperation I awkwardly stab the 'end' button. I put the phone down and try to speak. After a while I succeed in saying a few words and sound just about intelligible. Wispa watches me, ears pricked, curious and uncomprehending. When I can focus on my phone, I clumsily scroll through my contacts and find DCI Jones's number. She answers immediately and listens patiently to my slow and rambling account of what is happening. Then she tells me DS Kapoor and DC Montgomery are on their way. I put my phone down, relieved I've managed to express myself clearly enough for her to understand. Wispa's lain down by my feet again. I pull the blanket over me and close my eyes. After what seems like a second or two my doorbell rings, its fierce sound cutting through my stupor. My heart is pounding again. Wispa rushes to the hallway, barking. What to do now? I'm picking up my phone, when I hear someone shouting through the letter box.

'Ms Wright? Anna? It's DS Kapoor!'

DS Kapoor, what is he doing here?

'Hello,' I manage to squeak.

'Anna, do let us in!'

I try to get up, but the whole room sways and spins. I hold on to the sofa until the spinning slows down, then shuffle towards the hallway, my legs heavy and numb.

'Anna!' DS Kapoor pounds on the door.

'Just a minute,' I mumble.

I reach the hallway and move slowly along the wall towards the front door. I can see a blurred shape behind the glass, Wispa barking at it, wagging her tail. It takes me ages to undo the chain and open the door. There is a policewoman standing behind DS Kapoor. She's tall and blonde, her long hair tied back in a severe ponytail.

'Hello, Anna, this is DC Montgomery. Is it all right if we come in?'

I nod because it's too much effort to speak. They gently lead me to the kitchen and sit me down in one of the chairs.

'Can you try telling us what happened?'

This is hard, because I don't really know.

'Have you been drinking, Anna?' asks DC Montgomery. 'Have you taken anything?'

I look at her, uncomprehending.

'I don't know.'

'OK, not to worry.' DS Kapoor puts his hand on my shoulder. 'We'd like you to come with us, Anna.'

'Am I under arrest?'

'No,' he smiles. 'I'd like a doctor to have a look at you.' He speaks slowly and loudly. Too loudly. 'Nothing to worry about. But it would be good if you could come with us now. Can you do it for me?'

'Yes,' I say because I like him. 'But Wispa—'

'I'll look after her, don't worry. Can you stand?'

As I lean on the table and try get up the world spins again and fades to black.

I wake up feeling uncomfortable. I'm slouched on a hard, blue chair, DS Kapoor and DC Montgomery flanking me on both sides. We're in a hot and stuffy room, filled with people sitting in rows on blue chairs. There is a plasma screen on the wall in front of me, showing what appears to be a commercial for double glazing.

'Where am I?'

'A&E at the Whittington.' DS Kapoor smiles at me reassuringly.

'Have I had an accident?'

'You're OK. We just need a doctor to have a look at you.'

'Why?'

Before he answers, a swing door on the right opens and a nurse in blue uniform appears, saying my name. DS Kapoor and DC Montgomery hoist me up and I'm being led along a corridor to a small cubicle. There is a bed in it, I notice with relief. The nurse busies herself checking my pulse and blood pressure, then she puts a thermometer in my ear. It feels nice to be lying down.

I must've dozed off because I'm being woken up by someone new. He's tall and has the crumpled look of someone who hasn't slept for days.

'Hello, Anna, I'm Doctor Duval and I'm going to have a look at you.' He speaks with a strong French accent.

'Why am I here? Am I ill?'

'The two nice police officers who brought you here are a bit concerned about you.'

'What's wrong with me?'

'We'll do some tests and then we'll know more. Nothing to worry about, Anna.'

He takes my face in his hands and looks at my eyes. It seems extremely strange, but I let him do it. Then he turns towards the nurse and speaks to her in a quiet voice. I feel overwhelmed by tiredness and close my eyes.

I wake up in a different room and on a different bed. It's

quiet and the lights are dimmed. There is a drip attached to my arm, a bag dangling on a metal pole above my head, translucent liquid travelling down the IV line. I'm in hospital. In the semi-darkness I can see other beds; there are five of us in the room. The woman by the window is snoring loudly. Next to me there is an old, shrivelled lady, her face lined and tired, the shape of her tiny body barely visible under the sheets. I doze off again and am woken up by a loud voice. It's coming from the bed next to mine.

'And I shall be driving off in my Ferrari,' says the old lady.

A night nurse appears soundlessly by her side.

'You're not driving off anywhere, Margaret. You're in hospital.'

'Oh, sorry, pet.' The old lady sounds completely lucid.

'Not to worry, Margaret. Go back to sleep.'

'OK, pet.'

The nurse checks my drip, then disappears down the corridor. I fall asleep again.

Twenty-two Days Later

I'm woken up by the metal clatter of a breakfast cart. It's 7.30 a.m. and a choice of cornflakes or porridge is being served with milk. The nurses are bustling around, distributing drugs. A short queue of mobile patients forms outside the bathrooms. Two nurses tend to my neighbour Margaret, who is being washed in bed, her grey wisps of hair combed gently. A feisty nurse with a strong Eastern European accent checks my blood pressure, pulse and temperature, removes the catheter from my arm and tells me a doctor will come to see me shortly.

I must've dozed off again because when I open my eyes a tall man is standing by my bed.

'Hello, I'm Doctor Duval, you may not remember me from yesterday. I have good news. We are happy to discharge you today.'

'What was wrong with me?'

'We have found a concentration of diazepam in your system.'

'Diazepam?'

'Valium. You may have overdosed accidentally . . .'

'I don't use Valium. I've never taken it in my life.'

He purses his lips and exhales in a very French way.

'Well, we did find a concentration of benzodiazepine and its metabolites in your blood. Mixed with alcohol, it probably made you feel pretty lousy. But it wasn't a severe case and I'm happy to discharge you. Any questions?'

I can't think of any, so I purse my lips and exhale, imitating his French mannerism. He obviously gets the message, because he nods and moves on to the next patient. The feisty Eastern European nurse appears by my bed again.

'OK, dear? You're going home then? Your things are in there.' She points at a small locker by my bed. 'You can change here.' She draws the curtain around my cubicle. 'I think there is someone waiting to take you home.' She gestures towards the corridor.

'Who?'

She shrugs her shoulders and moves on, letting the curtain drop. I retrieve my clothes from the locker and dress hastily. Standing up proves to be more difficult. I have to hold on to the bed because of a wave of dizziness, but it passes after a few minutes. I open the curtain and tentatively move in the direction of the corridor. There is a man standing by the nurses' station. When he turns towards me, I recognize him. What the hell?

'DS Kapoor?'

'Nav, please. Morning, Anna! I've got your discharge letter.' He smiles at me and waves a piece of paper. 'All set to go?'

'Yes, I think so.' I look at him, perplexed. 'Why are you here?'

'I thought you needed a ride home. You looked pretty rough yesterday, I mean, you looked fine, but probably felt awful . . .' I look at him as he blabs on and I'm pretty sure he's blushing.

'Are you here in an official capacity?' I cringe when I hear myself, but I want to know.

'Well, it's my day off officially, but DCI Jones thought it would be good if I checked on you.'

'Oh, she knows.'

He nods. We proceed slowly through the hospital corridors, then Nav leads me through a modern-looking concourse to a pristine silver Fiesta parked outside. There is someone sitting in the front on the passenger side. When we get a bit closer I recognize her.

'Wispa!'

'Yes,' Nav beams at me, 'I went back to your place last night and took her home with me. I thought it wouldn't be fair to leave her on her own. I hope you don't mind . . .'

'No, thank you.' I look at him, overwhelmed with the feeling of gratitude. Anyone who's good to my dog must be a good person.

'Here are your keys, by the way.' He hands me my house keys and opens the car. Wispa jumps out, barking joyfully, and throws herself at me. I have to lean on Nav not to fall. Once the greeting dance is over, we're off, Wispa sprawled on the back seat of Nav's Fiesta.

'Hope she hasn't made a mess of your pristine car.'

'No.' He smiles at me. 'She's all right. I used to have a springer spaniel, he left his hair everywhere.'

'Thank you so much for looking after her.'

'No worries, Anna, I love dogs.'

When we get to my street Nav asks if he can come in for a minute and I say yes, relieved I won't have to enter the house on my own. I go straight to the kitchen and offer him a cup of tea, which he accepts.

'What do you remember about yesterday?'

'Not much,' I answer honestly, taking a sip of tea. 'I had a run on the Heath, changed the front-door mortice lock, had a visit from your boss who told me about Tom's arrest, went for a walk in Brick Lane, had a bagel . . .'

'Brick Lane?'

'I love the vibe of the place.'

Nav nods. 'My uncle has a restaurant there. I used to spend a lot of time in the area when I was a kid. Anything else you remember?'

'No . . .' I hesitate and then the memory of the encounter with Samantha hits me. 'Oh God . . .'

Nav listens patiently as I tell him about it.

'It must've been pretty stressful.'

'I meant to call DCI Jones and tell her about it, but I fell asleep.'

'Did you take anything to help you relax?'

'I did not!' I'm suddenly annoyed by his questioning. 'As I've already told the obnoxious French doctor at the hospital, I don't use Valium, I've never taken it and I don't keep it in my house!'

'I'm sorry, Anna,' Nav tries to placate me. 'We have to ask these questions.'

'Is this an official interrogation then?'

'No, no, no, it's not. I'm just trying to figure out what happened to you yesterday.'

I realize he has every right to be concerned. We sip our teas in silence.

'You didn't stop anywhere after bumping into Tom's wife?'

'No, I came straight home and curled up on the sofa with a nice glass of whisky—'

'Whisky? Do you still have the bottle?'

I shrug. 'It should be by the sofa. Aberlour, Speyside's finest.'

'Do you mind if I have a look at it?'

Nav is already on his feet when I shrug again. He comes back to the kitchen holding the bottle of Aberlour and my glass, using tissues he must've had with him.

'I'm afraid I'll have to take these away with me.' He suddenly sounds serious.

'Surely you don't think someone spiked my drink?' When he doesn't answer I add, 'In my own house? How?'

'You had some diazepam in your blood. We need to find out how it got there if you say you hadn't taken it yourself.' He's all business now.

'I drank from this bottle before and I was fine.'

'Exactly. Do you mind if I take this?' He picks up an empty Waitrose carrier bag and gently wraps the bottle and the glass in it.

'Go ahead.' I stop myself from shrugging again.

'I have to go now, Anna. Thanks for the tea.' He takes a business card out of his breast pocket. 'Here's my phone number, just in case. Do call if there's anything bothering you.' He goes to the door and stops. 'Oh, and do me a favour, take Wispa with you when you go out.'

'I won't leave her alone at home, I promise.'

'No, I mean, don't go out without her.'

'She's hardly a guard dog, Nav.'

'I know, but still.'

'OK, if you insist.' I smile. 'Thank you so much for everything, Nav, I do appreciate it.'

His smile is back for a moment and then he's gone. What a funny man, I think. I have a slight inkling his interest in me goes beyond professional. He seems to be always there when I need him. God, I hope it's not some kind of weird Munchausen by proxy syndrome . . . No, I don't think there is anything sinister in it. And, to be honest, I don't mind him going beyond the call of duty, I actually welcome it. Especially after he's been so nice to Wispa. Wispa my guard dog, bless him . . .

Aga Lesiewicz

I put the empty mugs in the sink, go to the hallway and put the security chain on, then go to the bathroom. A hot bath is exactly what I need after the night in hospital, and it feels heavenly. I luxuriate in the hot water full of I Coloniali Bath Cream for so long my fingers and toes begin to wrinkle. I'm in the mood for pampering myself. I smother myself with a body lotion enriched with Japanese yuzu fruit. As it says on the bottle, its aroma is supposed to chase away bad spirits. All the help I can get . . . I open the bathroom cabinet, looking for a face cream, and freeze. On the shelf right in front of my eyes sits a small rectangular box with the Roche logo on the side. Neat navy letters announce its contents: Valium, Diazepam, 10mg, 25 tablets. I hesitate, then reach for the packet and open it. The blister pack of baby-blue tablets inside is half-empty. I look closely at the pack: there is no sign of a chemist's sticker with the patient's name on it, just a white box, coated with my fingerprints by now, I realize belatedly as I put it back on the shelf. I'm covered with cold sweat, even though it's boiling hot in the bathroom. I wrap myself in a thick towelling robe and go down to the kitchen. I need to think and sitting at the kitchen table seems to be the best place for it. Someone's put a half-full pack of Valium in my bathroom cabinet, having spiked my favourite tipple with it. Was it an attempt to kill me or just a threat? Was I to stay unconscious while someone roamed my house, getting ready to do God only knows what with my helpless body? I pick up Nav's business card, then put it down again. Calling him now would feel like crying wolf once too often. Who could've done it? My thoughts go back to Friday night. Tom. Perhaps he wasn't trying to climb up the back wall, but was actually coming down, having left the Valium packet in my bathroom, which has a window facing the garden. Yes, but when would he have had the time and opportunity to spike my drink? Guilty or not, he's locked up and not a threat any more.

A sudden noise in the hallway makes me jump. My heart is instantly pounding as I get up, looking for something I can use as a weapon. Wispa lets out a single bark and trots to the hallway. I follow her, brandishing an empty wine bottle I grabbed from the recycling bin. There is someone at the door, trying to get in.

'Who's there?' I shout, hoping I sound in control.

'Hello, Anna? It's Pia. I can't get in.'

'Pia!' A wave of relief washes over me. I put the bottle down and unlock the door. 'So sorry. I had to change the lock again and haven't had time to make the spares.'

'No, worries.' She beams at me and I'm instantly wrapped in her positive energy. 'You all right?'

'Yes, I'm fine. Had a bit of a rough time lately . . .'

'I can see that.' She looks at the empty wine bottle by the door. 'Let's see how your garden's doing.'

For the next few hours I take on the role of Pia's assistant. I fill garden refuse sacks with dry leaves while Pia tidies the perennials, removes dead stems and tends to shrubs and trees. We work great in tandem. The garden transforms under her touch and her vibrant energy seems to push out all the bad vibes that have been hanging around in it since Friday. I feel I'll be able to enjoy it again. I go to the kitchen to make us a well-deserved cup of tea. As I take out a carton of milk from the fridge it occurs to me I have to get rid of all the opened bottles of drinks. The fridge is easy: the milk, apple juice and mineral water go into the sink. I hesitate for a moment in front of my drinks cabinet, but then a nearly full bottle of decent French cognac, half a bottle of Patron Silver Tequila, some Polish vodka and a splash of sherry end up in the sink as well. What a waste, but better safe than sorry. Thankfully, the rest of the bottles seem unopened. When I take a cup of tea for her, Pia shows me some loose panels in the fence at the back of the garden. The gap is big enough for a grown-up person to squeeze through. I fetch a drill and some screws and Pia fixes the fence with fastidiousness bordering on OCD, which I find reassuringly pleasing. Once she's finished, the garden seems safer than Fort Knox.

When I lock the door behind Pia I feel calm and in control. The bout of gardening has made me tired, but it's a good kind of tiredness. I heat and devour a pizza I've found in the freezer and wash it down with apple juice from a newly opened carton. I drag a heavy chair from the dining-room set to the front door and wedge it against the lock, the way they always do it in films. It may not be effective in practice, but it makes me feel better. I drag another chair to the kitchen door and barricade it as well, check all the windows are locked, draw the curtains and turn on the lights in the lounge and the hallway. Then I go upstairs, brush my teeth and climb into bed. It's not even four o'clock, but it's a dark, cloudy afternoon and it makes going to bed less of a crime. I fall asleep almost instantly, dreaming of nothing.

Twenty-three Days Later

I'm woken up by the buzzing of my iPhone. It's 9.15 a.m. and it's Gillian calling.

'Anna, darling, I'm just about to fire off our response to their redundancy offer.' I feel instantly awake. 'They want to avoid the unpleasantness of it dragging on as much as we do, so I've offered to strike a bargain for you to leave as soon as possible and with a minimum amount of fuss for a higher payout. One last detail I need to check with you: shall I include an offer of you signing a non-compete clause? Twelve or even six months would do.'

'Let's leave it out, Gillian.' I surprise myself by rejecting her suggestion. Even though I'm still adamant I'll never work in the media circus again, my gut instinct tells me not to limit my options.

'Fair enough. One never knows what awaits around the corner. I shall be in touch once we hear back from them. We shouldn't have to wait long.'

Gillian's positive energy is contagious and by the time I put the phone down I'm ready to face the world. The side effects of the Valium seem to have disappeared without a trace; I feel rejuvenated and alert. Wispa greets me excitedly, rushing to the front door and back, anticipating a run. I drink a glass of tap water, throw my running clothes on and am ready to accept her challenge. I drag the chair away from the front door and open it. It's a grey day, but at least it's not raining and it's quite mild. We tumble down Fitzroy Park, passing an elderly lady surrounded by a gaggle of small dogs in various knitted outfits. They all bark at Wispa, who ignores them magnanimously. The Heath is wrapped in fog, pierced here and there by bare tree branches. I inhale the damp air, ready to reclaim the park. It's as if Tom's arrest has dissipated the heavy negativity that hung over it, purifying the atmosphere and getting rid of menacing shadows. It's a beautiful open space again, nothing more and nothing less.

We run up the hill, Wispa keeping up with me bravely, her pink tongue lolloping about. It feels good to be out, to be active and unafraid. I pass a lone jogger going in the opposite direction and we exchange a little insider smile, sharing the joy of being Heath runners. At the top of the hill I turn right, following my old route. Even though the trees are almost bare now, it's much darker here, the lazy winter light not stretching this far into the woods. I slow down as flashes of images from the past start flooding in. The Dior Man, his wet T-shirt clinging to his chest, his hands on my breasts, our swim in the Ladies' Pond. Then another image muscles in, produced not by memory but my imagination. His body tangled in the bushes, surrounded by broken branches and trampled mud, lifeless and cold. I stop and bend over, trying to catch my breath. I've survived, but I'll always carry this awful image with me. A shiver runs through me; the damp air in the woods feels freezing. I hear a sudden noise behind me and I turn, instantly on guard. The elderly couple in matching green anoraks are making their way along the slippery path. They both stop, nod and smile at me, then continue their slow march. As they disappear down the murky path I shake off the feeling of inertia. I have to keep running, keep being alive. Wispa has stopped and is watching me expectantly, slowly wagging her tail. I force my body into a trot, then gather speed as my breathing returns to normal. I negotiate muddy puddles by the gate to Kenwood Estate, watching Wispa steam through them like a tug boat. We reach the open space of the West Meadow and my spirit lifts instantly. This is what I love about the Heath, the green expanse of freedom – peaceful, welcoming, relaxing. I turn right and run down a grass path along the edge of the meadow as Wispa overtakes me in a surprising burst of youthful energy, chasing a rabbit. Go for it, Miss Roly-Poly, I think, safe in the knowledge she'll never be able to catch it.

We run across the meadow, over a dilapidated wooden bridge and through the gate leading to Kenwood House. The scaffolding wraps the whole house now, neat, shiny and symmetrical, like a huge dental brace. I run up the steps and turn right, towards the cafe. I'm hoping it'll still be open and I can pick up a cone of strawberry ice cream. The gate at the top of the stone steps leading by the old bathhouse to the cafe is ajar and I trot down, debating whether I should go for a scoop of chocolate ice cream as well. But the cafe is closed and the whole place seems deserted. I'm just about to turn and run back up the steps when a sudden push from behind sends me flying forward. I stumble down the steep side steps that lead to the bathhouse, instinctively stretching my arms in front of me to soften the fall. Still, I land hard on the stone surface, the skin on my hands and my knees burning. I'm trying to get up when someone pushes my head down. My face hits the ground, my mouth filling with dirt and blood. Then I'm grabbed by the hair and lifted off the ground, dazed, semi-conscious. Someone kicks the wooden doors to the bathhouse open and pushes me in. It's dark inside and I stumble on the stone threshold, take a step forward, then gasp and move back. The deep hollow of the bath is right in front of me, its stagnant water covered in green scum. The door slams shut behind me and it gets even darker.

'Thank you for making it so easy for me,' a hoarse voice echoes in the cavernous space. I know this voice.

'James?'

I turn and he is right in front of me, gaunt and hollow-eyed. He is not well. And he scares me.

'James, what's going on? I thought you were travelling . . .'

He laughs, a harsh, almost hysterical sound.

'So you've been checking on me?'

'No . . . yes . . .' I don't know what he wants to hear.

'I should be travelling – seeing places, enjoying life – but you've destroyed everything for me!'

'James, I—'

'Shhh!' He raises his finger at me. 'Don't say a word. Just listen.'

I try to move away from him, but he pushes me violently against the cold, slimy wall.

'James, you're hurting me!'

He laughs again, the horrible cackle I've never heard from him before. The sound reverberates and distorts in the closed space.

'I am hurting you? But I haven't even started, my dear Anna.'

The way he says my name makes my skin crawl. I can hear Wispa's sharp bark somewhere outside, but I know she's not going to come to the rescue.

'That fucking dog of yours.' He's heard her, too. 'Stronger than I thought, fat bitch. It was a hefty dose of rat poison I gave her . . .'

'James, why are you doing this?'

'Why?' He lets out another deranged cackle. 'You don't know why? Let me tell you then. And you listen carefully, because it's your last chance to understand.'

He unbuckles his belt, slides it out of his trousers and wraps its ends around his knuckles.

'You know, when you dumped me I wanted to die. I thought of killing myself.' He pulls on the belt, as if testing its strength. 'You meant so much to me. My lovely, beautiful Anna. You made me happy, and then you took it all away. It was as if the whole world just froze, everything lost its colour, its sense of purpose . . .'

It looks as if he's about to cry, then he wipes his nose with the back of his hand and goes on.

'I drove to Cornwall, all the way to Land's End, to kill myself. And when I stood on the cliffs, looking at the ocean, I suddenly made a decision. I wouldn't let you go, I'd fight to get you back. I don't even remember driving back, I was so excited.'

I can hear scratching on the door and Wispa's quiet whine. She's found me. I try to shuffle slowly towards the door, but James blocks my way.

'You're not going anywhere. I want your *undivided* attention now!'

'I am listening, James, but I'm in pain – look.' I show him my hands, bloody from the fall. 'Let's go home, get it patched up—'

'Pain?' He pushes me and I stumble back, until I feel a recess in the wall and back off into it. 'You have no idea what pain is! Pain is sending you roses and then watching you go for a run with that guy. You knew they were from me, exactly the same as the ones I gave you on our first date!'

Shit, I remember now – James turning up with a bunch of red roses in his Audi, to take me out for a dinner at Hakkasan.

'I was waiting for you to give me a sign, to let me know you were thinking of me, that you knew it was me . . .' He starts laughing again, then punches the wall overgrown with green algae with his free bare hand and keeps punching until his knuckles are covered in blood. I instinctively move back deeper into the recess, which is like a small niche, with a statue missing. I am the statue now, and I'm trapped. Eventually he stops and looks at me, breathing heavily.

'And then I see you fuck that guy, suck him off . . . on your knees, like a cheap whore . . .' He suddenly retches, bends over the marble bath chamber below and throws up, then wipes his mouth with his bloody hand. 'And then you fuck him – and I know you're not my Anna any more, you don't *deserve* to be my Anna, you're a hideous, disgusting, selfish bitch and you need to be stopped.'

He approaches me, grabbing his belt with both hands again. He pushes me against the wall of the niche and raises his arms, the belt tight against my throat, his face, smeared with blood, by my face.

'So I kill you.' I smell vomit on his breath as he whispers, 'Except it's not you, it's that fucking dyke dressed as you . . . You make me kill her instead of you.'

The belt presses against my throat, crushing my windpipe, choking me.

'But next time I get it right . . . Do you want to know how he wheezed and snorted, thrashing about like a dying pig, when

I tightened the belt round his neck . . . not too fast . . .' His eyes glaze over and I know he's back there, with the Dior Man. 'He was strong – but I was stronger.' He is back, looking at me. 'It's the same belt.' He presses the belt harder and I fight for air, try to push him away. But he is stronger. I can feel his hot, stinking breath on my face. Dark spots dance in front of my eyes. Through the roar of blood in my ears I hear distant barking. Wispa, good girl, help me. The belt cuts into my skin, I can't breathe any more. I feel my legs give way, but he is holding me up with the belt on my throat. I'm going to die.

Sudden brightness hits me. So this is what death feels like. But then the pressure on my throat eases and I sink to my knees, fighting for my breath. I wheeze and cough, gulping the air in. Everything hurts. There is a commotion around me, I can hear Wispa barking madly. James is gone, but there is a man, kneeling in front of me.

'Anna! Look at me.'

I try to focus on his face.

'Anna, it's me, Navin. You're safe now.'

Other people gather round me, I'm being lifted off the ground, carried outside. As the fresh air hits me I'm beginning to recognize familiar faces. DS Kapoor, DCI Jones, some uniform guys, a couple of paramedics. I can see James being led away in handcuffs.

DCI Jones appears by my side, in a reflective waterproof jacket, combat trousers and heavy boots. When she reaches out to put her arm on my shoulder I can see she's wearing a black stab vest underneath her jacket.

'It's over, Anna.'

One of the paramedics, a rosy-cheeked big woman with a Yorkshire accent, helps me up and leads me to an ambulance parked nearby. She puts a plastic gadget on my finger, checks my eyes, my mouth, then slides an oxygen mask over my face.

'Take some deep breaths for me, love.'

She cleans the scratches on my hands and knees, puts something on my throat. As my breathing stabilizes and my heart regains its normal rhythm, I feel life coming back to me.

I'm in DCI Jones's office at the Kentish Town police station, sipping sweet, milky tea out of a Styrofoam cup. I feel exhausted and dirty, longing for a hot shower and my own bed. I've been thoroughly checked by the nice paramedic, who's given me the all-clear and warned I'll have a few nasty bruises. They'll take me home soon, DC Montgomery assured me, who's shown a much nicer, almost maternal side to herself today. But first I need to talk to DCI Jones, to make some sense of what has happened. She enters the room, her outdoor gear off, buoyant and buzzing with energy.

'As we have Tom Collins and James Morgan in custody, I can safely say that it's all over now. Mr Morgan has just confessed to killing Belinda Young and DCS Mark Thomas. We can put the Heath nightmare firmly behind us.'

I nod, looking at her.

'It'll take time to unravel all the details, but it seems James had developed quite an obsession with you.' She's telling me what I already know. 'He took leave from work, let out his apartment and rented a room in Highgate, so he could follow you. He was actually sharing a flat with Alden Jacobson.'

This I didn't know.

'He was Alden's lodger? Did Alden know who he was?'

'We're still in the process of building the whole picture, but it looks like James was determined to infiltrate your life, to come as close to you as possible, without you realizing it. He was keeping a very close eye on you, Anna.'

I feel sick and take a sip of the cold, sweet tea that actually makes my nausea worse.

'He watches you, he sees things he doesn't want to see, a switch gets flipped somewhere inside his psyche, a trigger that leads to the killing of Ms Young. We believe you were his intended target and Belinda an accidental victim. Wearing your raincoat, with the hood up, she looked remarkably similar to you. The murder of DCS Thomas was no mistake, though.'

'I know.' I put my face in my hands.

'Anna, you are not responsible for what has happened. You can't blame yourself for James's actions, whatever his initial motive may have been.'

'They died because of me . . .'

'No, they died because he killed them. And he would've gone and succeeded in killing you as well, if not for DS Kapoor's brilliant police work. Finding that GPS tracker in Wispa's collar was an incredible stroke of luck . . .'

'GPS tracker?'

'While he was looking after Wispa, when you were in hospital, Nav found a small personal GPS tracker in her collar. It's tiny, one of those prototype things that have a built-in sensor measuring speed and direction and provide the position even when the GPS signal is lost. So wherever Wispa went, she could always be located through a smartphone app. And wherever Wispa went, you went too.'

'So James followed Wispa through some application on his smartphone?'

'Not exactly.' DCI Jones leans back in her chair.

'But he followed me through Wispa, is that it?'

She looks away, as if making her mind up about what to say.

'What I'm going to tell you is confidential, Anna. It has to stay between us.'

'What is it?' I'm annoyed by her sudden reticence.

'It wasn't James who put the tracker on your dog. It was Mark . . . DCS Thomas . . .'

'The Dior Man?' It slips out before I can stop myself.

There is a flash of surprise or amusement in DCI Jones's eyes, then she goes on.

'DCS Thomas was tracking Wispa's movements.'

It all suddenly falls into place: the seemingly random meetings on the Heath, the precision with which I always bumped into him whenever I was out running with Wispa. I stare at the cup in my hand, dumbfounded. DCI Jones clears her throat.

'Nav matched the tracker to DCS Thomas's phone and was able to follow your movements when you were with Wispa on the Heath. That's how he knew where you were today.'

'And saved my life . . .' I whisper.

'I must say, I'm very proud of this young man. He insisted we didn't switch off the tracker, even though we had Tom Collins in custody. He took monitoring of your movements upon himself and, yes, he saved your life today.'

There is a knock at the door. It's DC Montgomery, who looks at DCI Jones expectantly.

'Are they ready?' DCI Jones gets up. 'I have to go, Anna. But I'll leave you in DC Montgomery's capable hands.'

'Let's get you home, love,' says DC Montgomery and leads me gently out of DCI Jones's office.

Twenty-four Days Later

They say you have to get up after a fall and keep walking, get behind the wheel of a car after a crash and keep driving. Otherwise you'll never be able to walk or drive again. That's why I'm up and about this morning. It's 7.30 a.m. and the sun is rising over the Heath. It's a glorious day, cold and crisp, and the clear blue sky is tinged orange in the east. There is a thin layer of fog hovering just above the ground that catches the first rays of the sun, suspending the light in the air. My rhythm is steady, my breathing regular as I run up the hill, Wispa trotting silently beside me. I took her old collar off last night and ordered a new one on Amazon, black faux leather diamante, in which she'll look fabulous and which she'll probably hate. I spent most of the evening yesterday thinking about my life. Assessing the damage. Dealing with the feelings of guilt. And eventually, reluctantly, giving myself permission to go on. Being on the Heath this morning is a test of my resolution. So far it's holding fast. I decide I'll order a bench in Bell's memory to go on the Heath. I'll get in touch with Candice. I'll go for my HIV test. I'll cut down on drinking wine. I'll swap my 4x4 for a hybrid. I'll spend more time with my friends. I'll stay single for a while.

On the way back I surprise myself by stopping at a coffee

shop in Highgate village, getting a latte and going through the morning paper, Wispa at my feet. I haven't done this for years and it feels good. To my relief I find nothing about yesterday's attack or James's arrest in the paper. I put the paper down and look out of the window. It'll take time for me to recover from all this. But I'll never be able to understand hatred so strong that it makes one want to kill another human being. I'll never see James again. I'll never know for sure who spiked my drink with Valium and why. But it doesn't matter now. It's over.

By the time I get home and have a shower it's already 9.15 a.m. There are five new messages on my phone, which I'd left on the kitchen table. Good sign, I think, the world hasn't forgotten about me yet, even though I'm out of the game. The first one is from Gillian, short and to the point.

'Anna, I've received a new redundancy offer from your employer. I think you'll be pleased, very pleased.'

The second message takes me by surprise.

'Anna darling, it's Tamara, Tamara Ashley-Sharpe. I think it would be rather beneficial for both of us if you cared to join me for lunch. I have some interesting offers I'd like to discuss with you.'

The Big T is inviting me for lunch. It's an invitation no one in the industry would turn down and I must say its prospect quickens my pulse.

The third message is from Michael, who tells me Tom and Samantha's lawyers have dropped all the charges against Giorgio. Good. He seems like a fine man and I hope Michael will find long-term happiness with him. Tom and Samantha. I wonder if she'll stand by him, regardless of what the outcome of his court case might be. Having seen the vehemence with which she attacked me while defending him, she probably will. Oh well, all monsters deserve someone who sees something good in their ugliness. Actually no, not all of them . . .

The fourth message I delete instantly, without listening to all of it. It's from Ray. But the last one makes me smile.

'Anna, it's Nav . . . Navin Kapoor. I'm calling to check how you are . . . and . . . I was wondering if – if you fancied going out for a drink or something at some point. It's absolutely fine if you don't feel like it, but it would be . . . really great if you did. Oh, by the way, I left something for you by your front door this morning . . . it's hidden behind the rubbish bin. It's just a little something . . . Hope you'll like it. Bye . . .'

Sweet man, I think as I go to the front door and open it. There is a gift bag wedged behind the rubbish bin. I untie a red ribbon and look inside. A small, stuffed toy dog with white snout and big brown eyes is looking at me from the nest of soft wrapping paper.

Acknowledgements

I would like to thank my agent, Jane Gregory, and editor, Stephanie Glencross, for picking my manuscript out of the slush pile; Trisha Jackson, Editorial Director at Pan Macmillan, for believing in me and my book; my fellow writer Caroline Gilfillan for her invaluable advice over the years; Anna and Alex for being my consultants on many subjects; and Jola for pushing me in the right direction.